the Christmas he Loved Her

JULIANA STONE

 sourcebooks
casablanca

Published by Sourcebooks Casablanca, an imprint of Sourcebooks, Inc.
P.O. Box 4410, Naperville, Illinois 60567-4410
(630) 961-3900
Fax: (630) 961-2168
www.sourcebooks.com

Printed and bound in the United States of America
VG 10 9 8 7 6 5 4 3 2 1

For the Mudslides. You all rock and are truly the best girlfriends in the world.

Chapter 1

THE CEMETERY WHERE HIS BROTHER RESTED WAS A desolate place in late November. It sat upon a drab green hill surrounded by a forest of pine and birch. In the distance, Crystal Lake shimmered through skeletal tree limbs like wisps of blue silk as a cold wind drew whitecaps on the water.

Jake Edwards pulled his Jeep over to the shoulder, cut the engine, and slowly exhaled. His fingers gripped the steering wheel so tightly they cramped, and though he stretched them out and tried to relax, it was no use. He was wound tighter than a junkie in rehab, and he drummed a methodical beat along the dashboard as he gazed out the window.

This particular cemetery was the oldest in town, and many of Crystal Lake's founding families were buried within its borders. Grand mausoleums and tombstones rose against the dull gray sky, painted dark like a macabre city skyline. He stared at them for several long moments, eyes hard, mouth tight, as a light rain began to fall. It was nothing more than a drizzle, really, and created a mist that hung over the cemetery, though he only had eyes for the row just beyond the large oak tree.

Row number thirty-six. Jesse's row.

The darkness in him stirred, leaving the taste of bitterness on his tongue. He let it settle. He let it burn. Hell, these days it was the only thing that told him he was still alive—even if he did feel half-dead most of the time.

A crow flew lazily in the sky, slicing through the haze until it swooped low and settled on top of a large stone angel not far from him. It cocked its head, then turned and stared at Jake—its small beady eyes steady as it slowly blinked.

Jake held its gaze for several more seconds and then jerked his chin up as if to say *Fuck you*. The crow cawed, rotated its head, and flew off once more, out over the lake.

Abruptly, he turned the key and put his Jeep in gear. He continued down Lakeshore Road because he sure as hell wasn't ready to deal with the cemetery yet.

His parents were expecting him, but first he had one more stop—a certain someone he needed to see. A certain someone he was damn sure had no desire to see him, and he didn't blame her one bit. Not after the way he'd left things.

Jake had screwed up, and now it was time to set things right.

Five minutes later he stepped out of his Jeep and slung a worn leather bag over his shoulder as he glanced up at a small cottage set back a few hundred feet from the road. At one time it had been a carriage house and was a solid structure built entirely of large blocks of gray, weathered limestone. A simple white-spindled porch ran the length of it, with empty baskets hung at each corner, their usual treasure of deep-red geraniums long dead.

An old, rickety rocking chair moved gently on its own there, the legs squeaking as it moved back and forth, pushed either by the crisp breeze that rolled in off the lake or the ghost of Josiah Edwards, an ancestor said to haunt the woods.

Jake pulled the collar of his leather jacket up to his chin and shuddered as a strong gust of wind whipped across the still-green lawn, carrying with it the remains of dead, rotted leaves and anything else it managed to shake free.

He took a step forward, eyes narrowed, as his gaze took in an expensive Mercedes parked near the house next to a rusting and faded yellow Volkswagen. He wasn't sure who owned the Mercedes, but the rust bucket he knew well. The ancient Beetle had been a broken-down mess when she had first bought it.

The car belonged to his sister-in-law, Raine, and in a world gone to shit, at least the car hadn't changed.

Jake slowly perused the property. He spied a weather-beaten bench near the tree line and knew that if he took the path that led through the woods to his right, he'd end up at his parents' home—eventually. It was still a hike, several miles to be exact, but this parcel of land, boasting an acre and a half of prime waterfront along with the stone cottage, had been severed years ago from his parents' property. It had been a wedding present to his brother Jesse and his then-new bride, Raine.

A familiar ache crept across his chest, and for a moment he faltered, his eyes squeezed shut. He pictured the three of them, Jake, Jesse, and Raine, decked out in their wedding finery. It had rained that day, a good omen, according to some, and Raine's dress was tattered along the hem from dancing outdoors in the mud, while his brother's tuxedo had remained crisp and clean. Jake's

tux, however, was as ruined as the bride's dress. They'd
posed for a picture, the three of them, there by the bench
beneath the ancient oak.

Jake sighed and opened his eyes, resting them once
more on the empty bench. It needed a fresh coat of paint.
He shook the melancholy from his mind and strode toward the house.

It had been a year and a half since he left Crystal
Lake. And even though he was pretty sure Raine
Edwards wanted nothing to do with him, he was going
to try his best to make amends. It was the least he could
do. For Raine. For Jesse.

And maybe, for himself.

He stepped up onto the porch, his eyes settling on
the newly painted white trim that encased the door—a
door that was no longer the green he remembered, but
a deep, dark red. He heard voices inside and his gut
rolled nervously. She had company. Maybe now wasn't
a good time.

His dark eyes drifted toward his Jeep. Ten seconds
and he could be out of here before anyone knew better.
He took a step backward, weighing his options, his jaw
clenched tightly as the all-too-familiar wave of guilt,
anger, and loathing washed through him. *Coward*.

Jake ran his fingers through the thick mess of hair
atop his head and tried to ease the tension that settled
along his shoulders. He hadn't seen Raine since the
Fourth of July, well over a year ago, and they hadn't
parted on good terms. They'd both said some things…
hurtful things…but he'd made everything worse by
taking off for what he meant to be only a few weeks
to clear his head. The few weeks had turned into

months, and those months had bled into nearly a year and a half.

It had been much too long, and he still wasn't sure he was ready to face the ghosts of his past. Yet here he stood.

Jake blew out a hot breath and reached for the door, when it was suddenly wrenched open and a bundle of gold streaked past his feet and barked madly as it did so. It was a ball of fur that ran crazily down the steps, with a chubby frame that was barely able to manage them. He stepped back, and then the puppy was forgotten as he stared down into the face that had haunted him his entire life, it seemed.

Huge round eyes the color of Crystal Lake on a stormy day widened, while the small bow mouth fell open in shock. Her skin was pale, the kiss of summer long faded, and the angles of her face were sharper, more defined. She looked fragile. And beautiful. And delicate. And…

"You cut your hair," was all he managed to say—barely.

Her fingers twisted in the uneven, ebony ends that fell a few inches past her jaw but didn't quite touch her shoulders. It was a reflex action, and damn if it didn't tug on the cold strings still attached to his heart. She pulled on a long, curling piece, tucked it behind her ear, and settled her hand, tightened into a fist, against her chest.

She wore a pink T-shirt, *Salem's Lot* etched across her breasts in a bold, black font. The old, worn jeans that hugged her hips looked tattered and done for, the ends rolled up past delicate ankles, leaving her feet bare, her toenails painted in chipped blue polish.

For a moment there was nothing but silence, and then she moistened her lips and exhaled slowly. "Your hair is longer than it's ever been."

The sound of her voice was like a returning memory, one that filled the emptiness inside and stretched thin over his heart.

He nodded, not quite knowing what to say. He'd officially left the military six months ago, and hair had been the last thing on his mind. The closely cropped style he'd sported his entire adult life was no more. Now it curled past his ears.

"It's been…a long time." Her words were halting, as if she wasn't sure she wanted to speak.

He held her gaze for a moment and then glanced away. The old wicker chair still rocked gently in the breeze, and the golden bundle of fur that had shot out of Raine's house was sniffing the ground near his Jeep.

"Yeah," was all Jake managed, and even that was hard.

"Nice that you made time for your father." A touch of frost was in her voice now, and he glanced back sharply.

Awkward silence fell between the two of them as he stared down into eyes that were hard. Had he expected anything less?

"He's been sick for a while now." Her chin jutted out. "You know that, right?" Accusation rang in her words.

A spark of anger lit inside him. So this was how it was going to be. "Yeah, Raine. I know."

Her mouth thinned and a flush crept into her pale cheeks. "Well, why the hell did you wait so long to come home to us?"

"I couldn't get away," he said flatly.

She arched an eyebrow and shivered. "Couldn't? Or wouldn't?"

He took a step closer and reiterated. "*Couldn't.*"

He knew part of it was bullshit. If he'd really wanted to come home earlier, he could have. The guys would have understood. But he'd never admit that it was only his father's health taking a wrong turn that had finally brought him back. Because that would mean admitting the reason he'd stayed away for so long was right in front of him.

All five feet four inches of her.

Her toe tapped against the shiny wooden planks at her feet, and her eyes narrowed into a glare that told him everything. Raine Edwards was pissed.

She cleared her throat and raised her chin.

She was more than pissed.

Jake squared his shoulders. This was good. He'd rather she was mad as hell than weepy and soft. Mad he could handle. Soft and needy, not so much. Not from her, anyway.

"You going to invite me in, or are we going to have it out, here on the porch?" Jake arched an eyebrow and waited. Nothing was ever "easy" and "gentle" between him and Raine. There had always been that friction.

She and his brother, Jesse, had been like yin and yang, while Jake and Raine were like oil and water. They didn't exactly mix and rarely saw eye to eye.

From the time they were kids... How many nights had Jesse given up and gone to bed long after the two of them argued over every last detail of whatever the hell it was they happened to be discussing? From Scrabble to politics to music and everything in between.

Raine's mouth thinned and she stepped past him, clapped her hands, and yelled "Gibson" as she did so. The puppy's head shot up, its round body quivering as it answered her call. The dog ran toward the house, chasing a leaf, weaving an intricate path until it climbed the stairs and barked at her feet.

She scooped the puppy into her arms and laughed as it struggled to lick her face. Something inside him thawed in that moment. Something that he'd encased in a wall of ice. It was painful, and the dread in his gut doubled. He'd known this was a bad idea, but it was a bad idea he needed to see through. He owed it to Jesse, even if he was a year and a half late.

And he owed it to Raine, after the way he'd left things.

She stepped back and cleared her throat. "You planning on spending the night?"

"Excuse me?" Jake answered carefully, not understanding her angle.

Raine licked her lips, the heightened color in her cheeks a healthy pink in an otherwise pale face. She pointed toward his bag. "Did you pack extra boxers and your toothbrush?"

"No." Jake shook his head. "This is just…"

She turned before he could finish and indicated that he follow her inside as she strolled down the hall with the puppy still in her arms, her hips swaying gently. He couldn't help himself. His eyes roved her figure hungrily, taking in every inch, from the top of her head to the bottom of her bare feet. His mouth tightened, a frown settling across his brow because he sure as hell didn't like what he saw. She was too thin. Too pale.

Too much like the ghosts he'd seen wandering the

base at Fort Hood—war widows and widowers, distraught families, friends. All of them had that look. Christ, he saw it every day he looked in the mirror, but Raine…damn, he wanted more for her.

Then maybe I should have done something about it. He winced at the thought, mostly because it was the truth.

The house was brightly lit, the sun that shone in through the windows creating warmth against the rich oak floors. For a second, Jake faltered as the heaviness of the moment slipped over him. So many memories he'd tried to forget. He'd helped his brother restore the entire main floor the last time they were home on leave nearly two years ago. It was the last time all three of them had been together.

Voices echoed in his head, echoes from a past that would haunt him forever, and he forced himself to *move*, noting that the kitchen sported a complete redo— gleaming antique-cream-colored granite, dark chocolate cabinets, and shiny stainless-steel appliances. No doubt a gift from his parents, because the last he knew, working at the youth center in the neighboring city didn't pay much. Not that it mattered. Aside from the sizable life-insurance settlement Raine had been entitled to, the Edwards family looked after their own.

She would never want for anything.

Raine had been a part of their lives from the time they were kids. Raised for the most part by her Aunt Jeanine, she'd been on her own since the age of sixteen, when her aunt died. Her mother, Gloria, traveled extensively, doing missionary work for the church. It was mighty charitable of her, though Jake had never understood the

need some people had to help others when it meant ne-
glecting their own.

His face heated when he realized that was exactly
what he'd done for the last year and a half. He was no
better than her mother—worse, even—because Raine
had always counted on him and he'd let her down when
it mattered most.

She'd become an extra member of the Edwards family, the third wheel in a lot of the Edwards boys' she-
nanigans, and it had come as no surprise to anyone when
she'd married one. The serious one, Jesse.

A male voice interrupted his train of thought, and
for a moment the hot flush of something fierce washed
through him. He jerked his head, hackles up, and stared
at her in silence, hands fisted tightly at his sides.

Raine paused in the doorway that led to the living
room/dining area and glanced over her shoulder—eyes
still questioning, mouth still tight.

"Look what I found on the porch," she announced
and walked into the living room. Jake took a moment
and then followed suit, halting just inside the room.

"Son of a bitch!" Mackenzie Draper, one of his oldest buddies, set his beer onto the low-slung table in
front of the sofa and rose, a smile splitting his face wide
open. "You didn't say anything about coming home for
the holidays."

Jake grinned. "It wasn't in the plans last time I saw you."

"Wait a minute," Raine interrupted. "When did
you see Jake?" Her gaze focused on Mac, who shifted
uncomfortably.

"I had business in Texas a few months back, and we
got together for a drink."

"Texas," Raine muttered. "Right."

She turned stormy eyes his way, and Jake flinched at the hurt and accusation that colored them a darker hue. He felt even more like a shit.

"Nice that you have time for *some* of your friends, Jake."

"It wasn't planned, really," Mackenzie began. "I had a couple of extra days and we got together."

Raine set the puppy down. "That's a hell of a lot more than I ever got." She didn't bother to hide the bitterness in her words.

Jake ignored the taunt and remained silent, his eyes locked on to Mackenzie's. His friend was dressed in an expensive suit tailored to fit his tall frame, the charcoal gray a nice choice against the plum shirt. Though his collar was loose and a thin black tie lay on the table in front of him, Mac always looked *GQ* ready. With his thick dirty-blond hair and vibrant green eyes, he'd been labeled a pretty boy his entire life.

Mackenzie, Cain Black, Jake, and his brother Jesse had been the best of friends from the time they were five years old and Mackenzie had come to school with his front teeth missing and a shiner the color of rotted grapes. It had impressed the hell out of the Edwards twins, though they were too young to appreciate the darkness and violence it represented.

It was good to see him. "You home for the holidays too?" Jake asked.

Mackenzie shook his head. "Nah, I don't think Ben would appreciate it if I crashed his long weekend. I had business in Detroit and thought I'd squeeze in a visit with my mother, but…"

"But?" Jake prodded.

Mac shrugged. "Same old same old. I called ahead and it's not gonna work. Ben's already home and liquored up. I guess his long weekend has an extra few days tacked on to it. Mom snuck away and we had coffee." Mackenzie's mouth tightened. "She'll never change. There's always some reason for the bruises on her arms or the soreness in her side. He beats the crap out of her and she stays."

"She'll wake up one day, Mac," Raine said carefully.

Mackenzie turned to her, with a bitter smile. "I doubt it. In spite of everything, she loves him. How fucked-up is that?" He glanced at his watch. "Anyway, I gotta hit the road. It's a good ten hours until I hit New York."

"You sure you don't want to stay for Thanksgiving? I've got—" She halted and cleared her throat. "Well, the spare room isn't usable right now, but the sofa is yours." Raine prodded gently, "Maybe Ben will…I don't know…"

"Do us a favor and kick the bucket?" Mackenzie shook his head. "That son of a bitch will outlive us all." He enveloped Raine into a bear hug and kissed her on the cheek. "Thanks, but I'd be crap company anyway."

Mackenzie paused a few inches away, his eyes intense as he studied Jake in silence. "You look like shit, soldier."

"I'm not a soldier anymore."

"No, I suppose you're not." The two men stared at each other for several moments, and then Mackenzie lowered his voice. "I miss him too."

The band of pain that sat around Jake's chest tightened and he nodded, a lump in his throat. "Yeah," he muttered.

They shook hands, but when Jake would have pulled away, Mackenzie held on for a quick hug. "Don't be such a douche bag, and stay in touch." Mackenzie stepped back and cocked his head to the side. "Give your dad my best. He's a tough son of a bitch, so I wouldn't worry too much."

Jake nodded. "Will do."

"It's good you're back."

Jake nodded but remained silent.

Mackenzie smiled a million watts at Raine, his green eyes crinkled with warmth. "Take care, gorgeous, and I'll think about Christmas."

The door closed behind Mackenzie, leaving silence in his wake and the oppressive weight of two ice-blue eyes shooting daggers at Jake. Now that Mac was gone, she didn't make any effort to hide her anger.

Jake turned to her, set his leather bag onto the coffee table, and waited for the hammer to fall.

"I should kick your ass all over Crystal Lake, you know that, right?" She blew out a strand of hair that caught at the corner of her mouth. "And maybe I will, but first I'd like to hear all about your yearlong vacation."

Vacation?

Okay, so now anger burned beneath his leather collar. Fort Hood was no fucking vacation. The nightmares in his head were no fucking vacation. The guilt and pain that lived with him every single day were no fucking vacation.

"Are you serious?" He asked so softly, he knew she barely heard him, or else she might have taken the hint and backed off. "You think the last year has been a vacation?"

Instead, Raine took two steps forward and thumped him in the chest with the palm of her hand. "Yes, I do," she spat. "You took a vacation from life for the last year and a half while the rest of us slugged it out in the trenches." Her eyes shimmered with unshed tears, and she'd never looked more fierce. Never looked more delicate and frail or so damn lovely it made his stomach ache. "It's time to come clean, Edwards. Why have you stayed away so long?"

The hammer, it seemed, was heavy, and it didn't take long to strike.

Chapter 2

Raine didn't know if she wanted to strangle the man in front of her, slap him across the face and order him out of her house, or hug him. And by the looks of it, Jake Edwards needed more than just a hug. Judging from the bleak, haunted look in his eyes, he hadn't fared well over the last year and a half. But then again, had any of them?

She tore her gaze from his, her heart pounding, her cheeks heated. God, she was so angry with him.

He stood in front of her, hurting so badly it fell off him in waves, and yet all she could think about was the fact that he had been in touch with every single person they shared a bond with, except her.

She'd received exactly six emails from him since he left Crystal Lake. And one drunken voice mail, which she'd never erased and would listen to from time to time when she was feeling more down in the dumps than usual. How sad was that?

Raine exhaled sharply and took a step back, eyes critical as she took him in once more. He was dressed in faded jeans and black leather, a deep blue turtleneck sweater offering some bit of warmth against the late November chill. His hair, so much longer than when she'd seen him last, was wavy, the thick espresso curls now touching his collar. The coffee-colored eyes that stared back at her glittered with a hardness in their depths she didn't like. His strong jaw, slightly crooked nose—broken when he was twelve and his brother dared him to jump off the bridge near the dam—and full, wide mouth hadn't changed.

He was still as handsome as ever, and she supposed some women would find the hard edge he'd picked up even more attractive. He looked dangerous, very much a bad boy—as if Jake Edwards needed any more weapons in his arsenal. Women had always flocked to his side like bees to honey. Heck, he'd been as much a horndog as Cain Black, back in the day.

He's so different from Jesse.

They were fraternal twins, so while physically they looked different—her husband had been lighter in coloring, with blue eyes instead of brown, and dark blond hair—there'd still been enough of a resemblance between them that anyone would know they were brothers. The Edwards twins. The Bad Boys.

She closed her eyes as a familiar wave of pain rolled through her. It stuck in her chest, tightening like iron claws, and she took a step back, hating the sensation more than ever.

She much preferred the numb cocoon she usually existed in. It was just easier when everything was coated in ice and frozen over, smooth as the lake in mid-December.

"Are you all right?"

Raine's eyes shot open. "What kind of question is that?" She turned, grabbed Mackenzie's empty beer bottle, and headed toward her kitchen. She rinsed the bottle out and set it on the counter, aware that Jake had followed her.

Keeping the granite island between them, she glared

at him. "Why wouldn't I be all right? I'm a thirty-year-old widow who lives alone, though I suppose Gibson counts for something." She paused and glared at him. "Gibson would be my puppy." Then she continued. "My mother is back in town and wants to spend the holidays with me, and really, she's the last person I want to see. Most of my friends are either too busy or too weirded out by my situation to come around anymore. I'm scared, pissed off, and…"

She went quiet as her thoughts wandered toward the dark place inside her. The empty place. The one that would never heal.

I'm alone.

Jake's eyes narrowed and the bleakness in them intensified. She knew exactly what he was thinking about, and for a moment she was back there with him. Back to that crazy night when the darkness inside both of them had exploded.

The night they had reached for each other in pain. The night they had used their bodies to try and forget Jesse's death—her husband, his brother. But it had backfired, and their pain had been too great, their last words bitter. Jake's had rung in her head for many, many nights.

I can't stand to be around you.

His gaze moved downward and settled on her stomach, for just a second, before he nailed her with an intense look. "So you never went through with it?" he asked bluntly.

"With what?" she managed, wanting to hear him say it. The one thing he'd been so pissed about.

"Having Jesse's baby."

Raine glared at him, even as her heart split wide open.

She couldn't fall apart. Not now. She didn't want to talk about it, not with him. That time had come and gone, and he'd been nowhere to be found.

"Besides the fact that it's none of your business…" She paused and grabbed an empty glass off the counter. "Do you see a kid running around here?"

Raine crossed to the fridge and yanked open the door. She grabbed a large jug of water, and then everything inside her stilled. Jake had moved and was inches from her.

"You're wrong about that, Raine."

She forced herself to pour the glass and then shoved the jug back into the fridge before turning around. He looked so hard and fierce and hurt that for a moment all she wanted to do was wrap him in her arms and ease his burden.

The moment fled as quickly as it had come. He would push her away. It's what Jake did, and besides, she was so raw inside, she was no help to anyone. Especially Jake. He'd disappeared from her life when she needed him the most, and she wasn't sure she'd ever be able to forgive him for that.

I'm so sorry for what happened. I never meant for any of it. Please, are you there? I can't stop thinking about you. About what we did that night. God, Jesse must hate us.

His drunken words, still on her voice mail, echoed in her head, but she shook them away, feeding on the cold anger inside her.

"How's that again?" she asked and then shoved her way past him. Gibson happily followed in her footsteps and jumped onto the sofa as she stood in front of the large window overlooking the trees out back. Blue patches of water glittered through the oak and linden trees, and she shivered, hating the emptiness—the bareness—of everything.

It was November, a month of dormancy, when all the living, green things wither and die and disappear until spring. She shook her head and drained her glass. She was just like the big old oak tree that stretched above the bench out back. Dormant. Existing in a state of sleep. And yet, unlike the tulip bulbs that lay beneath the earth in front of her home, she wasn't entirely sure she'd ever be able to thrive again. She sighed.

Half the time she didn't know if she *wanted* to.

"Jesse made it my business when he asked me to look out for you."

Raine closed her eyes, glad that Jake couldn't see the pain in them. He wouldn't understand. No one would. Hell, she didn't even understand the breadth of her emotions sometimes.

"And you've done such a bang-up job of that, haven't you?" Raine whirled around. "I haven't seen you since a month after Jesse's funeral. And I can count on one hand…" She looked at her outstretched fingers and snorted. "No, hold on." She held her middle finger up and shoved it in his face, a big fuck-you. "*This* is how many times I've heard from you." Suddenly the hurt inside was too much and her body shivered from the force of it. "Once." She laughed harshly, ignoring Gibson as the puppy began to whimper, sensing his master's anguish.

"That's bull. I emailed you more than—"

"One phone call is all I got, Jake, and you were drunk," she said hoarsely. "Emails don't count. Not for me. I deserve more than that." Her voice broke. "You have no idea…"

His face whitened and he took a step. For one crazy moment Raine thought he was going to reach for her, and she leaned forward, like a fool…like a starved fool who hadn't been touched by anyone in so long. God, she just wanted to lean on someone. Lean on someone strong, and forget.

Marnie and Steven were so fragile, still dealing with the loss of their son and Steven's illness; Raine didn't want to add to their burden. So she acted as if everything were all right. She let them spoil her however they wanted, because she knew it gave them comfort, but mostly because it was just easier to let them. But it wasn't enough for Raine, and with her closest friend, Maggie, gone to LA with Cain…there was no one.

After months of walking through life in someone else's shoes—some false facade she'd built up—Raine felt the cracks beneath the surface. She felt them every day…getting larger, deeper…and knew that if she didn't deal with them soon, they'd swallow her whole.

If she disappeared down the rabbit hole, Raine was pretty sure she'd never find her way back.

Funny, some days it was all she wished for.

"Are you still considering having Jesse's baby?"

Something about his tone got to her, and Raine glanced up sharply, her pain forgotten as anger replaced it in one fast, hot thrust. "What do you care, Jake?" She shook her head. "And don't tell me it's because you're going to"—she made quotation marks with her fingers—"*be here* for me. If you cared enough, you wouldn't have left in the first place." Her eyes narrowed. "Besides, I know what you really think. You thought I was nuts to consider having Jesse's baby after he died. In fact, if I remember correctly, you told me I couldn't even look after a goddamn cat."

Gibson chose that moment to bark sharply, his head going back and forth between the two of them, his tail wagging at half-mast. He knew the humans in the room with him were on edge. Raine glanced at the dog. *Gibson, you have no bloody idea.*

"Guess I proved you wrong, Jake. I've had Gibson a whole four weeks, and other than one trip to the vet because he ate a necklace, we've been fine."

"A dog is a whole lot different than a baby."

Raine took a step closer, the anger and pain inside her begging for release. "Really? I must have missed the memo on that one. And here I thought all I had to do was invest in a couple packs of pee pads and another dog crate."

"Raine, I didn't mean—"

"Yes you did," she interrupted and held her hands up. "You know what? I'm not doing this with you, Jake." Suddenly she was defeated. "I can't do this. Not with you."

Gibson stared up at the two of them from the coffee table, and even though he wasn't allowed on it, she didn't have the heart or the strength to push him away. In fact she wanted nothing more than to crawl back into bed and go to sleep. She glanced outside into the gray, overcast sky. It was only four in the afternoon. Was it too early to go to bed?

"Hey, I don't want to upset you." Jake sounded as tired as she felt.

But you do.

"Shouldn't you be with your parents? Why are you here, Jake?"

He ruffled the fur behind Gibson's ears, and she watched as her puppy wiggled outrageously, angling to get closer without falling off the table.

He nodded toward the leather bag he'd arrived with, which she now noticed he had set on the edge of the coffee table. "That belonged to Jesse, and after all the craziness with…" She watched him closely as he paused, his eyes on the bag, and for a moment, she knew he wasn't with her anymore. His eyes went darker, his mouth tighter. "It was left behind in Afghanistan and sent back to base, and I knew…Jesse would want you to have it, even if it's taken me forever to get it to you."

He stepped back when she bent forward. Raine's fingers trailed along the bag, lightly touching the strap that was bound with travel tags. "What's inside?" Her voice, barely a whisper, was rough, but she was thankful that she was able to hold it together. She clamped her teeth together as her stomach roiled. She *needed* to keep it together.

At least until Jake left.

"I don't know."

She looked up sharply. "You didn't open it?"

He shook his head but remained silent, his dark, intense eyes shiny. "It's not mine to open."

"Okay," she said finally. "So, what—"

The sharp ring of a cell phone cut her off, and Jake looked startled as he reached into his pocket. He withdrew the phone, glanced at it, and frowned. "Sorry, I gotta take this, hold on."

Raine nodded and took a step back. She scooped Gibson into her arms and ran her fingers through the dog's fur as she pretended not to listen to Jake's side of the conversation.

"Hey." He paused and glanced her way. Raine brushed past him and walked toward the kitchen, though her ears were left somewhere behind her.

"Yeah, I'm done here. I'll pick you up."

His conversation was none of her business, but listening to him tell whoever it was on the other end that he was done with her made Raine feel even less important than before. She couldn't lie. Even as angry and disappointed and upset as she was with him…she still wanted to matter, and his dismissive tone hurt.

There was a long pause as Raine busied herself refilling Gibson's water bowl, even though she'd done it a few hours ago.

"All right. I'll be there in fifteen minutes." He pocketed the cell, and Raine leaned against the counter as he entered the kitchen.

"Who was that?" she asked bluntly.

Jake shoved his hands into the front pockets of his jeans and shrugged. He didn't quite meet her eyes, and she knew something was up.

"A friend."

A friend. She didn't like the way he said it. She didn't like the guarded look that crept into his face. Call it women's intuition, but Raine had a feeling there was more to the story.

"What kind of friend? An army buddy?" she asked casually.

"No."

His dark eyes focused on her with an intensity that made her uncomfortable, and his one-word answer pissed her off more than it should. "You gonna elaborate, Edwards?" she pressed.

"What is this, twenty questions?"

She shrugged and pasted what she hoped was a sweet smile to her face. "No," she said slowly, as if talking to a child. "It's only one." She paused. "Are you going to answer it?"

His face was flushed now and a feeling of unease clutched at her stomach. Which was ridiculous—she didn't give two shits about who he traveled with.

"Lily was at loose ends for the holidays, so I invited her along."

"Lily?" Raine's eyebrow shot up. Since when did Jake have a *Lily* in his life?

She grabbed Gibson's water dish and emptied the water she'd just filled it with. Turning on the tap, she kept her eyes on the bowl and tried to keep her voice neutral. "Your friend is a female?"

"You already did that."

"What?" she snapped and turned so quickly, she spilled water all down the front of her T-shirt.

Jake pointed to the water bowl. "You already filled that."

Raine set it on the counter, her cheeks flushed as she grabbed a cloth and dabbed at the large wet stain on her chest. "You're staying for the holidays?"

He was silent for a few moments. "Yeah, I'm staying for the holidays. Thanksgiving is a big deal to my folks, and with my dad…well, with Dad being sick, it was time."

"And you brought a woman, this Lily person."

"Yeah, I brought a woman. A woman named Lily." Jake's tone was sharp and he cocked his head to the side. "That a problem?"

"Not at all. You can bring whoever the hell you want. Your social life isn't my business." Lips tight, Raine set Gibson's water bowl back in its spot, aware that Jake had moved toward the front door. She followed him out to the porch, wrapping her arms around her body and trying to find some bit of warmth. He stood at the bottom of her steps and glanced up once more.

There was no warmth in his eyes. In fact, there was nothing. Jake Edwards looked as frozen as she felt inside. He glanced at his Jeep. "I should go. It's been…it was nice to see you again, Raine."

Raine's chest was so tight, she was afraid to speak. She nodded and managed to get a few words out. "I'll see you Thursday." And then she turned, disappearing inside the house. She leaned against the heavy oak door, her breaths falling in short, tight spurts as she listened to Jake's Jeep roar to life and eventually fade until nothing but silence surrounded her.

Down the hall, the late afternoon was long in the tooth as new shadows crept over her floors. It was nearly dinnertime and she supposed she should eat…

Instead, Raine locked the door, took her phone off the hook, and with Gibson following behind, climbed into bed without bothering to change. She pulled her heavy lime-green comforter up to her chin, shivering violently as she lay facing the empty pillow beside her.

She heard the wall clock tick from the hallway. The wind rustling branches against the house. The creaks of her wood floors as the house shifted. These were the sounds of her life. The sounds that filled her world.

Eventually she closed her eyes and prayed for sleep.

Chapter 3

WEDNESDAY IT POURED BUCKETS.

All day long, wind and driving water lashed at Raine's windows and shook them in their frames. The world outside was drenched in a palette of gray that consisted of fog and water. It looked like the end of the world from where she huddled beneath the heavy pile of blankets.

Even Gibson preferred to hunker down in her bedroom, and it was an effort to get the dog out of the house to do his duty. Though, if she were to be truthful, it was more of an effort to get her own butt out of bed. But she forced herself because, given the choice, she'd rather not deal with doggie mess in the house.

Wrapping herself in a heavy coat and walking the dog outside would prove to be the extent of her exercise for the day, not that she cared. The funk that had been hanging over her head for months was slowly getting bigger, thicker, and she just didn't have the energy to deal with it.

So she chose not to. As Scarlett O'Hara had once said, tomorrow was another day, and she'd deal with it later. Raine let the cloud of fatigue and cold settle on her shoulders and huddled beneath her covers with the dog as midmorning crept into late afternoon.

She dozed off and on, her body sluggish, her limbs cold. At one point she crawled from beneath the heavy blankets and changed out of her jeans and T-shirt, throwing on a pair of thermal pajamas that drowned her slight frame but offered a modicum of warmth.

She was so damn cold, and no matter what she did, she couldn't seem to get warm. Gibson cuddled with her when he wasn't tearing around the room, his puppy growls and excited barks incredibly annoying. He brought her chew toys, squeaky things that she'd bought him, but she pushed them away or tossed them over the side of the bed. She ignored him for the most part and fell back asleep as the storm continued to shake her windows.

Much later, when the gray shadows outside fell into her room, draping everything in early evening gloom, she woke with a start. Rubbing her eyes, Raine blinked rapidly as she stared at the neon-green display from the clock beside her bed. It read six thirty.

She groaned and stretched her tight muscles. Had she really been in bed all day?

Gibson jumped up beside her and whimpered, his huge dark eyes staring at her solemnly, his chubby tail wagging crazily as he lunged upward, trying his best to lick whatever part of her face he could reach. She grabbed him and held him close, drinking in the puppy smell that still clung to his thick golden fur. For a second he settled in her arms, his cold nose wet against the crook of her neck, his warm body still.

The lump that had sat in the back of her throat since the night before swelled and she nearly choked from the size of it. Tears welled in her eyes as Gibson nuzzled her neck and made those adorable puppy whimpers that she'd come to love.

Had she even fed him?

With a groan, Raine slid from the bed and for the first time became aware of someone pounding on her front door. She pushed a mass of dark hair from her eyes and shuffled down the hall, Gibson following dutifully behind her.

The wooden floors were cold beneath her bare toes, and she shivered as she entered the kitchen and flipped the light switch. The warm glow that fell from the new ceiling fixtures made her wince, as did the increased ferocity of the pounding that came from her foyer.

"Jesus, hold your horses." Irritated, Raine marched down the short hallway and undid the dead bolt. Almost immediately, her door was thrown open, and she took a step back as a gust of wind pushed hard, bringing with it raindrops that hit her face so hard, they felt like ice pellets.

"My God, Raine. I've been calling for hours. Are you all right? I was worried."

Raine stared at her mother and fought the urge to slam the door closed. The woman stood before her dressed from head to toe in vibrant yellow rubber. From the tip of her rain hat and coat to the bottom of her knee-high wellies—the woman looked like a giant rain-slicked condom.

The door closed behind her mother, and Raine watched silently as she shrugged out of her wet gear. She hung her jacket on the coatrack, left her boots on the small area rug in front of the door, and wrung out the long braid that fell over her shoulder. The ends were drenched, and a good amount of water fell onto the rug.

Gloria Delgotto's olive skin was pale, her lips pinched,

and Raine wondered how long she'd been standing on her porch.

"Raine…" her mother started quietly.

Here we go.

"I've been calling all day. Is there something wrong with your phone?"

Raine turned and headed toward the kitchen, mostly out of habit, since she wasn't hungry and had no intention of eating. She grabbed the phone off the counter, aware of her mother's eyes on her, and very carefully, with much exaggeration, placed it back on the cradle. She reached for the kettle and filled it with water.

"Are you having tea, Gloria?" Raine knew it bothered the woman that she refused to call her mother and yet how could she? Gloria had been on another continent for most of Raine's life, taking care of someone else's little girls. She hadn't called Gloria *Mother* or anything like it since she was fifteen and Gloria had left for the Sudan for the tenth time in as many years. Gloria Delgotto was no more a mother than…

Than I'll ever be.

Raine cleared her throat as she turned to Gloria. Vibrant blue eyes stared back at her, though at the moment they were shadowed with what she supposed was concern and maybe more than a little dose of gratitude.

"Tea would be lovely." Gloria moved until she was on the other side of the island and pulled out one of the rich-brown pub stools. She settled onto it and watched in silence as Raine grabbed two mugs and two tea bags from the cupboard.

While waiting for the water to boil, Raine filled Gibson's food dish, feeling a little guilty as the puppy dove in with gusto, his eyes full of appreciation as he wolfed down his meal in between whimpers of delight.

Big fail on her part as she realized not only that she hadn't fed the dog, but that his water dish was bone-dry. A sigh escaped her lips as she filled his stainless-steel bowl. Maybe Jake was right after all.

"Have you eaten today?"

Raine glanced at her mother sharply. "What?"

Gloria's eyes widened and she opened her mouth to speak, but then paused and stared at Raine in silence. Her scrutiny made Raine uncomfortable, and she blushed when she looked down and realized she'd buttoned her pajama top incorrectly. The ends were misaligned and there were gaps between the buttons.

Her hair was a tangled mess, and if she were brutally honest, she'd have to admit that she didn't exactly smell all that good either.

"Raine," her mother said gently. "Have you eaten today?"

Raine ignored her mother and fixed her pajama top before pouring the steaming water into their cups and tossing the tea bags inside. She grabbed milk and sugar and set them on the countertop—if memory served, her mother liked her tea sweet, with loads of milk.

The hot mug felt wonderful in her hands and she took a tentative sip, her eyes lowered, her mind racing for ways to get rid of Gloria as soon as teatime was over. She just didn't have the energy to deal with her, and even if she had…she didn't want to.

"Raine." Her mother's voice was sharper, and with a sigh, she glanced up. She really was too tired for this.

"Look, Gloria, I know you think at some point over

the next little while we're going to miraculously bond or something, but honestly, it's not going to happen, so…"

Gloria took a sip of her tea and set the mug down. "You didn't answer my question."

Irritation sliced through Raine, bringing with it a wave of dizziness. She exhaled slowly and held on to the mug, focusing on the warmth. "What do you care if I've eaten or not?"

Gloria paused. "You look awful, Raine."

"Gee, say what you mean, already." Raine pursed her lips and glared at her mother. Seriously, what gave her the right? "I've come down with a bug."

"Would this bug be called depression?"

Okay, now the woman was getting more than a little too familiar. Who the hell did she think she was, anyway?

"No, it would be called the flu."

"The flu."

"Yep."

"Well, that's not very pleasant. Why don't you let me look after you?" Gloria took another sip, though her eyes never left her daughter.

Raine knew where her mother was going with this, and it wasn't going to work. She'd done just fine without Gloria Delgotto for most of her life, and there was no way in hell she was going to swoop in and play Nurse Nightingale at the eleventh hour because of some guilt trip that had taken thirty years to materialize.

"Nope." Raine shook her head. "It's more like the twenty-four-hour thing. I'm good."

"You don't look good."

The irritation inside Raine exploded, and she slammed her mug onto the counter so hard her mother winced as hot tea sloshed over the side and pooled on the granite.

"Gloria, let me share a secret with you. I don't have to look good for anybody. I live alone, and Gibson doesn't care what the hell I look like as long as I rub his belly now and again and feed him on a regular basis." She leaned closer. "I don't care that I look like crap, and neither should you."

Her mother moved around the island and grabbed a cloth from the kitchen sink. Raine stepped out of the way and watched sullenly as Gloria cleaned up the spilled tea.

"I hear Jake Edwards is back in town."

"Didn't take you long to plug in to the local grapevine."

"Mrs. Lancaster saw him downtown yesterday with some blond woman, and she told me when I stopped in for prayer meeting last night." Gloria faced her daughter. "I know he means a lot to you. Has he been here? Have you seen him?"

Raine clenched her teeth so tightly that pain radiated along her jaw. None of this was her mother's business, but she knew Gloria enough to know she wouldn't leave until she got what she came for. Raine decided to cut to the chase.

"I'm not discussing Jake Edwards—or Jesse for that matter—with you, so if there's anything else…"

"You're not all right."

No shit.

"What I am"—Raine leaned forward and spoke carefully—"is none of your concern."

She saw the pain in her mother's eyes, saw how they filled with the shiny, unmistakable sheen of tears, and still she plunged forward. She couldn't help herself.

"I haven't been your concern for a very, very long time, Gloria, so let's stop pretending. I don't need you."

"I'm your mother and I'm trying—"

"I don't need you to hold my hand. Not now. I needed that a long time ago." Raine gripped the edge of the granite countertop for support. "I needed you when I was eight and Auntie Jeanine's dog was run over by the school bus. I saw the whole thing and cried for days. I needed you when I was in ninth grade and got my period during gym class. Everybody knew, including Liam Atkinson." Raine paused as the old memory washed through her mind. She'd been teased mercilessly by some of the more popular girls, and Liam had dumped her like a hot potato.

"I needed you when Auntie Jeanine got ill. When she was puking every hour on the hour because she couldn't take the chemo. *That's* when I needed you."

"Raine, if I could have been here, I would have, but I couldn't leave the Sudan. Our mission would have fallen apart, and all those children… I couldn't…I couldn't let that happen."

But what about me?

Raine shook her head. "You keep telling yourself that."

Gloria carefully folded the cloth in her hand and set it on the countertop. "You're never going to forgive me."

"Is *that* what this is about? Your need to be forgiven?" *Unbelievable.*

Raine shoved past her mother and paused near the short hall that led to the bedrooms at the back of the house. "You'll never change. Your being here isn't about me. It's not about whether or not I look like shit or that I feel a hundred times worse than I look. It's not about Jesse dying and leaving me alone. Or about Jake, or wanting to know when I ate last. It's not about the fact that my life disappeared and I've never felt so lost or so useless." Gibson rested his butt on her feet and she scooped him into her arms. "Those are the things that a real mother would worry about."

"Raine." Her mother's voice broke.

"I can't do this with you, Gloria. You're only here to ease your conscience, and I can't help you with that." Raine took a second, afraid that she'd break down as the pressure inside her built. "In order to forgive you, I'd have to care, and I'm sorry but I just"—she shrugged—"I just don't."

Gloria's face whitened.

The hole inside Raine yawned open, and she knew she needed to disappear before her mother figured out what a big fat liar she was. "You can let yourself out."

She escaped down the hall, shut herself in the bathroom, and let Gibson down. For several long moments she leaned against the door, eyes closed, breathing erratically, until slowly she straightened and turned on the tap in the bathtub.

It filled with hot, steaming water, and after locking the door, Raine slipped beneath the soothing surface and emptied her mind. Everything drifted away except the silky hot liquid that melted her bones and massaged sore, tight muscles. Nearly an hour later she wrapped herself in a thick, bright pink, terry robe and made her way down the hall back toward her kitchen.

Outside the rain and wind still pounded her home, and inside her soul the conflicting emotions she'd warred with her entire life still raged.

Raine glanced into her kitchen. The lights were on low, casting warmth over the cool, shiny surface of stainless steel and granite. A plate sat in the center of her island, boasting a triple-decker sandwich wrapped in plastic and a note.

There's chili in the microwave. Homemade from Dante's Grill.

Mom.

She stared at the sandwich until it blurred, and she sniffled loudly as one solitary tear wove its way down her cheek. With Gibson running around her feet, she settled into one of the pub chairs and, though she wasn't hungry, reached for the plate.

Chapter 4

THE SMELL OF TURKEY GREETED JAKE AS HE MADE HIS way downstairs. It was barely six in the morning, yet he'd been up for hours. Sleep and Jake Edwards were pretty much at odds these days. Hell, most nights he dreaded closing his eyes, because he couldn't deal with the images burned into the back of his brain. It was why he worked out like a dog, pushing his body to the point of exhaustion in the hope that when he finally relented and hit the sack, his mind would shut off too.

But even then it was a gamble. How many nights had he been ripped from sleep, drenched in sweat with the smell of fear in his nostrils and the taste of agony on his tongue?

With a sigh, he ran his hand over the rough stubble along his jaw. As an Army Ranger, his mind and body had been honed into a weapon that worked with little or no sleep, yet sometimes, he'd have given his left arm for one undisturbed night in the sack. For some small measure of peace.

"Not today," he muttered.

Outside, the early November morning still darkened the large bay windows in the dining room. The sun came late to these parts of Michigan at this time of year, and with storm clouds still lingering, it was darker than usual.

Jake cleared the bottom step out of habit and avoided the squeak with ease, a rare smile claiming his mouth as he did so. How many times had he and Jesse come home way too late or way too drunk and struggled to avoid the loose bottom step as well as the second one from the top?

He shook his head. More times than he could remember.

There was a soft glow from the kitchen and he paused, watching his mother work. She was surrounded by mixing bowls and a host of ingredients, her dark hair pulled off her face with a clip, and a smudge of flour on her nose. She worked carefully, methodically, with the same ease she put into everything, as she kneaded the dough and stretched it out across the large wood surface.

There were new lines around her mouth and eyes, carved deeper into her flesh than he'd have liked, and he supposed he had a hand in them as well. On top of his brother's death, there was his father's illness to deal with. The prostate cancer had been caught early, but still, it was a worry. In a crap year that had seen him disappoint many, his mother was the one person he wished he'd been stronger for.

Liar. There was also Raine…

She looked up suddenly and smiled. "Coffee's on, honey."

Jake dropped a kiss on her cheek and poured them both a cup before settling across from her. "Bird smells good."

Marnie nodded. "Sure does."

"What did you name it this year?"

Her hands stilled as her smile widened, and for a moment he fell backward into a pile of bittersweet memories.

"Mommy, I don't like Victoria. That's a sissy name for a sissy bird, right Jesse?"

His brother ignored Jake, angling closer for the real prize—the one cooling on the counter next to their mother.

"Now you listen to me, young man. Victoria is far from a sissy name. In fact, your great-grandmother's name was Victoria, and though the two of you don't remember her, she was a very, very strong woman."

"I still don't like it." He turned to Jesse, who was perched at the counter, reaching for the fresh baked pie and the flattened crust sprinkled with brown sugar and cinnamon. "You got any ideas?"

Jesse snuck a piece of crust, stuffed it into his mouth, and thought about it for a moment. "Why don't we call it Vicki?"

"No way, dodo head, that's even more sissy than Victoria." Jake scrunched his face together, mind whirling with all the possibilities. "I got it!" He high-fived Jesse and beamed up at his mother. "We'll call the turkey Vic."

"Jake? Did you hear what I said?"

The pictures in his mind faded quickly, the colors bleeding into gray like the fog that drifted beyond the window. Only the echoes of voices remained, long-dead whispers of another time and place, and he shook his head in an effort to clear them.

"Sorry, what was that?"

His mother stared at him for several long moments, her eyes shadowing in the kind of pain he knew all too well. She whispered softly, "Franklin."

"Franklin?" Jake nodded slowly. "I like it."

"Good." She smiled once more and continued to knead her dough. "Good, I'm glad."

"How's Dad this morning?"

"He sleeps a little later these days, but he's doing all right." Her eyebrows swept low. "He's going to be okay."

Jake took another swig of coffee and then slid to his feet. "Is there anything I can help you with?" It didn't feel right to sit and watch her do all the work.

Marie glanced toward the baking pans behind him. "You can grease those for me, so I can get these buns to rising."

They worked in silence, mother and son, and he'd just finished greasing the last pan when she cleared her throat. It was a subtle, careful hint, but he knew it for what it was. She wanted to talk, and judging by the serious glint in her eye, she sure as hell didn't want to talk about Franklin the turkey.

She poured them each a second mug of coffee, set the cream and sugar in front of him, and sat down.

"So," she began.

Cold sweat ran down Jake's neck, and for a second, the hard fist of pain twisted inside him. He concentrated on doling out the required sugar and cream, dreading what was coming. They'd never discussed Afghanistan, and he was sure she, as a mother, wanted to know exactly what had happened to Jesse, not what had been in some official report. She'd want to know the circumstance…the cause and effect.

Jake just didn't know if he was man enough to tell her the truth.

She leaned in close, her eyes earnest. "You have to tell me about this girl you've brought home."

Jake swallowed a mouthful of coffee and wiped the corner of his mouth as he grabbed a muffin from the basket in front of him.

Shit, damn, and fuck. Okay. This wasn't what he had expected. He thought after he'd escaped the night before with only a few questions, there wouldn't be any more.

Miscalculation on his part. He began to pick off the raisins, contemplating his reply, but his mother beat him to it.

"She's…" Marnie began and then paused as if searching for the right words. "She seems…nice."

Jake smiled at that. Leave it to his mother to sugar-coat it. Lily St. Clare wasn't *nice*. She wasn't warm and fuzzy, and she certainly didn't inspire thoughts of puppies and rainbows. He took a bite of his muffin and spoke. "Lily is an acquired taste."

Actually, she was more than an acquired taste. The woman had more walls around her than anyone he knew, except maybe his buddy Mackenzie. Lily was from old Boston money, the kind that breeds anxiety, paranoia, and plain old-fashioned craziness. She'd told Jake once that it was a direct result of the Southern blood that had infiltrated the family back in the 1800s. There was some sort of scandal, and the bloodline had been tainted.

Or at least that's what she'd been told.

Yes, Lily St. Clare appeared as cold and brittle as the crisp blond facade she presented to the world, but Jake knew better. At a time when he'd been drowning in darkness, on the edge of free-falling down endless bottles of tequila, she'd been the one to pull him out. She understood pain. And loss.

They were two of a kind, with skeletons rattling hard and scars beneath the flesh that only X-ray vision could see.

"Where did you meet her?"

Jake paused, swiped the mess he'd made on the counter into the palm of his hand, and rose. "I met her in a hospital in Texas."

He felt the weight of his mother's eyes on him as he tossed the crumbs into the garbage and then turned, his hip leaning against the edge of the sink as he contemplated his next words. "Her brother was in my unit. He was hurt in the incident that, uh…" Jake cleared his throat roughly, hating the weakness—the tightness—inside him. "He was hurt in the incident that took Jesse."

"And he was brought back to Texas?"

He nodded. "Yes. I'd sit with him every day for hours at a time, just shooting the shit, talking nonstop." Pain pressed hard into his chest and he exhaled. "Hell, I talked so much, I got sick of hearing my own damn voice, so when this blonde showed up and took over, well, let's just say we bonded in that small, sterile hospital room."

His mother rinsed out her mug. "So are the two of you…" She picked at an invisible crumb and swept it into the sink. "I mean, you never said anything when I showed Lily to the guest room last night, but you're a grown man, and if the two of you are serious…"

Jake smiled—a full-on, wide-eyed smile—and cocked his head to the side. "What are you trying to say, Ma? That it's okay if I want to score me some action in your house?"

"What?" Marnie's eyes widened and she blushed a pretty shade of pink that just about made his day. Hell, it made his whole week.

He couldn't help himself. "Because I'd be fine with that, if Lily and I were involved, but we're not, so"—he patted his mother's shoulders—"you can relax. She's just a friend who was at loose ends for the holidays and I didn't want her to be alone, so I figured the more the merrier. I didn't think you'd mind."

"No, of course not. No one should ever be alone on Thanksgiving." His mother's forehead furled and she bit her lip as if contemplating her next question. He could have saved her the bother, because he sure as hell knew where she was headed, but he loved watching her.

"Is she really…" Marnie found another invisible crumb, which she promptly took care of. "Well, your father told me she was on one of those silly reality television shows. Is that true?"

Jake shook his head. "No. That would be her sister." He gave his mother a quick hug. "I'm going to head out for a run before I shower."

"All right, honey. Dress warm, you don't want to get a chill. And Jake?"

Jake paused in the doorway. "Yeah?"

"How is Lily's brother?"

His hand fisted at his side as all the tension inside him reared up and grabbed hold as tight as it could. "Blake is still in the hospital." He paused as an image of the young soldier flashed before his eyes. Hair as blond as Lily's, matted through with blood and gore. "He's in a coma, and the doctors aren't sure he'll ever wake up."

"Oh." His mother turned and began to fill her pans with the dough she'd kneaded earlier. "I'm sorry to hear that."

"Yeah." There was nothing to say. The lightness of the morning was gone.

Jake grabbed a jacket from the closet in the laundry room and less than a minute later ran outside, inhaling great gulps of fresh, cold air as the wind continued to howl and buffet the area. He followed the path that ran alongside the lake and after a while was able to clear his mind and concentrate on putting one foot in front of the other.

He ran hard and fast, slipping through the dense bush that carpeted most of his parents' property, and though there wasn't any conscious thought, he wasn't surprised when nearly an hour later he paused there at the edge of the forest along Raine's driveway. He was drenched in sweat, his body hot and loose, and small puffs of mist fell from his nostrils as he watched the house in silence.

He inhaled sharply as the front door swung open and Raine appeared on the porch. It was past daybreak, though the cloud of gray still held sway, and she stood in the shadows that fell along the front of her house. Carefully she let a wiggling ball of fur loose and crossed her arms as she watched her puppy slide down the steps and rummage around the front yard in an effort to find the perfect place to pee.

God, she looked incredibly frail, and the big robe she wore did nothing but emphasize the fact.

The dog ran in circles and barked crazily for several minutes while Raine hugged herself and shivered in the early morning dampness. Jake shook his head. She was going to get sick if she didn't get her butt back into the warmth of the house soon. He took a step forward but something stopped him. What was the point?

They'd only fight. It was what they did. They pretty much disagreed about everything.

Suddenly Gibson stopped barking and turned his head in Jake's direction, his tail wagging, nose sniffing madly. Jake froze, hoping the shadows between the trees were deep and dark. He had no desire to be caught lurking in the bush like some deranged stalker by a ten-pound bag of fur.

Raine turned in his direction and his eyes locked on to the mess of dark hair that tumbled around her pale face. She pushed it out of the way and called for the dog, her voice falling like dead stones. The puppy yelped at him one more time before whirling around and running for his master. Raine opened the door, and with one last glance around, disappeared inside the house.

Jake let out a long, tortured breath and turned abruptly, his mind a mess of jumbled, half-formed thoughts. With renewed vigor he tore through the brush, needing to push his body to the limit. Needing to think about something other than the only thing that had been on his mind for months.

For years.

How fucking pathetic. After all this time he was still a mess when it came to the one woman he could never have. The only woman he'd ever loved.

His brother's widow.

————

Marnie Edwards covered her pans with tea towels and arranged them neatly on the counter. The buns would need a few hours to rise before baking, and for the moment she was done. Franklin smelled wonderful, and after basting the large turkey, she shoved him back in the oven and reduced the heat. Steven was still in bed, and for moment she relished the quiet. It had been a tough few months with her husband in treatment, and she found herself craving alone time, or rather time for herself.

She grabbed another cup of coffee and wandered into the family room, which was just off the kitchen. It was a large open space and in a house of many rooms was the one place everyone gathered. It was homey, colored in buttercream yellow and sage green, and boasted an impressive wall of glass that brought the outdoors inside. With the lake glistening a few hundred feet away, it was her favorite spot.

She tucked herself into a large overstuffed chair that she'd had reupholstered many times. It was one of the first pieces of furniture she and Steven had bought, and though the sofa that had come with it was long gone, this chair had always been special, the one she felt most comfortable in, and she refused to give it up.

She'd fed her babies in this chair. Read to them. Cuddled them. And loved them.

She sank back into the soft, caramel fabric and closed her eyes. The coffee mug in her hands provided a bit of warmth, but she drew a thick throw blanket across her hips and tried to relax. But it was so hard.

With one son lost to her and the other drowning in pain, Marnie's insides were all twisted. She'd heard Jake in the night and had followed in his footsteps as he disappeared into the basement.

At first she'd thought he couldn't sleep and was in the mood for TV—she had almost joined him—but then she realized he'd gone into the exercise room. She'd sat on the top step and listened, arms crossed over her chest, mouth trembling as the clang from the weights echoed into the silence. Over and over...and over.

She'd winced at the grunts of pain as her baby worked out like a demon, and her heart broke a little more with each harsh echo.

It was then that she knew there wasn't a thing she could do for him. Gone were the days when she could wrap Jake into her arms, kiss his boo-boo, and make it all better. If only life were that simple. If only childhood remedies worked on adults.

Her world would never be all right again, but there had to be hope in there somewhere, or else what was the point of it all? Why would God take one of her sons and leave the other broken?

The front door slammed shut and she jumped, nearly spilling coffee all over herself as she straightened in the chair. Jake was back from his run.

She listened as he tossed his dirty clothes into the laundry room and at least one shoe banged against the side of the washing machine, followed by a muffled curse. It brought a bittersweet smile to her face and a deluge of memories that were a little less painful to remember than they had been even a few weeks ago.

It was then that Marnie Edwards realized something. Maybe she wasn't so helpless after all. Maybe she could help her son and, if she was lucky, help herself and Steven as well. There *was* hope all around, if you knew where to look. Jake was hope. He was here and he was alive. Hope lived inside him, buried beneath layers of pain—he just didn't know it yet.

She thought of the woman upstairs, a woman he claimed was just a friend, and her mind wandered, thinking of all the possibilities. Was this Lily St. Clare the key? He cared enough about her to bring her back to Crystal

Lake with him. Surely that meant something more than "just friends." Maybe this Lily was Jake's hope.

A plan began to form in her head and excitement rolled in her belly for the first time in months, though she bit her lip as she sprang from the chair. She'd need help from someone who cared about Jake as much as she did, and though her husband Steven was as concerned for their child as she was, Marnie knew he'd never agree to what she had in mind.

Besides, he had to focus on getting well, not worry about his wife's plan for their son.

No, she needed a much more devious kind of mind. A feminine kind of mind. As Marnie headed back into the kitchen to throw her pies in the oven, she smiled, her steps light for the first time in months. She knew the perfect accomplice.

And she was coming for dinner.

Chapter 5

THE TUBE OF MASCARA WAS MORE THAN A LITTLE goopy, but it would have to do, because it was all she had. Raine squinted into the mirror and applied it as best she could, taking care not to leave any clumps behind. It had been ages since she'd taken the time to do her makeup. Ages since she'd worn anything other than jeans or sweats. What was the point? Anything more complicated than spandex and cotton was more of a bother than anything else.

But it was Thanksgiving, after all, and the Edwardses loved to make a big deal out of the holidays. This year, with Steven's recovery and Jake's return, Marnie would no doubt go all-out. It was a distraction she needed, as well as a celebration.

She twirled the mascara wand inside the canister and applied one last coat. Damned if she was going to show up and meet Jake's new girl looking anything less than spectacular, and though it might be silly of her to feel that way, she wasn't about to overanalyze her feelings. Besides, there was nothing wrong with wanting to look good.

She stood back and stared at her reflection critically. Nothing wrong at all.

She'd successfully covered her pale complexion with a light dusting of bronzer and blush. With a touch of smoky shadow—along with the goopy mascara—her eyes had a dramatic, exotic look to them. A whisper of gloss on her lips and she was good to go.

She'd thought of flat-ironing her hair, but realized the ends would look jagged, a direct result of her dumb idea to cut it herself. So she left it to wave around her face and angled her head for a better look. She supposed the waves softened the more pronounced lines of her cheekbones and jaw.

She tucked the one piece that always curled the wrong way behind her ear and sighed. What the hell had she been thinking? Answer? She hadn't.

Shit, Raine, the next time you're feeling blue, do not pick up the scissors. Cutting hair isn't the answer. Reach for the wine bottle instead. Wise words from her friend Maggie.

Raine dabbed a hint of Escape behind her ears and searched her closet for her black Pradas. They'd been an extravagant impulse purchase the last time she'd been to Detroit, but damn, they looked good and added to her height. She tossed them in her bag along with a pair of flats, and she was ready.

Raine stood in front of the long mirror that hung on the back of her bedroom door and studied herself with a careful eye. She'd lost some weight in the last few months for sure, but the padded bra did wonders for her bustline, and the dress she'd donned didn't look awful.

The bodice was a sleeveless boat neck in ice-blue silk, while the dark navy skirt clung to her body and fell a few inches above the knee. She smoothed the soft fabric over her hips, and for a second her fingers faltered as an image of strong male hands over hers flashed in her mind. She inhaled sharply, felt the heat and the whisper of a caress. An ache so intense it nearly brought her to her knees spread through her body, and a whimper fell from her lips as she struggled to keep it together.

Her hands lingered at her waist, and her vision blurred as the emptiness inside her expanded into fragments of hurt, despair, and longing. She bit her lip. She couldn't let it linger. She knew from previous experience that if she did, it would consume her and she'd never make it out of the house.

Gibson chose that moment to come barreling into her bedroom, barking happily at her feet, and it was enough to break the spell. Raine exhaled a long, shuddering breath and ran her fingers across his soft back, digging in slightly as she murmured, "You ready, fella?"

The dog took off for the foyer, Raine following in his steps, and after she slipped into a pair of boots, she grabbed her purse off the hall table along with a bottle of wine and headed out into the crisp, cool air. The rain had finally stopped earlier that morning, though it was still cold and damp. Dead leaves scattered her yard, their wet carcasses dressing the grass and pathway in a blanket of gray-brown sludge.

She picked her way toward her car, avoiding mud and slimy leaves, though she was pretty sure Gibson wasn't as careful. Not that it mattered. She didn't exactly drive a limo. She let him into the backseat, where he promptly turned in a circle before settling onto an old, ratty blanket.

The car was an ancient Volkswagen she'd bought when she was eighteen after working two entire summers at The Hut, a local ice cream joint. Jesse had hated the damn thing and refused to even sit in it, referring to it as a Barbiemobile. She smiled at the thought, though it quickly faded as she glanced toward the passenger seat. It was as empty as it ever was, the moss-colored vinyl seat held together with duct tape. She'd thought of getting it repaired, but then, what was the point? No one ever sat in it.

With a sigh she reversed out of her driveway and headed toward the Edwardses'.

The trip didn't take long, as her in-laws basically lived around the corner—though out here it meant they lived down the lake. She followed the twisting road, catching sight of the water through the trees to her left, and ten minutes later pulled up next to Jake's Jeep. She noticed another car parked on the other side of it and frowned.

A tattered bumper sticker with an overly religious slogan—Raise Your Hand for Jesus—was barely discernible from age, but it sure as hell looked like her mother's compact sedan.

Great. It would be just like Marnie to invite Gloria for dinner. The woman had a heart of gold and a soft spot for anyone and everything.

Gibson yapped happily and followed her up the steps toward the front door. She opened it and whispered for the dog to sit, but of course Gibson was like any other man she knew. His selective hearing kicked in and he ignored her completely, running madly toward the back of the house, where the kitchen was.

Where the food was.

And from the sounds of the voices…where all the people were.

Raine picked out Jake's low timbre immediately, and

as she slipped off her boots and tucked her feet into her heels, she wondered how the hell she was going to get through this day. Between Jake, his lady friend, and her mother, Gloria, she just might end up bat-shit crazy.

Gibson must have found the humans—Marnie's squeal of delight echoed down the hall—and that brought a smile to Raine's face. Her mother-in-law adored the puppy and had insisted she bring him for the afternoon.

"There you are!"

Raine had just hung up her coat when she turned and was immediately enveloped by her father-in-law's tight embrace. Steven Edwards was a tall, burly bear of a man who had no trouble showing emotion. A man of contradictions, he wasn't afraid to wear his heart on his sleeve because he didn't give two shits about what anyone thought of him. He lived for his family and loved his wife with blind devotion, but when it came to business, he was known as a ball breaker.

"You look beautiful." He stood back and nodded—his pale eyes so much like Jesse's, crinkled around the corners. His large, open face was a tad gaunt from his surgery. And though he too had lost a bit of weight, the man was still sturdy. They stared at each for several seconds, her eyes misting at the pain reflected in his. Jesse was gone, but his presence was still larger than life, and she knew Steven missed his son terribly.

He cleared his throat. "Can I take that?"

She handed him the bottle of wine. "You look pretty handsome yourself."

"Bah." He waved his hand. "I look like crap, but I'm feeling better."

"Raine, we were just going to send Jake after you."

Marnie Edwards joined her husband, a smile on her face. The woman was small, a few inches over five feet, with a slight frame. She always looked put together and today was no different. Her simple cream dress, a Dior by the look of it, was fabulous, and her dark hair, perfectly kept and shiny, curved expertly against her jaw. Red and black jewelry complemented the ensemble.

"Well, I'm here, so there's no need to send the cavalry."

"Come on in, we're just having drinks, and dinner is ready when we are." Marnie threaded her arm through Raine's. "I hope you don't mind, but I asked your mother to join us."

"No." She smiled tightly. "I don't mind at all." They entered the kitchen and turned toward the family room, which was to the left.

Gloria sat on a deep leather sofa the color of cured tobacco, a tremulous smile on her face. She wore a simple black dress with a single strand of pearls that she rolled between her fingers nervously. Her long hair was pulled off her face and pinned loosely on top of her head. She looked elegant and beautiful and every bit the mother that Raine used to dream about. But those days were long gone.

The woman on the sofa was a stranger.

Raine nodded at Gloria but remained silent as she glanced at Jake, who was a few feet away, near the wall of glass.

He stood in the corner by the fireplace, hands shoved into the pockets of faded jeans, expression guarded as he looked in her direction. His wide shoulders were dressed in a slate-gray-blue sweater with a white collared shirt beneath it. His stance said casual, but the darkness in his eyes and the firm set to his mouth screamed anything but...

What happened to you Jake? What happened to us?

Gibson sat at his feet, wagging his tail as if Jake Edwards was his entire world, and a shot of resentment rifled through Raine.

Traitor dog.

"You must be Raine."

Startled, she tore her gaze from Jake and turned around. A tall, willowy, blonde thing—one who belonged on the pages of a fashion magazine, not standing in the middle of the Edwardses' kitchen—had spoken. As if the Red Sea itself had parted for her, the woman stood alone, and Raine swore that the only beam of sunlight to appear all day broke through the clouds and filtered in through the windows—just for one second—to halo her head in a ring of golden glory.

Crystal-blue eyes stared at her from a face that could only be described as perfection. Cold perfection, mind you, but flawless nonetheless. It looked as though a zit had never had the audacity to grace her chin. Long hair hung in perfectly coiled waves down her right shoulder—artfully arranged that way, no doubt. The dress she wore was stunning, a perfectly molded black creation with a plunging neckline that showed off every curve—and the curves, they were substantial. The woman was a cross between Marilyn Monroe and Barbie, truly every man's dream.

Apparently, Jake's dream.

Raine disliked her on sight, which might not have been fair, but there it was.

The blonde arched an eyebrow, as if sensing Raine's

feelings, and a smile stole over her features—one that showed off plump *Playboy* lips and a row of perfectly straight, perfectly white teeth. Fake. Fake and fake.

She looked familiar, and a tingle of apprehension wove its way down Raine's spine.

"Oh, my goodness. Where are my manners?" Marnie tugged her forward and nodded. "Raine, this is Lily, Jake's friend."

The woman—Lily—held her hand toward Raine as if she were a queen and Raine was the damn maid. She ignored the hand, and the smile on Lily's face widened like the one on the Cheshire Cat from *Alice in Wonderland*. She withdrew her scarlet-tipped fingers and bingo, a lightbulb lit up in Raine's mind.

You've got to be kidding me.

She glanced over at Jake. What the hell was he thinking?

"Lily…your last name is St. Clare, if I'm not mistaken?" Raine asked sweetly as she accepted a glass of pinot noir from her mother-in-law.

The blonde's eyes narrowed at Raine's tone; a slight tightening pulled at her mouth, but it was gone in an instant. She nodded coolly. Diamonds sparkled at her ears, peeking through the silken sheets of hair, and they shimmered like raindrops breaking on water.

"Of the Boston St. Clares?" Raine added.

Again, another tight nod. The woman was uncomfortable. Good.

Raine smiled toward Jake once more. "I can't wait to hear how our very own Jake Edwards from lil' old Crystal Lake managed to hook up with one of the St. Clare sisters." She paused. "So which one are you anyway? The one who's famous or the one who's infamous?"

Lily was silent for a moment, her eyes glassy like newly frozen ice. Raine held her gaze. She wasn't a pushover, some backwoods country girl in awe of the big-city trust-fund baby.

"Neither." Lily didn't elaborate and Raine pursed her lips wondering…just how many St. Clare sisters were there?

"Well, then." Marnie spoke quickly as if sensing the tension and nodded toward the dining room. "Franklin's ready, so let's eat!"

Raine watched Steven and her mother, Gloria, follow in Marnie's steps, while Lily glanced toward Jake, nodded slightly, and then followed suit.

Jake joined her in the kitchen, eyes hard and mouth set into a firm line that told her a bunch of stuff she didn't want to know.

While she'd spent the last year and a half worrying about him, he'd been doing God knows what with Lily St. Clare. *Of the Boston St. Clares*. He *cared* about this woman, and for him to bring her back to Crystal Lake for a family holiday, well, that meant he cared for her a whole hell of a lot.

She glared at him, hoping he could see the anger she felt inside. He'd chosen Lily St. Clare over his family.

Over me.

The thought was selfish and snuck in quicker than she could blink it away.

Jake leaned close, his breath a warm whisper against her cheek, though the steel in his voice was as cold and hard as an arctic blast. "Don't be a bitch. She's not what you think."

"How would you know what I think?" Raine grabbed

his hand, wanting to pull him aside and tell him exactly what was on her mind, but all conscious thought fled. The only thing that settled inside her brain was how warm he felt and how rough the pads of his fingers were. Heat poured into her like lava rippling over the side of a volcano.

It was the kind of heat that made you dizzy. The kind that made you crazy.

She yanked her hand from his as if she'd been burned, her body trembling, her breath caught in her throat.

Jake's face whitened. "Hey, I'm sorry. I didn't mean to get in your face…" Jake's voice trailed off as he stared down at her. He ran his fingers through the waves that curled near his collar. "Shit, Raine. I…"

"I'm good," she said tersely. "Let's eat."

She pushed past him, escaped to the dining room, and slid into the seat beside Steven, with Gloria to her right, only too aware of the empty chair at the end of the table. Her eyes rested on it for a moment, and then she focused on one of the biggest centerpieces she'd ever seen. It was a cornucopia filled with fresh flowers, gourds, and baby pumpkins, yet it was nearly lost among the huge assortment of food.

God, there was so much food. The smell nauseated her and Raine quickly topped up her wineglass, ignoring the little voice inside her head—the one that said slow the hell down. She was staring down the barrel of the Thanksgiving from hell, and if a little extra fortification was needed, then so be it.

Because Lord knows, it was.

Gloria kept trying to make small talk, all the while piling more food onto Raine's plate as if she weren't going to notice. Across the table, Lily studied her covertly from her spot beside Jake, and Raine wasn't sure what made her more anxious—Lily's all-knowing gaze or Jake's dark, brooding glare.

The next hour passed in a haze of conversation that Raine would never remember. Steven and Marnie were gracious as usual, making polite small talk with Lily while including Gloria as much as they could. But Jake was quiet, his dark eyes never far from Raine, and she tried like hell to ignore him.

Just as she tried to ignore the empty chair at the end of the table. It was a huge reminder that she didn't belong to anyone anymore.

She was well on her way to finishing her third glass of wine—or maybe it was her fourth—when Marnie asked for her help in the kitchen. Something about the pumpkin pie and the triple-chocolate trifle, and Raine was only too happy to oblige. Anything to get away from her mother and the blond Barbie...and Jake.

She just wished her stomach would stop rolling and that Marnie would turn down the heat. It was hot...so, so hot. She grabbed a cloth, ran it under the cold water, and then pressed it against her forehead. Her hair was damp, the short length of it curling madly against her neck.

She must look like a wilted flower.

"Raine," Marnie whispered as if afraid anyone would hear her.

Raine exhaled slowly and turned from the sink. "Yes?" Her heart raced and it took more than a little effort for her to remain still...to keep her head up and not wobble on her four-inch Pradas. Damn, she *knew* better. She was a lightweight when it came to wine.

Marnie snuck a look into the dining room and clasped her hands together. "I need to ask you a favor."

Raine dabbed the wet cloth against her throat, not caring that large drops fell down the top of her dress, staining the silk. She leaned back against the sink and concentrated. "A favor? Sure," she said carefully, her tongue thick. "Anything, Marnie."

"Isn't it wonderful to have Jake back with us?"

Raine nodded. "Peachy." The room spun a little bit, but she gripped the edge of the counter and managed to stay upright.

Marnie gave her a strange look. "Are you all right?"

"Never been better." She hiccupped and pressed the cloth against her cheeks once more.

"You just looked a little peaked, dear."

Raine didn't say anything, mostly because she was concentrating on her stomach.

Marnie cleared her throat and spoke quietly. "I think that this Lily person means a lot more to Jake than he's let on, and…"

"You think?" She'd gone for a sarcastic retort, but it was lost on Marnie.

"I know you've got a few things to work out with Jake. I know he upset you when he left, but I'm hoping you can put that aside. I'm hoping you will help me with something."

Oh God, Marnie needed to get to the point, because Raine didn't think she could stand much longer. She padded the wet cloth along her forehead and down her neck once more and hoped the floor would stop moving beneath her feet.

Maybe she should have switched her Pradas for her flats.

"It's hot. Don't you think it's hot?" Damn, she could barely concentrate. And she definitely should be wearing flats.

"Oh." Marnie looked surprised. "It's...normal, I think, but I can check the thermostat if you like."

Raine nodded. "That would be good."

A surge of laughter drew their attention to the dining room, and Marnie moved closer. She clasped Raine's hands within her own. "I think that this Lily could be just what Jake needs, don't you?"

Sure, like a bad rash.

The room was still spinning, just off its axis by a bit, but if she could just get some fresh air, she'd be good. "Um, I'm not following." She paused. "Maybe we should open a window."

"Can you talk to him? About Lily? Maybe encourage him to…"

The rest of Marnie's words were lost, because she was speaking way too fast and whispering way too low. Or maybe it was because Raine had had one too many glasses of wine and just couldn't listen and stand at the same time.

Her belly rolled once more and sweat broke out along her forehead. "Marnie, just tell me what you want and I'll do it, but I really need to sit down."

Marnie paused for a moment. "You and Jake have always been so close, like best friends." She smiled a sad, wistful smile. "At one time, I even thought…"

The white noise that buzzed around her head receded as Raine stared at her mother-in-law. "Thought what?"

Marnie's eyes softened. "I thought you and Jake would end up together."

"Jake and me?" Raine was silent as shock rolled through her. "Why would you…why would you think that?"

Marnie smiled softly and shrugged. "I guess it was in the way you two always fought and then made up. Reminded me of Steven and myself, but what do I know? You and Jesse proved me wrong." She licked her lips nervously as she glanced toward the dining room once more. "The one thing that I *do* know is that you care about him and I know you want him to be happy. I think this Lily could be his happy."

Raine really didn't like where this conversation was headed. She frowned and shook her head. "You want me to encourage Jake to hook up with Lily St. Clare?"

"Well, that makes it sound kind of dirty, but yes." Marnie smiled. "I need your help. He can't see what's right in front of him."

Raine stared at her mother-in-law for several long moments and tried like hell to keep it together. What was Marnie thinking? Lily St. Clare was all wrong for Jake. She opened her mouth, intending to tell it like it is, but then her stomach heaved and it was too much.

She whirled around, leaned over the sink, and scraped her hair out of the way just in time.

Then promptly lost all four glasses of wine.

Chapter 6

"EDWARDS, WOULD IT BE TOO MUCH TO ASK FOR YOU TO drive a little slower?"

Jake rounded a sharp curve on Lakeshore Road and glanced toward the passenger side of his Jeep. "Thought you were passed out."

Raine struggled into a seating position and shot a dark look his way. "I wasn't passed out."

"No," he countered. "The snores told me you were wide awake."

"I don't snore," she muttered, and her eyes narrowed slightly before she glanced over her shoulder. "Where's Gibson?" She exhaled loudly and then collapsed back onto the seat.

"Mom kept the dog. She thought you might not want the distraction 'cause you're shit-faced drunk."

"I am not"—she hiccupped and swore—"drunk."

"Keep telling yourself that, sweet cheeks, but from what I saw, you were guzzling pinot noir like it was grape juice."

He knew how much she hated the nickname but couldn't stop himself. Earlier she'd pulled away from him as if he had leprosy, and the sting of that one action had pretty much ruined his night.

"Whatever," she muttered.

Jake maneuvered the Jeep up her driveway until he stopped a few feet from her front door. He cut the engine and stared up at the house, his gut churning with an anger that had burned inside for hours. It was irrational, this anger, and one he didn't want to analyze too closely. But it was there nonetheless. Christ, he'd been home a little over twenty-four hours and nothing had changed.

She still got under his skin. Still made him ache and burn. But then, had he really expected it to go away?

His jaw clenched. "We're here."

"I can see that."

His brow furled even more. He turned to Raine, his gaze rolling over her slight form. She was pressed against the door, her head lowered, her mad mess of dark curls damp against her neck. She'd refused her coat back at his parents—*naturally*—because contrary to what bullshit her brain was feeding her, she *was* piss drunk.

Her dress rode up her thighs, leaving way too much leg on display, and he swallowed thickly as he looked away from the dark crevice between them. Her feet were bare, and the insanely high heels she'd worn were on the floor, where she'd slipped them off.

Vulnerability rolled off her in waves, and his chest tightened painfully. What the hell was he going to do about her?

He'd left Crystal Lake because he knew he couldn't be around Raine without going crazy. The woman had pushed every button he owned for as long as he could remember. And though it killed him, he'd convinced himself that Jesse's dying wish didn't make sense. Raine didn't need him. She'd always been a firecracker who traveled her own road and had no problem being on her own. Christ, most of her marriage had been solo, and last year he'd told himself she'd be fine without him hanging around.

And yet…she wasn't fine. Jesse had been right. Raine was a mess.

His gaze lingered on the blue silk top, there, where her collarbone met the hollow of her neck. Her pulse rose and fell rapidly, and for several seconds he couldn't look away as the wall of emotion inside him threatened to bust open.

He closed his eyes, his jaw still tight. He remembered the damn dress. Remembered the last time she'd worn it. He remembered what it felt like to hold her.

He and Jesse had been home on leave just in time for their cousin Katelyn's wedding. It had been a hot August evening, one filled with the promise of rain and the chaotic song of the cicadas.

He'd taken Tammie George, a local girl and one of his go-to dates, along to the wedding. The four of them had ripped it up but good. Of course by the end of the evening, Jesse was done and Tammie had had one too many beers. They'd been about to leave when the band had broken into some crazy song—an Irish jig, if he remembered correctly—and Raine had claimed him as her dance partner.

How could he say no to her?

The two of them had danced like there was no one watching, and he would have danced with her all night. Would have held her close and inhaled her scent. Taken her home and made love to her.

But she wasn't his.

And now…now the world was a mess, and some of the things that should have changed never had. Damn, but he'd thought the pain would lessen with time. Instead, it seemed to have sharpened.

Jake sighed and ran his fingers across the stubble along his jaw. "Let's get you in the house."

A groan was his answer, and he slipped from the Jeep, slamming his door shut as a fresh wave of anger rolled over him. The darkness inside him was pressing hard and he clenched his hands in an effort to squelch it. He couldn't afford to let it win, because the fallout would be nasty and Raine would take the brunt. And damned if he'd do anything more to hurt the woman than he had already done.

He took a second and got hold of his emotions. The air was chilled with the smell of snow on the breeze. He exhaled twin plumes of mist as he stared up at the house, which was in darkness—not even the porch light was on. Jake glanced around, suddenly very much aware of just how isolated she was out here. As far as he knew, she didn't even have an alarm system. Any kind of sick bastard could be lurking in the shadows.

Jake shook his head, his thoughts darkening. It wasn't right that she was out here alone. Hell, it wasn't right that she was alone.

Damn you, Jesse.

He yanked the door open and cursed as Raine pitched forward. He caught her deftly, ignoring her groan as he balanced her so he could grab her shoes and bag. Her head lolled back and her eyes opened briefly, two round balls of midnight blue, and she stared up at him in silence.

Several moments passed as the cold wrapped around them. Jake's world narrowed until all that filled it was

Raine. Her eyes misted, the corners shimmering with moisture, and her hand rose, but something snapped inside him and he jerked his head back.

Her eyes widened for a second and then her hand dropped weakly as he turned and headed up the stairs.

"Where's your key?" His voice was gruff and echoed into the dead air that swirled around them.

"Purse," she muttered softly.

She leaned against him, her small frame shivering in the cold as he rummaged in her bag. He found the key, and a few seconds later they were in. The house was in darkness, the shadows long, but he knew his way—hell, he'd practically lived here when home on leave—and he headed down the hall toward her bedroom.

The light near her bed had been left on, however, the glow soft and muted.

"Oh God, the whole damn world is spinning," she murmured next to his throat. "How much wine did I drink?"

"I'd say the whole bottle."

She groaned. "Jake, why didn't you stop me? You always stop me."

His mouth tightened and he let her slide from his arms. She stood facing him, swaying unsteadily as she pushed the tangled mess of hair from her face. Her skin was pale, like vintage porcelain, and her eyes were large, exotic. She stepped backward and nearly fell onto the bed, and then cursed while trying to reach the back of her dress.

She glanced up at him and he shook his head at the question in her eyes. Not a chance.

"Just go to bed, Raine."

"I will." Her brow furled as she continued to stumble

around and tug on her dress. "As soon as I get this off. It smells gross."

"You can barely stand. Why the hell do you care what your dress smells like?"

"When did you become such a big fat grumpy head?" She giggled at that and nearly fell over, but he caught her.

On reflex, her hands moved forward and splayed across his chest as his large hands wrapped around her waist. Her hips poked into his groin, and the feel of her softness and the scent of her did all sorts of shit to him that he didn't want. Every muscle inside him tightened, and he loathed the fact that he was instantly hard.

Jesus Christ, he needed to get a grip.

Jake gritted his teeth and stared down at her, hating the way his body betrayed him. Hating the way she felt so right.

Raine slowly raised her head, totally unaware of the effect she had on him, and giggled once more. "Jake, you look like someone pissed in your cornflakes this morning."

"Well, that would be wrong," he ground out, irritated.

"I don't think so," she slurred.

"I don't eat cereal."

She stared up at him for the longest time, and he shifted his weight in an effort to alleviate the stress between his damn legs. Something changed then—a softening of her eyes, a charge of electricity in the air. Whatever it was, it put him on edge and he glared at her, resenting the effect she had on him.

"That's right," she whispered. "You're an egg-and-waffle guy." She paused. "Jesse liked his cornflakes."

Her hand drifted toward his face once more but he pulled back so that she couldn't quite reach. Her finger brushed the air between them before falling back to his chest. She swallowed, and her eyes never left his, their shiny recesses full of something he couldn't name, though he sure as hell recognized it.

The same damn thing was reflected in his own eyes.

"You look…lost, Jake."

A muscle worked its way across his jaw. "I've been lost for a long time, Raine. There's nothing new in that."

"No," she answered softly. "I guess not." A sad, wistful smile claimed her lips, and his heart beat erratically as she gazed up at him. "But you're home now. We can be lost together."

Silence filled every single nook and cranny around them. He didn't know what to say to that, so he said nothing and the two of them stood like stiff soldiers, staring at each other for God knows how long. But it was long enough that the cold claimed her and her teeth began to chatter as it took hold, leaving goose bumps across her flesh and shudders rolling over her slight frame.

"I'm tired, Jake. Can you just unzip me?" She turned in his arms and bent forward, though without his support, she'd have taken a header onto the floor.

He clenched his jaw tight and reached for the zipper, trying his best to ignore the provocative display. The fact that it wasn't contrived or staged made it all the more hot. Her neck was bare, the fine curve of her spine bent in a way that would make any man think of things he shouldn't be thinking of. Not when the woman in your arms was your brother's widow.

Carefully he tugged her dress down and kept her steady while she shimmied out of the damn thing, until she stood in a black lacy bra and matching panties. Sure, it covered as much as a bikini, maybe more— but still, seeing Raine like this was different. There was something much more intimate about a woman in her underwear. Her pale skin was luminescent beneath the glow from the lamp beside her bed, and he was struck once more with how incredibly fragile she looked.

Her hip bones jutted out a little too much, and the hollow at her stomach wasn't right. A woman's belly should be softly rounded. Raine had always been on the thin side, but she'd had more of an athletic build. This... this was something else entirely. She was too thin. Too pale and...

"Don't look at me like that," she whispered hoarsely, her eyes filled with tears.

"Raine, you need to take better care of yourself." A pinch of anger bled through his words, and she wiped at her face roughly as she backed toward the bed. "You're not eating."

"I eat." She yanked on the covers and drew them back. She stumbled a bit. "When I'm hungry. Not my fault I don't look like your Barbie doll."

"My Barbie doll?" He moved closer to the bed as she scrambled between her covers and pulled them up to her chin, her teeth chattering crazily in the quiet.

"Lily St. Clare."

"Lily isn't my Barbie." Christ, if Lily were here, she'd have had one of those cool grins on her face because, as he knew only too well, Lily St. Clare belonged to no one. She was even more emotionally damaged than he was—which was saying a lot about the woman.

She ignored him. "We'll talk about her tomorrow."

Raine had always had her nose in his business. It used to amuse him, but now? Now it irritated him to know she still thought she had a say in his life.

"Lily isn't something I want to talk about. Especially with you."

Raine rubbed her eyes. "We *will* talk about her, because I don't care what your mother thinks." She struggled to hold back a yawn. "That woman is all wrong for you."

Shit, now his mother was poking her nose into his business? "Really," he retorted gruffly.

"Really," she murmured.

Her eyes drifted shut and she flung a hand above her head, turning slightly toward the empty pillow beside her. The one that had held his brother's head.

His gut churned as all the dark, tortured feelings inside him rose to the surface. Every single wrong thing about his situation, about Raine's reality and his parents' loss, came crashing back and he took a step backward, surprised at their intensity. He realized in that moment that running away from everything hadn't accomplished squat. It hadn't dulled the pain or improved his outlook. Every shitty thing was still the same.

A strangled sound escaped him as he ran fingers through the thick hair at his nape and across the stubble that graced his chin.

His brother was dead and nothing could bring him back. The images from that terrible day, the smells and sensations, were never going to leave him. They shadowed him, following in his footsteps, and rested beside him at night. He knew as surely as the sun would rise in a few hours that he would be haunted by them until he drew his last breath.

So where did he go from here?

His parents weren't whole. They were dealing with both the loss of his brother and his father's illness. Hell, they were barely getting by, but at least they had each other. He closed his eyes. Raine was right.

Jake was lost.

In the first few weeks after Jesse's death, he'd survived on a steady diet of pure, raging adrenaline. Then as the weeks had passed into months, the adrenaline had dissipated and he'd been left with nothing but the bitter taste of disillusionment. Of pain and emptiness. Of the knowledge that if only he'd…

"Jake," Raine mumbled.

"Yeah." Jake's eyes flew open and he wiped at the corners of his eyes.

"I'm just…I'm just so tired."

He glanced down at the bed. Raine's eyes were still closed.

"I know. Try to get some rest."

He turned away and faced the door.

"Jake?"

He cocked his head to the side. "Yeah?"

"Don't go."

For one second, his mind emptied and the need he thought he heard in her voice called to him. He turned back to her. He couldn't help it. Jake Edwards was that weak.

"Please stay. Don't go back with her."

"Her?"

"Barbie."

Jake sighed and left without another word. He closed the door to Raine's bedroom and, instead of leaving, wandered into her kitchen. He flipped the light switch and stared at the perfectly organized, clean space. He crossed to the fridge and yanked it open, his anger expanding at the sight of how poorly stocked it was. A carton of milk, some eggs, cheese, a near-empty bottle of ketchup, and a takeout box of half-eaten chili from in town. Her pantry was no better. Hell, she had more food for the dog than she had for herself.

He left the kitchen and lingered in the family room, his gaze settling on the bag he'd brought back from Texas. It was still where he'd left it on the coffee table, and from what he could tell, Raine hadn't poked around inside it.

His fingers ran over the worn leather and he lifted it off the table. There was some weight to it, and though he'd wondered what Jesse had stowed inside, he'd never opened the damn thing—for the simple fact that it wasn't his to open.

For several long seconds he stared down at the bag, and then his gaze drifted to the window, out into the starless, cold night. The security light that sat near the edge of the forest was on, its stark circle of illumination sparkling among the snowflakes. Huge, fluffy flakes drifted toward the earth in a lazy dance until they fell to the ground.

By morning the grass would be covered with a blanket of the cold, frozen stuff. Winter had finally arrived, it seemed.

He eyed the sofa and then glanced down the hall toward the front door. Indecision ate at him, but before he could analyze things any more, Jake sank onto the sofa and dropped his brother's bag onto the floor beside it. There was no point in heading back to his parents'. He wouldn't sleep anyway. Better to hang here in case Raine needed him.

It seemed as if some decisions came easier than others.

His eyes drifted back to the snowflakes and he stretched out his long legs. There was a time when the first snowfall was like a gift from the gods. It meant snowmobiling through the brush with his brother and their buddies, Cain and Mac. It meant nights of bonfires, beer, and girls. Reckless stunts, racing across frozen lakes, and skiing by firelight.

He'd been invincible then. All of them had. Untouched by tragedy, with the innocent mind-set of youth. Never in a million years had he ever thought Jesse would be dead at the age of thirty.

His gaze moved from the snow up to the ceiling as the emptiness inside him, ate through the cold shell of his heart. Call it what you will—a twin thing, a sibling thing—the moment Jesse had passed, Jake had been cut open, and he'd been bleeding ever since. He didn't think it would ever stop.

God, he was so tired, but sleep was a monster that left him utterly wrecked. The nightmares, the cold sweats… the rage…they were his constant companions these days. No matter that outside a white wonderland was slowly shaping up, deep in his heart and mind there was only bleak, never-ending darkness. There was desert and sand, heat and death.

Jake tried to relax, hell, he even closed his eyes, but his thoughts kept him awake long after the clock circled around again. And again. And again.

He thought of those snowy nights from his past. They were a lifetime ago, and contrary to what some people thought, there was no going back.

Chapter 7

WINTER CAME WITH AN ARCTIC BLAST AS IT HAD A habit of doing this time of the year in northern Michigan. One day, the smell of fall was still in the air and the next, winter's kiss claimed the terrain. The snow had fallen steadily through the night, and when Jake finally rolled off the sofa, more than a little stiff and cranky, there were nearly four inches of the white stuff outside.

He'd dozed off and on but hadn't succumbed to sleep. He couldn't do it. Not here, with Raine. No one would hear how pathetic he sounded when ripped from sleep by the darkness inside him.

Especially not her. His pain would lead to questions never asked, to answers never given, and he didn't know if he was strong enough to deal with that right now.

Jake stretched, rolled his neck and shoulders, and went in search of coffee. Considering the meager offerings he'd seen the night before, he wasn't expecting anything but was pleasantly surprised to discover that though Raine hadn't much use for food, apparently caffeine was still on the menu. And even though he was more of a cream kind of guy, there was two percent milk in the fridge with a sell-by date he could live with.

It was just after five in the morning, and while he waited for the coffee to brew, he filled a tall glass with water and rummaged through the cupboards until he found some painkillers.

Raine was still asleep and pretty much in the same position he'd left her in, though he couldn't see her face from the mess of wild curls across it.

Jake placed the water on the table beside her bed and made sure it was in reach, along with two shiny, extra-strength red tablets. He paused for a moment, his chest constricting as he gazed at her, and gently moved the tangles from her face. Her nose twitched and she groaned softly, her legs moving as she burrowed deeper into the mattress.

He froze as her eyes fluttered open, dream filled and sleepy. For one second, a smile lifted the corners of her mouth and something inside him lightened. But then shadows fell into her eyes as memory returned, and the smile disappeared.

"Hey," she murmured.

"Hey, yourself."

"You stayed." Her voice was hoarse, and a wince accompanied her words.

"Yeah."

"Oh God," she groaned once more. "My head hurts."

"I expected it would. Take the pills, they'll help." He straightened and moved away, annoyed that her vulnerability was enhanced tenfold by the sweet remnants of the sandman.

"Jake?"

He paused at the door and waited, but after several long moments realized that she was out cold once more. He closed the door, grabbed a coffee, and left Raine deep in dreamland, hopefully with more than enough painkillers for the hangover that was about to pay her a visit.

—∿—

"You look like shit, Jake."

"Thanks." Jake threw his jacket across one of the kitchen chairs and scowled in Lily's general direction. "And in case you're wondering, I sure as hell feel worse than I look."

Dawn had fully arrived, spreading a wash of sunlight across the fresh snow that reflected back so brightly, it made him squint. He walked over to the bay window that encircled the breakfast nook and stared out across the lake. It was much too early for the lake to freeze, and the water looked rough as it rolled onto the beach, pushed forward by a cold north wind. In the distance, he saw the sprinkling of cottages lining the water, but for the most part, this side of Crystal Lake was isolated, with homes that were considered estates nestled among forest and privacy.

Only those with deep enough pockets could afford to live here.

"It's pretty."

He nodded. "It sure is."

"Do you miss it?" Lily was beside him now, her willowy frame covered in bright pink flannel pajamas that hid a hell of a lot more than Raine's bedtime attire.

"I used to." His eyes followed a squirrel as it frantically dug through the snow at the base of one of the oak trees that bordered his parents' estate. When the darkness of Afghanistan was overwhelming, thoughts of home had always got him through. Memories of the lake, his family. Raine.

"You don't anymore?"

He shook his head. "Not really." *Liar*.

His abrupt tone would have put most people off, but Lily wasn't most people. She had an innate ability to see and hear only what she wanted to.

"Coffee?" she asked.

He'd already had two cups but… "Cream?" He lifted an eyebrow.

"Damn straight. Is there any other way?" Lily grinned and settled back into her chair. She grabbed the newspaper he'd brought in with him. "Can you pour me a cup while you're at it?"

"Sure thing, princess."

He fixed them each a cup and grimaced when he caught sight of his face reflected in the window. With his overgrown hair and scruffy chin, he looked nothing like the soldier he'd once been. Christ, if his unit could see him now, they'd think he'd gone Hollywood. They'd call him a pussy and have every right to do so.

"Your parents are nice." Lily set the paper down and stared at him in that direct way that she had—the one that put most people on edge. With her face free of makeup and her hair thrown back into a ponytail, she looked younger, fresher than the woman she portrayed in public. "They're so normal…nothing like the circus I grew up with."

"I gotta agree with you," he said drily. "They're pretty damn special."

Lily folded the paper just so and tugged the edge of her flannel pajamas down to her wrists. She settled back into her chair, all prim and proper, and took a sip of coffee as she stared at him.

"What?" he said abruptly.

The woman had radar for all kinds of shit, but he didn't know if he was in the mood for any of it right now. Sure, they'd bonded over a shared bottle of tequila on one hell of a crazy night at the Sundowner in Texas, but two fractured human beings didn't always make for the best sort of company.

"So, your sister-in-law, Raine…"

He cut her off before she could go any further. "We're not talking about her."

"You're in love with her."

He glared at her, though he didn't bother denying it. What was the point? Aside from the fact that it was the truth, Lily St. Clare was tenacious and wouldn't let it go. It wasn't her nature, especially since sticking her nose in his business gave her something to focus on other than the sad state of her own personal affairs. When it came to a fucked-up past, she was running neck and neck in that race with him.

But this was hitting a little too close to home.

"Lily, I don't want to talk about her."

She made a face but relented, though for how long was anyone's guess. He tossed the remainder of his coffee into the sink and glanced at the clock. It was now nearly seven, and he knew he'd better hop in the shower and do something about the state of his appearance, or his mother was going to worry. After everything she'd been through, that was the last thing he wanted.

"Your dad is feeling up to an outing, so your parents invited us to some"—she smiled at him—"*thing* in your little town this afternoon, and I said we'd be more than happy to go with them."

Shit, here we go.

Friday after Thanksgiving meant only one thing. The town-wide Black Friday extravaganza. Every single store would be open, filled to the brim with overzealous shopping crowds out for the best deal they could find, and overzealous townsfolk all wanting to know where the hell he'd been for the last year and a half.

Jake could not think of any other place he'd rather *not* be.

"Why the hell would they do that?" His brow furled into a thunderous line, hating the feeling like he was being fenced in, forced into a corner he couldn't get out of. And that made him feel even more guilty than he already did. He should have been chomping at the bit to spend more time with his parents. They deserved it, and deep down he knew that he needed it. The precipice he'd teetered on for months was starting to crumble, and he needed something solid and concrete to hold him steady or he was in danger of falling.

He thought back to Texas. If he fell again, he wasn't so sure there was anyone who could bring him back. A cat only had so many lives, and he was pretty sure he'd used all of his up.

Lily shrugged. "Your parents love me."

"They barely know you," he muttered, still confused by the back-and-forth his emotions were putting him through.

"Are you trying to tell me that I'm not lovable?" She pouted cheekily.

She knew damn well she wasn't lovable, or cute. She was beautiful—striking, really—but definitely more Nordic chill than warm and fuzzy. Lily St. Clare was one of the most prickly females he'd ever had the pleasure of meeting, and her cool blond looks exemplified the glass shell she liked to hide beneath. Tequila had allowed him to see beneath the surface, and after their failed attempt to find comfort in each other's arms, something else had happened. Something unexpected but much needed for the both of them.

Friendship.

"I couldn't say no. Besides, I'm pretty sure your mother thinks we're involved, and I didn't have the heart to set her straight on that one."

He groaned, thought of Raine's words, and shook his head. "What the hell is up with that?"

Lily bristled at his tone. "They care about you, jackass, and obviously the thought of having a woman in your life makes them happy. They're concerned and have every right to be. You're a mess."

"Guess that's why we get along so good." Jake glared at the blonde, not in the mood for her high-handed attitude. All he wanted was a long, hot shower. It wasn't too much to ask for, was it? Hell, he'd spent the night *not sleeping* on a sofa that didn't exactly fit his long frame. The least Lily could do was get the hell out of his way and let him by.

"Look." Lily stood and faced him.

So much for getting out of my way.

"This was your idea. I was perfectly okay staying in Texas for the holidays, but you needed backup, and I get that."

"Lily—"

"I'm not finished."

Irritated, Jake folded his arms across his chest and hoped that she'd make this quick. Over the last year, as he'd got to know the woman, one thing about her had become pretty apparent. She liked to talk. And she liked to be right. In some ways she was a lot like Raine, which wasn't surprising, since it seemed to be his bad fortune to surround himself with females who annoyed the hell out of him.

"Your mom and dad think that we're sleeping together."

"I told my mother we weren't."

"She obviously didn't believe you."

"Unbelievable." Jake made a strangled sound. "Women accuse men of having selective hearing all the time, and you know what? We do! Because you guys only hear what the hell you want to hear, so why should we bother?"

"Whatever, Jake. Honestly, what did you think your mom would think? You bring a woman home for Thanksgiving, it's not that far off for them to assume we're sleeping together."

"It's all bullshit."

"*I* know it's bullshit. *You* know it's bullshit." Lily shook her head and smiled. "But your parents don't and neither does Raine."

"What are you getting at?" Christ, it was too early in the morning for this kind of crap.

"I'm here for a few more days. What's so wrong with us"—she smiled in that way that instantly put Jake on alert—"pretending we're together, if it makes your parents happy?"

Jake's irritation grew by leaps and bounds. What the hell was up with the women in his life?

"That's the most insane thing I've ever heard." He'd barely got the words out when his mother and father walked into the kitchen, both bundled up in matching plum-colored terry robes and huge, fluffy slippers.

His father's complexion was pale, his cheeks gray, but there was a lightness in his eyes that set Jake at ease. Jake glanced down at his father's feet and then back up to his father. His expression said, *Don't ask*, which of course meant Jake couldn't let it go.

"Nice slippers." He couldn't help it and his face broke into a wide grin as the tension inside him slipped through the cracks.

"Thanks," Steven said airily as he reached into the cupboard for two coffee mugs.

"Aren't they different?" Marnie stuck her foot out, twisting her ankle. "I saw them in one of my catalogs and knew Steven would like them as much as I did. They're so warm and comfortable."

Jake nodded. "I see that." He glanced up at his dad again. "They're, uh…really furry."

His dad tipped his head to the side. "They are."

"And really purple."

Steven poured his coffee. "They are that too."

"They match your robe."

His father's eyes narrowed. "We could go on all day I suppose, but let's just stop right about now, son, sound good?"

Jake chuckled and nodded. "Hey, I wish I had a pair."

"I could order you some, if you like."

He glanced at his mother and shook his head. "Nah, I'm good."

Marnie took a sip of her coffee. "How's our Raine?"

At the mention of his sister-in-law, the lightness of the moment vanished. "She's going to have one hell of a hangover, that's for sure." A thought crossed his mind. "Where's her dog?"

Jake had forgotten about the puppy until now.

His mother's entire mood lightened, and for a second he just drank in the sight. "Gibson is asleep on our bed."

"Your bed?"

Okay, his parents were definitely going crazy. For as long as he could remember, dogs were strictly meant for outdoors. They'd had a collie one summer, a mangy animal that Jesse had found down at the pier in town. They'd brought it home, ignoring its general unease and nastiness, convinced their father would fall all over himself with joy at the thought of his sons gallivanting through long hot summer days with a white and black collie following in their footsteps.

The reality was much different. Steven hadn't budged, and they'd had to beg for permission to keep it until an owner could be found. The dog was eventually named Puppy and spent the summer in the boathouse, roaming the woods that surrounded their property and turning up for food every night. Near the end of that summer, Puppy didn't show up for his dinner, and they'd never seen the dog again.

Jake shot a look toward his father, who shrugged. "I've learned to pick my battles, son."

"Did Raine have a bad night?" his mother asked softly.

Jake turned back to his mother, unhappy to see her smile gone. The worry that creased her forehead was ingrained deeper than he liked, and it twisted his gut something fierce to see the pain she tried so hard to hide from him.

"I got her to bed but didn't want to leave her alone, so I slept on the sofa."

"Did you get any sleep?"

Jake's gaze rose to just above her head. He couldn't look his mother in the eye and lie, and he sure as hell didn't feel like sharing the pain and nightmares that visited him during the night.

"Yeah," he said simply. "I got a few hours." Silence wrapped around all of them and he flashed a smile—one that belied a state of mind he didn't feel at all.

"So." He arched a brow. "Black Friday?"

His mother linked her arm through his dad's and nodded, a smile once more leaving her eyes glistening. A smile that lightened him inside, if only for a moment.

"Sounds great," he murmured, ignoring the satisfied look on Lily's face. "Guess I should shower, then."

Chapter 8

MARNIE BROUGHT GIBSON HOME SATURDAY EVENING, and though it took everything Raine had just to drag her butt out of bed, when Marnie asked for a hot cup of tea, she didn't have the heart to say no.

While her mother-in-law plugged in the kettle, Raine splashed some water onto her face, threw on an old faded gray sweatshirt that hung nearly to her knees, and scraped her hair back into a messy ponytail. The sweatshirt had been Jesse's—sent back with his things—and after his funeral she'd worn it to bed for weeks.

Raine smoothed the soft and thinned fabric. She couldn't remember the last time she'd worn it and just now had grabbed only it because it was the next clean thing in her drawer.

With a sigh she glanced outside. It was after six, dark as sin, and the wind howled as it swept by her home. Being this close to the lake didn't afford much shelter when the weather was bad, and it looked like another stormy night was in store.

It didn't bode well for the annual football game scheduled the next day in town, but Raine had no plans to attend, and even as the fleeting thought occurred to her, she moved on. She didn't care.

She returned to the kitchen and rummaged through the cupboard, looking for anything she could serve with tea. But there wasn't much to choose from, and she tried to hide her embarrassment when all she could muster was an open box of shortbread cookies. Raine took a bite and made a face before throwing the entire contents into the garbage.

"Sorry, Marnie. They're a little stale."

"Oh, I'm fine, dear. We didn't really get a chance to chat the other night, and I just wanted to see how you were doing. A spot of tea seemed like a good idea."

Raine avoided the woman's probing gaze and fixed her tea, grateful that Jake hadn't finished what little milk she had left. If she skimped a bit, there should be enough for the both of them. The date wasn't the best, so she sniffed the carton first and then froze for a second as realization hit.

I just sniffed the carton because I have no idea if this is usable.

I'm serving my mother-in-law tea with milk that expired a week ago, and I don't even have cookies to offer her, because they're stale.

A lump formed in her throat, one that took a bit of effort to clear, and the hot sting of tears settled in the corners of her eyes as she tossed her tea bag and cradled her mug between cold fingers.

I'm a pathetic mess.

"Don't worry about the milk. I take it black, hon."

Raine nodded and set the carton of milk onto the counter. For the first time, she was going to take it black as well. She slid into the chair opposite Marnie, and the two women sat in silence for the longest time, each seeming to be lost in thought or maybe more than a little wary of what the other was feeling.

The silence grew heavy, uncomfortable. It thickened

and took shape, becoming so loud that it pressed on Raine's ears and chest, and she exhaled loudly in an effort to alleviate the stress. She knew panic would set in if she didn't manage to calm herself, so she stared at her fingers. At the chipped blue nails and the bruise still dark on her forefinger from when she caught it in the cupboard the day before. Or was it two days ago?

"We're worried about you, Raine."

Marnie's quiet words nearly undid her—the tears in the corners of her eyes sharpened—but Raine stared down into her cup and forced them away. She swallowed the lump in her throat and slowly exhaled. The abyss she'd been sidestepping for the last year and a half was closer than ever. It would be so easy to just step into it, and yet...

She stirred her tea, even though it didn't need stirring, and avoided Marnie's gentle gaze. She knew that if she looked into Marnie's eyes, she'd fall apart, and as much as she didn't care about most things, she didn't want to add to her mother-in-law's burden.

She focused on the china cup in her hands. At one time there'd been eight cups, the bone-white china adorned with a delicate pattern of indigo blue roses. Now only five remained. The set was broken. It was unfinished. Kind of like Raine.

"You know I don't usually say much or get too involved in the lives of those I love. I've always been of the mind that generally people need to come around on their own. But, Raine—" Marnie's voice deepened and she paused.

Raine's bottom lip trembled. Still she refused to look up at her mother-in-law.

Marnie cleared her throat and grabbed Raine's hand, her fingers warm against Raine's cold skin. "You're *not* coming around, and I'm afraid for you. I thought that with Jake home and the fact you actually came to dinner the other night…I thought you might have turned the corner, but honey, I have to be honest with you. I'm worried."

"Marnie, I'm fine."

The words sounded hollow, even to Raine.

"You're not." Marnie's voice broke a little. "You're not fine at all."

Her face was hot and the urge to wrench her hands from Marnie's grasp strong, but Raine kept still, afraid that if she moved an inch, the wall of emotion inside her would break and her plan not to upset Marnie would blow wide open. It was so hard, though. The pressure inside was fierce, like a geyser about to explode.

"I know you've had a really tough time, the last six months especially so, but you're much too young to have given up hope, and I—" Marnie's voice wavered and slowly Raine met her gaze. Marnie squeezed Raine's hands. "I can't lose you too."

"I'm not going anywhere, Marnie."

"That's my point, sweetie. You're standing still, and if you don't start moving forward, time will pass by with no regard, and before you know it, you'll be looking back at wasted years."

Raine's heart beat faster as the blood rushed through her body, making her dizzy. The cracks, it seemed, were seeping. "It's not that easy." She withdrew her hands from Marnie and wiped her forehead. "I lost *everything* last year. I can't…" She shook her head, having a hard time articulating the thoughts that filled her mind.

"Everyone grieves differently, Raine. I won't pretend to know what you're feeling, but I do have some perspective. I lost a son and pieces of my heart are broken…pieces that won't ever be repaired. No matter how hard he tries, Steven can't fill the gaps, and neither can Jake. They're the scars that Jesse left behind, and I had to find a way to live with them. I had to find a way to go on for the ones left behind."

Raine wiped at her face slowly and whispered, "It's just so damn hard."

No one slept beside her at night. There was no one there to listen to her sobs, or wipe away her tears. No one to hold her when she was cold, or tell her that things were going to be all right. No one to tell her she was pretty or interesting…or that she mattered.

But the truly sad thing was that there were some nights Raine didn't even know why she cried. She just did.

"I know it's hard, Raine. But you have to try to find something to hold on to…something to anchor you. Even Jake—"

Raine's head snapped up. "Jake?" An image of his dark, tortured eyes solidified in her head. "You think Jake is okay? That he's over whatever the hell it was that happened over there?"

Raine slid from her chair and began to pace. Gibson whined and sat near Marnie's feet, his tail at half-staff, his large brown eyes fixed on Raine as she crossed to the window and looked out into the darkness.

Her heart hurt. Her throat was tight, and she felt as if she was going to throw up. "Has he ever told you what happened?" She barely got the words out and stared at Marnie's reflection in the window. Tears began to fall down her cheeks and she wiped them away angrily. "Because he's never said anything to me. Nothing."

Marnie shook her head slowly, her voice barely above a whisper. "No."

For some reason, her quiet manner revved up Raine's anger. Something gave way inside her as she whirled around, pushing back the strand of hair that never stayed put. "Don't you want to know? Don't you want to know exactly how Jesse died?"

Marnie's gaze didn't falter. "No."

"I do. I want to know every single detail," Raine continued, as if Marnie hadn't spoken at all. "I don't care what the official report says. That's just a lousy piece of paper with a bunch of words I don't feel a connection to. I don't care that it tells me it was fast, or that he wasn't in a lot of pain. I don't care that a fucking bullet tore through his aorta, while a piece of shrapnel sliced through his jugular." Tears flooded her mouth, her nose—and something inside Raine burst open until pain lanced across her chest and flushed through her in a hot thrust that left her clammy. She was about to fall apart, and there wasn't a damn thing she could do.

"I don't care about any of that, because they're just words on a piece of paper that some stranger I've never met wrote up. They don't mean anything to me." Her entire body shook violently, and for a moment the world darkened. All color fled her vision until there was only gray, and white noise filled her ears.

When Marnie flew to her side and wrapped her arms around her, Raine went still. It had been so long since she let anyone touch her like this.

The space inside her expanded and for a moment she

couldn't breathe. The pain was much too intense. She closed her eyes and slumped into Marnie's arms, suddenly so utterly defeated and weak that if not for her mother-in-law, she would have fallen to the floor.

"I need to know everything. I need to know how it happened. Why it happened. I need to know if the sun was shining or if they were in the middle of another sandstorm. Did he sleep all right the night before? Or did he have one of those god-awful nightmares he had whenever he was home? I need to know that he was okay in the end. That his pain…that his fear was dealt with. I want to know why he was acting so out of it and weird that last time he was home on leave."

There it was. The dirty little worm that had been digging into her heart and her mind for so long. "He wasn't right," she whispered.

Raine shuddered and disengaged herself from Marnie. She took a few steps, wavering slightly because she felt so weak. So damn tired. "I need to know what his last words were…that he wasn't scared or sorry."

"Don't do this to yourself, Raine."

Raine faced her mother-in-law, totally spent. She crossed back to the island and slid into the nearest chair. She took a sip of her tea and said the one thing that had haunted her for the last year and a half. "I want to know if he left for Afghanistan knowing he wouldn't be coming back, because I'm not even sure he wanted to."

She saw that Marnie was shocked by her words, and for one second she wished that she could snatch them back. But the moment passed, and for the first time in forever, it seemed, a bit of the weight that had hung on her shoulders seemed to dissipate.

Marnie stood in the middle of the kitchen for the longest time, looking so small and lost that Raine had to look away. She felt like an absolute ass. Why had she opened her mouth? Where had all those words come from? What the hell had happened to *not* hurting the one woman on the planet who had only ever shown her love and kindness?

Gibson rubbed his furry body against her legs. She bent down, scooped the dog into her arms, and held him close. His puppy smell was familiar and safe. She inhaled his chubby goodness, drank in his warmth, closed her eyes, and whispered, "I'm so sorry."

There was a long pause, and for one scary moment Raine was afraid she'd done too much damage and that Marnie would just up and leave. If that happened...

"Don't ever be sorry for saying how you feel. You can't keep all this darkness inside you, Raine. It's too much for anyone to bear."

Relief flooded Raine, and she gripped Gibson so tight that he whimpered in protest and squiggled madly until she let him go. She swallowed and gathered one more shot of courage. "Jake's *not* okay. You know that, right?"

Marnie was silent for a few moments, her eyes filling with tears as she struggled to speak. She nodded. "I know my son is hurting," Marnie acknowledged wearily. She ran her hands over her face and closed her eyes. "I know that he doesn't sleep at night, and when he does, I can only imagine the horrors that haunt him. I know that he felt the need to stay away from us for far too long, and now that he's back..." She exhaled harshly. "Now that he's back, I can't lose him." A slow, sad smile crept over her features. "But my boy is strong and he's making an effort. I know he doesn't want to live in darkness any longer, and you could learn from that."

Ouch. However much it hurt to hear those words, Raine knew they were true.

She grabbed a box of puppy treats from the cupboard and tossed a few to Gibson. She tried to keep her voice casual but wasn't altogether successful. "You *really* think this woman…Lily St. Clare…is what Jake needs?"

Marnie shrugged. "I don't know if she's what he needs, but I do know that he's home after all this time, that sometimes he smiles and I've seen glimpses of the old Jake. For whatever it's worth, I'm fairly certain she has something to do with it."

Raine's mouth thinned. Marnie couldn't be more wrong. Jake Edwards wasn't a big-city-trust-fund-baby kind of man. He was…hell, she didn't know what he was anymore, but she knew with every fiber of her being that Jake Edwards and Lily St. Clare didn't belong together.

"I know you'd like me to encourage Jake in regard to this woman, but can we agree to disagree?"

"Why don't you like her?"

"It's not that I don't like her, I don't know her. I just…" Her voice trailed off, because she really didn't know how to answer the question. She shrugged. It was more a feeling that she couldn't put into words.

Marnie's face softened. "Okay. I think you're wrong. But okay."

The lump returned big-time, settling into the back of her throat once more. She would have given anything to wipe away the pain she saw reflected in Marnie's eyes.

"I'm so sorry I dumped all that onto you. I don't know what came over me."

Her mother-in-law crossed the room in three strides and hugged her tightly. They clung to each other for several long moments. "I miss him so much," Raine whispered.

"We all miss him, sweetie."

Raine squeezed her eyes shut as a wave of guilt washed over her. It wasn't Jesse she was speaking of.

Marnie gave her one more hug and stepped back, her features relaxed into a slow grin that warmed Raine's heart. "I've got some good news."

"You do?" Raine gathered up the cups and rinsed them under the water in the sink.

Marnie nodded, reached for Gibson, and scratched the puppy under his chin, grinning as the dog rolled over onto his back and offered up his soft belly.

"Jake's bought the old Wyndham Place."

"What?" Raine was shocked. "But it's in ruins."

Marnie nodded. "Yes, it is."

Raine set the cups on the drying rack and leaned her hip against the counter, biting her lip thoughtfully as she gazed out the window into the darkness. The Wyndham mansion had been built by one of the founding families of Crystal Lake back in the early 1800s, during the lumber boom.

A palatial antebellum home on the water, Michael Wyndham had presented it to his new bride, a Southern belle who'd defied her family and married for love. It had been passed down through several generations until the last Wyndham left Crystal Lake for a brighter future somewhere else, leaving it to fall into disrepair sometime back in the 1970s. The last anyone knew, it was owned by some distant relative and had become both an eyesore and a liability.

The Wyndham mansion was been a virtual playground for Raine when she was growing up. A place to pretend and explore. A place to find love and fantasize about the proverbial knights in shining armor. When she was younger, Raine used to pretend she was the lady of the house and play inside the ruins for hours at a time.

It was where she'd stolen her first kiss.

"I always loved that house. I didn't know it was for sale." She turned back to Marnie.

"We ran into Brad Kitchen at the hardware store yesterday during the Black Friday sales and he told Steven he'd just listed it. Something went off inside Jake—I saw it in his eyes. We all went out to see the place, and even though it needs a lot of work, he put in an offer last night and found out a few hours ago that it was accepted."

"Oh." She couldn't help but feel left out, and though she tried to keep her bottom lip from trembling, she wasn't wholly successful. "I would have gone…" she managed, "if I'd known."

"He called you," Marnie said quietly, "but you didn't answer your phone, and we just figured…"

Raine blushed as her mother-in-law took in the tangled ponytail, ratty old sweatshirt, and the mismatched socks on her feet.

"Honey, we just figured you still weren't feeling all that well."

"Oh, right. There's a bug going round. That's fine," Raine mumbled, hating the hot sting of tears that scorched the corners of her eyes. She squared her shoulders and put on a fake smile. "What's he going to do with it?"

Marnie's smile widened. "Why, my dear, he's going to bring it back to life."

Chapter 9

"YOU KNOW YOU'RE CRAZY, RIGHT?"

Salvatore Nuno, owner of the Coach House, shook his head and placed a beer in front of Jake. Moisture gathered along the top of the brown bottle—it was cold, just the way he liked it—and Jake grinned as he took a swig and waited for another sermon.

Salvatore's forehead was beaded with sweat and the man huffed with a lot of effort as he rubbed at the edge of the worn, wooden bar top. "Wyndham Place is one helluva undertaking, my friend. You ever see that movie, *The Money Pit*?" Sal's bushy eyebrows twisted together as he leaned over the bar. "Huh? With that there guy… you know, Forrest Gump?" He tossed the rag over his shoulder and shook his head. "*That* is what Wyndham Place is, my friend—a money pit. And only a fool would think otherwise."

Jake set the bottle back onto the bar and tried not to laugh at the outraged expression on the man's face. "Don't hold back, Sal. Tell me how you really feel."

Salvatore shook his head and ran his fingers over his smooth, shiny, bald head. His faded gray T-shirt stretched tight over his belly, and his dress pants hung dangerously low, held up by an ancient leather belt that looked to Jake to be on its last legs. "I'm just telling you the truth. Everyone around here thinks you're crazy to spend that kind of money on a run-down estate that should be demolished. It's not just an eyesore, it's a god-damn safety hazard."

Jake ignored the comment, mostly because he'd been hearing nothing but the same kind of rhetoric since Saturday, when word had leaked out that he'd plunked down a sizable amount of cash for the Wyndham estate.

Sizable, and about all he had.

Crystal Lake was a small town, and considering Lori Jonesberg was with Brad Kitchen when the offer was finalized, he wasn't surprised everyone seemed to know his business. Lori owned A Cut Above, the gossip center in a town like Crystal Lake. Newly separated from her husband, she'd wasted no time getting herself on the market and was currently making the rounds with Brad.

"You got that wine ready yet?"

"Hmph."

Salvatore scowled and grabbed a wineglass from beneath the counter, or at least what passed for a wineglass hereabouts. The stem was thick, the glass dull. It was the farthest thing from crystal, but Jake knew how much Lily enjoyed her wine.

"I hope she likes it, because it's all we got." Sal poured a good amount into the glass, muttering loudly to himself as he did so. "Wine? Huh. No one comes in to the Coach House and drinks wine. Scotch maybe, or whiskey, but wine?"

Jake glanced back toward the far corner, where Lily sat. She stood out like a sore thumb, dressed head to toe in white, with her platinum hair curling down past her shoulders just so, emphasizing her considerable cleavage. He was sure she'd dressed that way on purpose.

Lily was a pro at garnering attention. In fact, he was

pretty damn sure there was an on switch inside her, and even though she claimed to like anonymity, he doubted she could turn it off even if she wanted to.

She'd drawn some curious stares—a group of young guys hanging near the stage kept glancing back, definitely interested. They nudged each other and whispered behind hands, but no one approached her.

He shook his head. Must be the arctic expression on her face. A man would have to have balls the size of basketballs in order to muster up enough courage to talk to her.

It was Sunday and her last evening in town. Lily was heading back to Texas in the morning. His parents had gone to Putnam's Landing, a neighboring town, to visit some friends, and feeling restless, Jake has suggested a trip into Crystal Lake.

For the first time in a long time, he was busting with excitement with the need to do something. He'd almost forgotten what it felt like to get up in the morning and look forward to his day.

The only damper was Raine. There was still a lot of unfinished business between the two of them, and now that he was sticking around, the sooner he got it out of the way, the better. He thought of everything he wanted to say—of everything he *needed* to say—and his gut tightened.

There was no way he could move on until he cleared the air.

He'd called Raine a few hours earlier, thinking he would swing by, but got her voice mail. He'd left a long, rambling message telling her about the house and not much else.

Jake sighed. A lot of memories at Wyndham Place.

"Here you go." Sal interrupted his thoughts. "And if she don't like it, well…" Sal shrugged as his gaze swung toward Lily, a glare lighting up his small, round eyes something fierce.

"I'm sure it will be fine, Sal." Jake grabbed the wine-glass and shoved off from the bar.

"It's not fancy like what she wanted, but it's all I got and it will have to do."

It was nearing nine o'clock, and the band would be going on soon. Jake wound his way through the mess of tables, most of them full, and nodded to the familiar faces that he saw.

"Here you go." He placed the glass in front of Lily and watched as she tried to hide her disdain for what was in front of her. Her nose wrinkled briefly, and then she sighed.

"It's…" She glanced up at him with a confused look in her eyes. "It's, uh, bubbly."

Jake slid in across from Lily. "I know."

Lily frowned and took a sip, her face screwing up as she shoved it away. "It's…it's…"

"Yeah, it's Cold Duck."

Lily groaned. "Seriously? This is all he had? I know it's a dark, smelly grease pit, but Cold Duck instead of real wine?" Lily stared at him. "Seriously?"

Jake leaned back in his chair and glanced at the stage. "Yep." He angled his head. "You want tequila instead?"

Lily narrowed her eyes. "Sure. Why the hell not?"

Oh Christ, here we go.

Jake's grin widened. "The last time we did tequila shots—"

"Don't you dare! You said you'd never bring that up again!" Lily was laughing loudly now, her chuckle unrefined and generous. "Hold on, redneck, I'll score us some real liquor."

Lily slipped from her chair and disappeared into the dark at the same time the house lights went down and the band took the stage. It was a local act, Shady Aces, and he was pretty sure they'd been around the last time he was home. A mix of blues and hard-edged rock, the young guys on stage were chock-full of energy and attitude.

Jake settled back into his chair and watched them. There was something wild and untamed about the group, and he found himself growing more than a little wistful at the camaraderie he sensed. He'd had that once. A long time ago, back before his world had imploded.

Back before the constraints and damage of adulthood had taken over.

Lily came back as the band ripped into their second song, with six shots of tequila on a small tray, balancing it like a pro. If he didn't know better, he'd have guessed she'd waitressed at some point in her life, but considering the golden spoon and all, he highly doubted it. She set it down in front of him, shoved three shot glasses his way, and sat down beside him.

She licked her lips, aware the guys in front of the stage had turned around fully, their interest in the band gone as soon a she'd waltzed by their table, swinging her hips in a way that would make any man look twice.

Carefully, dramatically, she put a glass of tequila against her lips, winked at him, and then tossed it back like a hardened barfly.

Jake did likewise. They settled into an easy hour of

music, and he let every dark thing inside him go. He knew it would come back, but when he was with Lily, it was easy for him to forget.

It was closing in on ten when the band finished their set and the DJ filled the empty noise with a selection of slower songs.

Lily leaned back and stretched. "I like this place."

Jake snorted. She was so full of shit. "Really."

"Yes, really."

"You just hate the wine."

She cocked her head to the side and looked at him as if he were crazy. "They don't have wine, remember? Cold Duck is not wine." She grinned. "Though I will concede, their tequila is as fine as a whore's tongue."

Jake shook his head and fingered the empty shot glasses. "That it is." The one thing most people would be surprised to know about Lily St. Clare was that the woman could hold her booze better than most men he knew, and on occasion she talked like a trucker.

Unlike Raine, who was a lightweight when it came to the hard stuff.

The thought of Raine was enough to kill his buzz, and Jake sighed as he ran his hand along the back of his neck.

"Don't you dare," Lily said loudly and stood.

Jake looked up at her in surprise. "Don't what?"

"Don't retreat into your dark place. Not now...not tonight." She held her hand out as a slow, melodic tune swept over the dance floor. "It's my last night and I feel like dancing." Lily moved her hips and giggled. "Come on, redneck, show the city girl how it's done out here in the boonies."

"I don't dance," he shot back.

"Sure you do."

He shook his head. "Not gonna happen."

Lily grinned as her hands went to the edge of her blouse. She gazed beyond him and paused for a second before she tossed her hair all over the place and rolled her hips suggestively. If he didn't know better, he'd have said she was gunning for an Academy Award. "Dance with me or I'll take my shirt off, and in case you haven't noticed, I'm not wearing a bra."

Jake gritted his teeth and glared at her. He knew her well enough to know she'd do it too. And she knew *him* well enough to know he'd never let her.

"You're not only crazy," he ground out, "you're a goddamn brat."

"I know." She beckoned him. "Now dance with me."

Jake rose and let her lead him to the darkened dance floor, where they slid among several couples moving slowly to the music. It was heavy on the steel guitar, a melancholy sound that tugged at something deep inside him. He'd never heard the song before, but the tone and feel of it reminded him of…

Raine.

He stilled and held Lily as they moved along the edge of the dance floor, both of them lost in thought and somewhere else. Her fingers dug into his shoulders and he knew that she was tense. As much as she projected a sex-kitten image, Lily wasn't fussy on being touched, and though it made him wonder why she'd wanted to dance, he pushed the notion aside. About a week after meeting Lily, he'd given up trying to figure out how her mind worked. So he held her lightly and tried to forget how good it felt to hold someone.

How good it had felt to cradle Raine against his chest the other night.

"Wouldn't it be nice if we…"

He angled his head and looked down. "If we what?"

Lily's eyes shimmered, and though she tried to hide the pain inside her, she couldn't. She swallowed and smiled, a small, sad smile. "I just thought it would be nice if we could have been more than friends. If you weren't so screwed up and I wasn't so broken."

Leave it to Lily to hit the nail right on the head. Hard.

"I would have wanted someone like you," she whispered.

Jake exhaled slowly, wishing he could ease her pain. He knew the secrets she kept hidden from the world. Her hands rose up and cupped his face, her fingers light. "I want you to be happy, Jake. You deserve to be happy."

He didn't know what to say, so he kept quiet. Happiness and Jake Edwards were at odds, and he doubted they'd ever be friends.

She leaned up and kissed him alongside his mouth, pressing her cheek next to his, and she whispered, "Promise me you'll tell her how you feel."

She let him go, took a step backward, and slowly her features relaxed into a smile that immediately put Jake on alert. She was a chameleon, and he'd seen that smile before. The woman was up to something, and he was pretty damn sure it was nothing good.

The song ended and silence filled the air around them as the couples on the dance floor slowly disengaged and returned to their seats. A few of them said hello on their way by and he nodded, though his eyes never left Lily.

She moved past him and he turned to follow, his long stride faltering as he caught sight of a woman standing alone near the edge of the dance floor, huge eyes trained on him. *Raine*.

Raine's pale face looked almost elfin beneath the muted lights and she licked her lips, a nervous gesture, as she gazed at him. For a moment she reminded him of a doe about to bolt, but then her chin lifted ever so slightly, and he knew she'd stay.

He covered the distance between them in seconds and cleared his throat, but she spoke before he could get a word out.

"Hey," she said softly. "I, uh, got your message and thought…" Her voice trailed into nothing as her gaze wavered between him and Lily. "Well, I thought…"

Jake watched her struggle to speak and hated that things were so uncomfortable and awkward between them.

"I'm glad you came out." His voice sounded strained. Jesus Christ, but he felt like a damn schoolboy.

"Yes, so good to see you got over that nasty flu bug," Lily interrupted as she joined them. "You didn't look so great Thursday night." She pointed to just behind Raine. "We're sitting there."

Jake followed the women over to their table, and Lily scooped up her coat, nodding toward the closest chair. "Take a seat, Raine. I'm leaving." She shrugged. "I could lie and say I'm exhausted, but truthfully, this place kind of grosses me out. It smells like stale beer and God knows what else, and my damn heels keep sticking to the floor. I've been dying to leave ever since I arrived, and now that you're here, you can keep Jake company while he drinks to that god-awful property he just spent way too much money on."

Jake's eyes narrowed. What game was Lily playing now? She'd practically done backflips when she saw Wyndham Place and was on her speed dial to some fancy-pants interior designer by the name of Melvin before he'd even made an offer.

"You don't mind, do you, Jake? I've already called a cab, so you don't need to worry about me."

Liar.

"I'll see you later, babe." Lily reached up and kissed him on the mouth. It was a light caress, one meant for show, and if they weren't in the middle of the Coach House, he'd have told her exactly what he thought of her meddling and games.

He arched an eyebrow. *Babe?*

She stretched—a long, drawn-out, exaggerated movement that had the eyes popping out of the heads of the guys a few tables over.

Lily tossed one more mischievous smile his way and whirled around. She strode toward the bar, pulling her cell phone out of her purse as she headed toward Sal. She leaned over and chatted with Salvatore for a few seconds, gave Jake one more wave, and then disappeared from view.

He turned back to Raine, who stared after the blonde with an unreadable expression on her face. He gestured toward the seat. "Guess it's just you and me."

Chapter 10

AN HOUR BEFORE, IT HAD SEEMED LIKE SUCH A GOOD idea to come out to the Coach House, but that was before seeing Jake and Lily St. Clare together—really together—had all but made her toss her cookies.

And now? Now she felt like an asshat. An outsider.

She restlessly picked at an invisible speck of lint on her jeans and she glanced away from Jake, trying desperately to keep it together.

She felt like someone who didn't matter.

Jake had called earlier but she had been in the shower, and pacing the floors, Gibson trailing after her feet, barking and yipping as he tried to catch her toes, she'd listened to his long, rambling message.

For that one moment, he'd sounded a lot like the old Jake—excited and filled with expectation, or maybe even hope. Wyndham Place was his, and she more than anyone knew what it meant to him.

When the restlessness inside her had threatened to spill over, she said, "Screw it," and had dressed hastily in dark navy jeans that weren't falling apart—thanks to the spandex in the material, they actually fit—and a moss-green sleeveless blouse. Four-inch heels, a speck of gloss and some shadow…and she was ready to go. Her hair was a tousled mess, but she was finally getting used to it and thought that maybe it was kind of…sexy.

Not that she was trying to look sexy, but it sure as

heck felt good to think she at least looked that way for a change.

She'd locked Gibson in his crate, ignored his mournful barks, and tossed him a cookie before leaving. The drive to the Coach House had taken less than twenty minutes, and she had sat outside for nearly twenty more before mustering enough courage to go inside.

Only to watch Jake suck face with Blonde Ambition. Ugh. It was enough to make her puke. The girl was totally wrong for Jake. Why couldn't he see it?

"You want something to drink?"

"No," she answered quickly. Her stomach rolled at the thought of alcohol. "Water, maybe?"

"Sure." Jake signaled the waitress.

Raine cleared her throat and glanced around the bar as she waited for the waitress to return.

Music played in the background, the DJ spinning some soft country song. Jake's gaze was shuttered, a small frown on his face, and she glanced away, hating the silence between them. God, there'd been a day when the two of them couldn't shut up. It used to drive Jesse crazy. Her late husband was the type to sit back and analyze things—people and places—while Jake and Raine were more in-your-face with their opinions. And their opinions rarely matched—in fact they most always clashed—and that led to arguments that on more than one occasion had sent Jesse packing while the two of them duked it out.

She hated this uncomfortable space between them. Hated it a lot, but for the life of her, she had no idea how to conquer it.

Melinda, the waitress, brought her water along with

another beer for Jake. Raine watched the way the young woman's eyes rested on him. She saw the hungry look and she also saw the questions. Melinda was wondering about Lily. Wondering about Jake's relationship with the blonde.

Join the club.

The water was tepid, and Raine made a face as she took a sip and watched Melinda weave her way around the tables on her way back to the bar. A few guys sat there, including Matt Backhouse. He caught her eye and nodded, his eyes appreciative in the way a man's are when he sees something he likes.

It had been so long since anyone had looked at her that way that for a moment she was startled. She'd been holed up for so long that she'd forgotten what it feels like to be appreciated. Raine smiled politely but not before Jake caught the look and turned around.

"Backhouse?" he said roughly. "Really?"

Raine glared at him. "What's that supposed to mean?"

"Backhouse is a skirt."

"A skirt?"

Jake nodded, his frown firmly in place. "Yep."

Raine gripped her glass a little tighter and took another sip, even though Jake's cold beer was looking a hell of a lot better than what she had in her hand.

"What exactly is a skirt?" she asked drily.

Jake looked at her as if she'd just dropped in from outer space. "You don't know what a skirt is?"

"I'm pretty sure my definition of a skirt is a lot different than the one in Jake Edwards's dictionary."

His frown relaxed somewhat as he settled back in his chair. "Well, let's see. Backhouse is divorced, right?"

Last she heard.

"You know he is."

"His wife left him for Pete Ramsey?"

She nodded. It had been quite the scandal at the time.

"Pete Ramsey is his best friend?"

Her lips tightened. "Since elementary school."

"And isn't that Pete he's sitting with?"

Raine glanced back toward the bar. Again, she nodded. "Your point?"

Jake took a long drink from his beer and stretched his legs out in front of him. "My point is, he's a skirt. If my woman left me for my best friend, you can bet your ass I wouldn't be having social beers with the guy. It would take everything in me not to beat his ass into the ground."

"Well that's a great way to solve things." She motioned toward the men. "Maybe they worked their issues out."

"I'm not talking about solving anything. I'm talking about code, a guy's code of conduct, and that"—he nodded back toward Backhouse—"is just wrong." He shook his head in disgust. "I bet he moved back in with his parents."

Raine gritted her teeth, but she had to hand it to Jake. He was calling it pretty close.

"Kind of like you?"

Jake's eyes widened. "That's different, and you know it."

Of course it was, but she couldn't help herself. Raine set her elbows onto the table and cocked an eyebrow. "How so?"

He leaned forward, his spicy, earthy scent floating in the air between them. Raine was aware her pulse

exploded and kicked into overdrive. And God, she was
so hot...hot and sweaty all of a sudden.

Jake stared at her for several long moments before
answering. When he finally spoke, his voice was low and
gruff. "Because I'm a grown man and I don't need my
parents to get me through life. I do just fine on my own."

No shit, she thought.

"You never used to be so..." She licked her lips and
glanced down at her hands. Her wedding ring and dia-
mond looked huge on her third finger, all the more so because she'd lost so much weight in the last few months.

"What?" he prodded.

Raine exhaled a long shuddering breath and whispered, "Hard."

His eyes pierced her. "Better that than a"—he nodded
behind him—"damn skirt."

"So"—Raine leaned forward—"when you say 'skirt,'
you're making a derogatory female reference, correct?"

Jake frowned. "Not really. I just mean the guy is
a wimp."

"And because I wear a skirt from time to time, I'm
somehow defective? Weak?"

"That's not what I meant—"

"Then what did you mean exactly, Mr. Edwards?"
A crack of something lit up inside her and her chest
tightened. God, she missed Jake more than she wanted
to admit.

The darkness in him seemed to soften and he cocked
his head to the side, a smile pulling on his mouth. "Well,
Mrs. Edwards, what I'm trying to say is that Matt
Backhouse isn't the guy for you. You'd scare the crap
out of him, and he wouldn't know what to do with you."

"I—" she sputtered, feeling strangely exhilarated.

And hot. And bothered.

"I would scare him? What the hell does that mean?" She grabbed her water and finished the glass, slamming it down onto the table as if she'd just downed an entire jug of beer.

"He's a skirt, and someone like you needs a guy with a hell of a lot more backbone."

"Really," she said carefully, not liking the way his dark eyes settled on her. "And why is that?"

He grinned at her just as the house lights dimmed and the band members resumed their places on stage. "Because a skirt wouldn't sit here and argue a point. He'd nod and agree with everything you say, and you'd be bored to tears."

She didn't get a chance to reply, because the band kicked into a raucous rendition of an old Lynyrd Skynyrd song that had half the bar tapping along to it and the other half trying their damnedest to sing along.

Forty-five minutes later, when the band was finally stretching out that last note, it was near closing time.

Raine sat back, feeling a little lighter—happier than she'd been in a long time. As she gazed around the room, she realized a few things, troubling things that needed to be dealt with.

First off, she had become a bit of a shut-in, and that had to stop. She needed to get out and try to breathe some life into her soul, because if not—she swallowed and glanced at her hands—if not, she would wither and die. Oh, her shell of a body could go on for years, but living without a soul wasn't a way to exist.

And Jesse would not have wanted her to waste away.

"Hey."

Jake's quiet voice grabbed her and she sat back.

"You all right?"

"I'm good." And she was.

"So"—she paused—"Wyndham Place."

Jake leaned back in his chair and nodded. "Yeah, Wyndham Place."

She reached over and grabbed his beer bottle, taking a good long sip from it as she organized her thoughts. But in the end, it wasn't so much being organized as it was just asking the question.

"Why?"

Jake studied her closely and she took another long drink from his bottle, emptying it along the way, and set it back in front of him.

Brad Kitchen appeared from nowhere with a more-than-a-little-tipsy Lori Jonesberg on his arm. The woman was sporting a vibrant red head of hair with shocking chunks of white blond fringing her bangs. The look was retro, loud, and on anyone else would have looked outrageous, but on Lori it looked cutting-edge and was actually almost tame, compared to some of the looks she'd sported over the last few years. As owner of the local salon, it was almost as if Lori felt she owed it to the town to show them exactly how cool they could look.

Except there were very few residents who could pull it off, Raine included.

Raine pretended not to notice the frown that settled on Lori's mouth as the woman eyed Raine's own impromptu cut. The frown deepened and Lori's eyes—slightly crossed from too much beer—narrowed as she teetered dangerously on her four-inch leopard-print boots.

"Good Lord, which one of my girrrlzz did that to you?"

Shit.

Raine fingered the one piece that never settled and tucked it behind her ear. "Uh, I kinda did it myself."

Lori's eyes widened in horror. Seriously. It was as if Raine had just told the woman she was terminally ill or something.

Thankfully, Brad saved Raine from the brunt of whatever the hell Lori was about to unleash.

"Congrats again, Edwards, on the Wyndham deal." Brad's arm snaked around Lori in order to keep the petite woman steady. "You never did say what you're going to do with the property. You gonna demolish it and build?"

Jake shook his head. "Nope."

For a moment, Brad seemed a bit mystified, and then his eyes widened incredulously. "That house was this close to being condemned, Jake. Are you seriously going to fix it up?"

Again, Jake nodded.

"Hell, that will take a small fortune and a hell of a lot of time and worry."

"I guess it will."

"Good luck with it, then."

Jake took the hand offered to him and shook it. "Thanks."

They both watched as Brad Kitchen led Lori away, though she did manage to peer over her shoulder and grimace at Raine once more, her hand to her ear as she mouthed *Call me* before Brad guided her out of the Coach House.

"Don't pay any attention to her," Jake said quietly.

Raine stopped fussing with the errant strand of hair and glanced back at him.

"You look good."

She stared across the table at Jake for so long that when he cleared his throat and looked away, she exhaled a shaky breath and pushed her empty glass back. He was so full of shit that if his eyes weren't already brown, they sure as hell would be now. She looked like crap and she knew it.

"You ready to go?" he asked, pushing his chair back.

"Yes," she murmured. "Do you need a ride, or are you okay to drive?"

"I'm good," he answered.

They both stood and once again the big, empty space between them yawned open.

"About your question earlier," he said, his hand at her back as he pushed her toward the door. They both waved at a beaming Salvatore, and when she stepped outside, the November air hit her so hard, her lungs hurt as she inhaled a crisp, cold shot of it.

She shivered and pulled her coat tighter. "Question?" she asked as she took a few steps before she realized he wasn't following. Raine turned around and waited.

Jake's expression was unreadable as he hunched his shoulders against the brisk wind, hands shoved into his front pockets. For several moments there was nothing but the sound of the wind through the trees and the scattering debris it whipped across the concrete parking lot.

"Your question about Wyndham Place. About why I would spend a crap ton of money on a home that half of Crystal Lake thinks should be demolished." A devilish grin spread across his face, and for the first time in what seemed like ages, Raine relaxed. She took a few seconds, content just to drink in the change in him. There was a bit of the old Jake in front of her.

"Dad asked me the same question."

"And what was your answer?"

His eyes glittered, the lines around them somewhat softened by the half grin that still claimed his lips. "Why the hell not?"

She smiled. "Why not?" she repeated softly.

She knew there was a lot more to it. Wyndham Place had been theirs. The Bad Boys and their tagalong fifth wheel, Raine. They'd spent way more time than they should have in the old house when they were teenagers, and a lot of stuff had happened there. Parties. Romances. Fights.

Her eyes misted. A lot of firsts.

"So, that means…" She exhaled and met his eyes. She needed to hear him say it. Needed to feel like maybe there was a chance for things to get back to good. "That means you're staying in Crystal Lake?" She licked her lips nervously as she thought of Lily St. Clare.

Jake's expression turned serious, his hooded gaze unnerving as he rolled his shoulders and rubbed the back of his neck. He wrapped a deep indigo scarf around his neck and nailed her with a direct look.

"I guess I am."

Chapter 11

WHAT THE HELL WAS HE THINKING?

The buzz he'd been feeling for nearly a week was starting to wear off—big-time—and he had no one to blame but himself. Wyndham Place was a hell of a lot more than just a run-of-the-mill fixer-upper. It was a massive undertaking and one that he'd gladly embraced in the heat of the moment nearly a week ago, but now…

Jake stared at the huge pile of crap outside the long rambling porch—a porch that was sagging in several areas—and he had to ask himself the question.

Was he crazy or just a sucker for punishment?

The last Wyndham who had actually lived on-site had taken steps to update plumbing and electrical, but even so, there were problems, and a good bulk of the electrical had to be replaced. Luckily the pipes were in good order, though the boiler that heated the old steam radiators was toast.

It was cold as hell, but he couldn't even use the fireplaces—and there were plenty of those—because the chimneys needed to be cleaned first, and he had a feeling they were home to more rodents than he cared to think about.

He scratched the five-day stubble that had grown along his jaw and gazed up at the house. It needed new windows, a roof, and exterior paint by the truckload. There were some serious framing issues on the main level, because some idiot had thought it would be a good idea to take out two load-bearing walls. Asshole. Those would have to be replaced and the subsequent flooring issues upstairs caused by the dumbass move dealt with.

And that was just a small dent in the list he'd been adding to daily. Jake Edwards was, if anything, a perfectionist, and if he was going to do this, he was going to do this right. No cutting corners. It was something he had learned from the best—his father. The family business, Edwards Lumber Company, had been a mainstay in the area for more than three generations, and Jake and his brother had cut their teeth working for their father every summer until they'd enlisted.

"Too bad there's a shit ton of corners," he muttered as he carried out another pile of crap.

He'd spent the day before ripping out the kitchen, and the mess before him was the fruit of his efforts. Old crappy cupboards, countertops, and appliances. The large refuse bin he'd rented had already been carted away and emptied twice, and he was waiting for it to be brought back and dumped in his driveway so that he could fill it again.

Jake rubbed the back of his neck with a gloved hand. He was hot and sweaty despite the cold November weather. It was nearly four in the afternoon and already getting dark. With most of the leaves gone from the surrounding trees, the place looked pretty damn bare. He inhaled a crisp shot of cold air, his chest tightening as he gazed across the expansive lawn toward a small stone cottage barely visible behind an overgrown cedar hedge.

Cedar… The smell settled in his lungs.

They say scent is what keeps memories glued

together, and Jake had been battling scent demons ever since he'd got back from Afghanistan well over a year ago. He'd never really left the desert, it seemed.

A few days after his brother's funeral, he'd taken off to the shooting range. Somehow he'd got it in his head that if he could just shoot the shit out of something, it would help relieve the stress and heartache that ate at him night and day.

Christ, had he been wrong. The sound of gunfire was bad enough—even in a controlled environment—but it was the smell of it, that certain metallic scent of hot ammo, that immediately grabbed him hard. He'd barely been able to get through his rounds and the hell away from the shooting range without losing his shit all over the place.

He glanced at the cottage again as the smell of earth mixed with the bits of snow at his feet. The cedar and the hint of winter in the air combined and brought a wave of memories over him. Before he knew what he was doing, Jake tossed his gloves and headed for the cottage.

When he came out the week before to see Wyndham Place, he'd had no interest in the cottage and hadn't bothered to look at it. The main house had been his concern and he hadn't thought twice about the smaller home.

At one time it had belonged to the Wyndham caretaker, and though at first glance it appeared to be as neglected as the main house, he was surprised as he got closer to find that it wasn't the case. In fact, all the windows that he could see were intact. He supposed the ones around back could be busted, but for the moment they looked good.

Jake walked up the stone path and hesitated at the door. His gut churned and he was sweating profusely.

Those damn demons were just waiting to get him. He knew this, and yet he was helpless to do anything but move forward. There was a reason, or two, as to why he hadn't bothered with the cottage the week before. He could say it was because the place didn't matter. He could tell himself that until hell froze over, but the simple truth was, it was bullshit.

"A heaping pile of bullshit, brother."

A wry smile crept over his face as the echo of his brother's voice sounded in his mind. Christ, the four of them, the Bad Boys, as they'd been called, had never shied away from calling bullshit.

"I nailed Rebecca Stringer last night."

"Bullshit."

"Hey, it was me who hit the grand slam in the bottom of the ninth, not Cain."

"Bullshit."

"No, really."

"I call bullshit."

Carefully he turned the knob and the door swung back slowly. Jake stepped inside the cottage. There were beer cans and bottles strewn about, as well as fast-food debris. Cigarette butts and empty bottles of wine and liquor littered the floor, and the only piece of furniture, a red and blue plaid sofa, was in the middle of the room, with an old rug on the floor in front of the fireplace. He was surprised it wasn't in worse shape.

He took a few more steps inside, letting his eyes adjust to the dim lighting, and crossed over to the kitchen area. The cottage was open concept, with high beams and a loft at the back that ran the length of the house.

The fridge door hung open and he closed it, wincing

as the hinges squealed in protest. He was surprised to find appliances. The oven looked to be in good shape, though the countertops were crap and something had used the sink as a nest. He glanced around. The bones were good.

Jake exhaled and took a few steps back, his eyes on the stairs leading to the loft. Before he knew it, he was taking them two at a time.

He paused on the top step, gazing around a large area that was pretty much devoid of anything, save for the old four-poster bed pushed up along the far wall. Tattered gray curtains hung from the two large windows, and an old painting of a large sailing ship rested against the wall, where it had fallen years ago.

His eyes narrowed as he turned in a full circle. There used to be a dresser tucked away in the corner and a… red velvet sofa between the two windows.

Slowly Jake walked over to them and peered below. The windows overlooked a decent yard, though at the moment it was overgrown, and beyond the cedar hedge was a thick stand of evergreens. There was a clearing out there among the spruce and fir where they used to have bonfires.

Jake closed his eyes, ready for the wave of pain that rolled over him. In his mind he saw Jesse—he saw all of them, Jesse, Cain, Mackenzie, himself, and Raine, together. They'd been young and crazy and, on occasion, out of control. But they'd been tight, and back then they had felt like kings. Back then there was no sorrow, or darkness.

Back then, no one died.

The ache inside him was intense, and he didn't know

how long he stood there like an idiot, eyes closed, hands clenched at his sides. The sound of wind chimes from below cut through the fog in his head, and he was helpless to stop a trip down memory lane. He remembered another time he'd been up here and that sound...that sound had filled his head. It had filled him.

And so had she.

Contrary to Jesse's calling bullshit, Jake *had* nailed Rebecca Stringer. It had been a hot July night, he had been seventeen, horny as hell, and she'd been all over him.

"Oh my God, Jake Edwards! You did not just have sex up here with Rebecca Stringer!"

Jake whirled around, having just tucked himself back into his jeans. Shit. Raine.

Rebecca smirked and adjusted her halter top as she stepped forward. She stopped a few feet from Raine and tossed platinum hair behind her shoulders as if she'd spent hours practicing the move. Which she probably had.

"What's it to you? Who invited you anyway? I know you're, like, the tagalong orphan or whatever, but seriously, Raine, aren't you a little young to be out here at a kegger?"

Raine ignored Rebecca. Instead her eyes were on him.

"I can't believe you," she said as if he'd just committed some god-awful crime. Jesus, he was seventeen. What the hell did she expect him to do when someone like Rebecca Stringer practically forced herself on him? Push her away and say *"No, Rebecca, this would be wrong, so let's just hold hands and we won't move past heavy petting, okay?"*

"Did you hear me, Jake Edwards?"

Embarrassed, he glanced at Rebecca, though he didn't much care for the way she was looking at Raine.

"Jake!"

Shit, was that hurt in her eyes? What the hell?

"Oh my God. Drama much?" Rebecca continued. "You weren't invited, so go back to wherever you came from and leave us alone." Rebecca glanced back at him, her lips wet and inviting. "I don't think Jake and I are done yet."

Raine's hair hung down to her waist and most of it was a wild, tumbled mess. Her eyes, huge and wide-open with disbelief, stared at him for so long and hard that he had to look away. What. The. Fuck.

Who was she to look at him as if he owed her something?

She was Raine Delgotto.

His heart pounded and blood rushed through him.

She was a buddy. The female guy in their group. Almost like a sister.

Shit, anyone would take a piece of Rebecca Stringer. The girl had sprouted tits in eighth grade and had been torturing every guy in Crystal Lake ever since. Cain already had had a piece, and probably Mackenzie too. Of course Jesse was too much of a pussy. Too fucking morally confused.

Jake glared at Raine, pissed and maybe a little confused at the differing emotions running through him. He noticed her T-shirt—the tight T-shirt that clung to her small, high breasts. U2 splayed across the front, and as she crossed her arms underneath her chest, it only served to push her breasts up. They were small, but hell, they were out there.

Something curled in him, something hot and fierce.

Raine was looking at him as if he were some kind of sleazy guy, when she stood there in a T-shirt that, in his opinion, was way too tight and a pair of shorts that barely covered her ass. The kegger was in full swing, and there were a shit ton of guys out there who would be more than willing to take a peek at what she had. Did she have any idea how dangerous it was for her here? What if some drunken asshole decided he wanted her? She was small, and there was no way she could defend herself.

He glanced around wildly. Where the hell were Jesse, Cain, and Mac?

She wasn't ready for that kind of shit.

His gaze slid down her body, pausing briefly at the soft skin visible above the waistband of her jean shorts, down to toned, tanned legs, and delicate feet shoved into pink flip-flops.

Holy hell. She wasn't even sixteen yet. When the heck had she...when had she started looking like this?

"Are you hard of hearing, Raine?" Rebecca spat.

Suddenly he was really pissed off and close to losing it big-time.

"Get the hell out of here, Rebecca," he said roughly.

"What?" The blonde whirled around, face wrinkled in anger. "You're kicking me out because of her?"

He didn't have time for this shit, and hell, it wasn't as if he was the one who had invited Rebecca up to the loft. This whole thing had been her idea. "Just leave, all right? We're done."

Rebecca gazed at him in disbelief, her eyes narrowed, her chest heaving. "Unbelievable." She shoved past Raine, muttered "Bitch," and then disappeared down the stairs.

"Rebecca Stringer, really?" Raine strode toward him, her eyes flashing in what little light there was from the lamp beside the bed. "You guys are just so stupid." She flung her hands out and shook her head. "All of you. Cain, Mac…" She bit her lip, eyes lowered, and he thought that maybe her bottom lip trembled a bit. "Why is sex so important to you?"

Jake didn't know what to say, so he stood there with his hands loose at his sides and said nothing.

"I mean, that's what this was all about, right? Sex?"

"Raine," he began, his throat so tight he could barely speak. He didn't understand what was happening.

"I don't want to hear it. I thought you were different."

What? That pissed him off even more.

"Different from who? What the hell has gotten into you, Raine? I'm not a fucking choirboy."

Suddenly she was inches from his face, her huge eyes looking up at him all shiny and…hold on, were those tears?

Jake stepped back, confused and overwhelmed with the shit going on inside him. What the hell had he done to her? When had she become this…this…hot chick? She smelled…soft and light. Like peaches and summer.

"I…" she started. "Don't you want… What's wrong with me?"

He was shocked and it showed. Raine would have pulled away, but he grabbed her forearm and held her in place.

"Raine, you're just…" Shit, what the hell was he supposed to say to that? "You're just…" His mind frantically worked to find the right words, because in that *moment he knew this was important. And why the hell did she have to smell so damn good? His gaze dropped to his hand, to the soft skin beneath his fingers, and that hot, fierce heat inside him erupted. It clutched his heart and squeezed hard, and he glanced into her eyes, surprised at the intensity he felt.*

This was Raine. This was wrong.

She made a weird noise and rose up onto her tiptoes, her right hand sliding behind his neck before he could stop her. Her soft, pliant lips touched his, first a hesitant stroke, and then as all the confused feelings inside him collided, he opened his lips and took the tongue that she offered.

His hands fell away, down to her waist, down to that barely covered butt, and though he knew it was wrong—she was so young—he couldn't help himself. The world had gone to hell. Upside down was right side up.

He kissed her with all the finesse a boy of seventeen could muster. His hands moved of their own accord over soft curves, and as his fingers crept up beneath her T-shirt, over soft, satiny skin. His head was filled with peaches and summer and Raine.

She whimpered beneath him, and the sound drove him crazy. When her other hand sank into his hair, when she pushed her hips into him and he felt the strain of his erection, he panicked.

He'd never in his life felt like this. Like his insides were on fire and his mind was gone. Jake was so hard, he was afraid he'd blow and embarrass himself, and when Raine grabbed his hand and slid it around so that he now cupped her breast—her naked and soft breast—he nearly did explode.

Something penetrated the fog—wind chimes from outside that hit the window—and he wrenched himself away.

"We can't do this. What the hell, Raine?"

She stared up at him, her eyes shiny with tears, and then she bowed her head—whether from shame or embarrassment, he didn't know. For a moment there was nothing but silence, and he groaned as the raging hard-on in his jeans threatened to destroy whatever bit of self-respect he had left.

"Why?" she whispered softly.

Jesus, didn't she know? Jake ran his hands through his hair and took a step back into the shadows. Oh God, he felt like an absolute shit.

Raine covered her mouth with her fist, her cheeks flushed red, that wild hair all over the place. Her eyes were huge, her mouth swollen from their kiss.

He'd never seen anything as hot as Raine Delgotto in that moment. It was then that he realized how much he wanted something he couldn't have.

"Jesse." He exhaled harshly. "We can't because of Jesse."

Chapter 12

HIS CELL RANG AND THE MEMORIES WASHED AWAY AS quickly as they'd come. How long had he been standing there? It was now nearly dark, and a shiver rolled over him as he turned away from the window. He was drenched in sweat and cold as hell.

Jake grabbed his cell from his pocket and took the stairs two at a time, not glancing at it until he was out of the cottage, and even then he took a few seconds before answering.

"Jake?" Raine's voice was warm in his ear.

"Hey," he answered, hoping he sounded somewhat normal. He didn't do the walk down memory lane real well, especially when either Raine or Jesse was involved.

"You sound funny. Where are you?"

Leave it to Raine to cut to the chase. He hadn't seen her since Monday afternoon, when she came by for a tour of the place. Lily had still been in town and was in the house taking all kinds of pictures for Franz, or Henry, or whoever the hell it was she'd called about decorating.

It was obvious that Raine didn't care for Lily—it was pretty damn hard to miss—and the short hour Raine spent with him had been plain weird. He wasn't sure if she was just being bitchy—a territorial woman thing—or if she was back there, back to the way they were.

It left him feeling like crap, because he'd hoped that after the night before, he and Raine had maybe turned a corner.

But the space between them was as big as ever and he had no idea how to bridge it.

"I'm at Wyndham, where are you?" He cleared the cedar hedge and made his way over to the pile of crap in front of the house he now owned.

"It's six o'clock," she said, a hint of impatience in her voice.

"And…?" he answered with an edge. He wasn't in the mood for Miss Bossy Pants and quite frankly was getting sick of walking on eggshells around her.

"You were supposed to pick me up for the turkey roll, remember?"

Shit. He had forgotten about the damn fundraiser. Why the hell had he let her talk him into that anyway?

Dumb question. He'd always had a hard time saying no to Raine, but the turkey roll? He knew it was for a good cause and all, but shit, every single available woman would be there—pretty sad when a turkey roll was the "big event" of the season—and they'd be gunning for fresh meat. He didn't have Lily as a buffer, since she'd left for Texas.

He clenched his teeth and ran a hand over his forehead as he gazed off into the gloom. "Sorry. Time kind of ran away from me."

There was a pause. "Are you still coming? Do you want me to come get you?"

He glanced down at his ragged jeans and dirty hands, and grimaced.

Aside from the single women out looking for love, the entire town would be there as well, and he'd had enough of them on Black Friday. He knew what some of them thought, the rumors as to why he'd left town not long after Jesse's funeral.

Some of the townspeople thought he had a drug problem. Others thought he was an alcoholic or crazy with grief or just flat-out certifiable. Soldiering would do that, they said. Make you crazier than you already were.

In fact, there was a bit of truth in all of those reasons.

"Jake?" Raine repeated.

"Yeah, I'm still here."

"Are you all right?"

No.

Jake rolled tense shoulders. Damn, he was tired. He hadn't hired any help at all. Hadn't taken up his father's offer to lend him some of the workers from Edwards Lumber, either. His plan was to work his ass off every single day until he fell into bed at night, exhausted. He wanted to sleep, for fuck sake.

Except his plan wasn't working.

His head was still haunted and he was lucky to get two hours of sleep at most. As a soldier, he was used to running on fumes, but a body could only do it for so long until it crashed and burned. He was there. On the edge.

"Jake?"

He scooped up his gloves, took the stairs up to the porch. "Yeah," he answered distractedly.

"Are you going to bail on me?"

He locked the front door and turned around. She was nervous. He heard it in her voice, and as much as he needed to go home and do whatever he had to do in order to sleep—at this point pills and booze were looking mighty good—he couldn't. He owed Raine so much more than that.

"No," he answered, heading toward his truck. "I'm not bailing, and neither are you."

"It's a turkey roll, Jake. I'm sure we can throw some cash at the committee and be done with it."

"No, I'll meet you there. I just have to run home and shower first."

There was a pause and he knew she was thinking of a way out. His mother had filled him in on how Raine had become somewhat of a shut-in, and though he got it—he understood the need to be alone—it wasn't healthy. If he could help her get through this, then maybe he could help himself.

Who the hell was he kidding? Jake was beyond help. His demons were bastards that wouldn't let go, but maybe Raine would be different. Maybe Raine would make it through to the other side in one piece.

"I'll see you at the arena." He pocketed his cell and headed for his Jeep.

———

"Raine Edwards, in the flesh. Wow, I heard there was a sighting last week, at the Coach House, of all places, but I didn't believe it."

Raine squeezed her eyes shut and bit her bottom lip. She had just entered the arena ten seconds ago and already she regretted her decision to come.

You can do this.

She pasted the fakest smile that she could muster onto her face and turned around.

Rebecca Stringer-Hayes stood a few feet away, her model-thin frame sheathed in soft brown leather with fur trim and pencil-straight jeans in a dark indigo. Knee-high brown leather boots—again, trimmed in fur—completed the smart ensemble.

"It's so good to see you!" Rebecca said with an equally fake smile in place, her platinum blond hair falling to just past her shoulders. Rebecca's eyes glittered as she shoved a long piece behind her shoulder. "I see having Jake back has brought you out of your shell."

Raine's facade cracked a little bit and it took a lot to keep her shit together. Rebecca Stringer had always pushed her buttons. A few years older than Raine, Stringer was a spoiled, selfish bitch.

And that was being nice, as far as Raine was concerned.

"So…" Rebecca moved toward Raine, her steps smooth like a dancer's. "What the hell is up with Jake and Lily St. Clare?" She winked and leaned closer as if she were Raine's best friend and confidant. "I heard they're about to get engaged. Is that true?"

She didn't wait for Raine to reply but plowed forward, running her mouth as if she were competing in the Olympics. "Oh my God, can you imagine? Crystal Lake is, like, the new in place for celebrities. Of course Cain has pretty much left us in the dust, but still, this could be great for our little town, don't you think? Maybe they'll do another reality show."

Raine's nails dug into the soft skin of her palms and she waited a moment, still trying to keep her shit from falling all over the place and very much aware that a good number of the people in the arena lobby were watching her and Rebecca.

"I don't know, Rebecca. Why don't you ask him yourself?"

Rebecca's eyes narrowed at Raine's insolent tone.

"He's right behind you."

Thank God.

Raine had delayed coming into town when she found out Jake would be late. Hell no, that was a lie. She'd almost said screw it and stayed in, but the thought of Jake facing the curious—though well-meaning—townspeople alone had been enough to make her get her butt into her car and drive into Crystal Lake.

Her timing was good, though she would have considered it a win if she'd at least managed to avoid Rebecca altogether.

Jake nodded to Mrs. Avery, the florist, and stopped just to Raine's left. She glanced up quickly and her heart squeezed a bit. The man was exhausted. Fatigue lines crept along his eyes and the expression inside them hurt her something fierce. He wasn't just exhausted. He was haunted.

And even though she was still holding on to a truckload of anger where he was concerned—anger over the way he'd abandoned his family. Anger over the way he'd left her alone to deal with the most heartbreaking year of her life.

She couldn't deny her feelings for him. Jake Edwards was her family.

Though if she was honest, he was more than that. Always had been. He was connected to her in a way no one else had ever been, not even her husband, Jesse. The problem was that the two of them clashed more than they got along, and she knew it would take a bit for them to get over the last year and a half.

But they would get there. They had to. There was no other choice.

Jake put his hand at Raine's back and smiled at

Rebecca. "Hey, it's been a while. How's Bradley doing these days?"

Rebecca licked her lips, and Raine scowled at the obvious sex-bomb ploy. The woman had more Botox and collagen than a freaking Hollywood starlet, and while she supposed Rebecca was still considered hot, there was something insanely wrong about putting that crap into your face when you were in your early thirties.

Fifty? Maybe. Sixty? Hell, yeah. No judging. There was nothing wrong with firming up a bit if you wanted to, but why mess with nature when you were still so young? She'd look like a freak by the time she was sixty.

"Jake, I was so glad to hear you finally came to your senses and are back home where you belong."

Rebecca waited for a response but none came, and an uncomfortable few seconds passed before Rebecca giggled nervously. "Now if only we could convince Cain and Maggie to return from Los Angeles, we'd have half the Bad Boys back in town and it would be like old times, don't you think?"

Raine felt Jake stiffen at her side and she stared at Rebecca, loathing everything about the woman. She did not have a brain in her head. It wasn't possible.

Raine waited for the explosion, the harsh, condescending words that would surely erupt from Jake's mouth, but he surprised her.

"I'm not real keen on going back in time, because I don't think things will ever be the same again. But then, that's the way it should be, no?"

Rebecca shrugged. "Sure, I hear you. I just meant it would be nice if everyone was home again, Cain, Mackenzie…" Her eyes moved to Raine. "And of course,

Jesse. None of us have forgotten him. He'll always be a part of us. Of this town."

Suddenly, Raine had had enough of the bullshit. Rebecca had meant nothing to Jesse, and she certainly didn't mean anything to Raine. And other than being Jake's fuck buddy when they were teenagers, she wasn't relevant.

She turned abruptly. "Let's go, Jake."

The two of them crossed the lobby, and Raine's tension increased in small increments as she said hello to Mrs. Lancaster, the pastor's wife, and then Mr. Lawrence, owner of Lawrence's Tackle & Bait, followed by the vet, Dr. Hannigan.

Her heart pounded and she heard each and every beat inside her head. What the hell was wrong with her?

She glanced to the left and then to the right.

Of course, half the town was out, because really, what else was there to do on a Friday night but grab hold of a frozen turkey and throw it down the ice at ten bottles of diet soda?

I don't want any of this.

For one moment she considered turning around, making an excuse, and getting the hell out of Dodge. The thought of her sofa, Gibson, and a brainless movie to take her away was almost more than she could take.

Raine hesitated. She was cold. And hot. She felt disoriented.

But then a warm hand traveled up her back and settled at the top of her spine. Long, male fingers. They gently rubbed along the corded muscles there and she held her breath, mouth going dry.

The sensation was bittersweet and so foreign to her that she wanted to cry. It had been that long.

"Hey."

Her breath held as Jake's mouth moved to near her ear. He was still behind her, and she supposed—judging from the covert glances tossed her way—they looked almost intimate.

"Let's buy some raffle tickets to support the community center, watch a game of turkey bowling, and get the hell out of here."

"Okay," she whispered. "Okay."

She hadn't done a big crowd in months, and she just didn't know if she had the strength to deal with everyone's well-wishes.

They entered the rink and bought a bunch of raffle tickets, all for the chance to win various sorts of prizes ranging from barbecue utensils to engine oil to bottles of booze.

Already a robust game of turkey bowling was under way, and the two of them slipped through the crowd, inching closer to the rink for a better look. Someone handed Jake a beer, but Raine declined, her eyes on the ice, already looking at the clock and counting down the moments until she could leave.

There were too many happy people around. Too many couples. Too many stolen glances, soft touches, and kids. Holy Christ, the kids. They were everywhere.

Raine swallowed hard and was about to bolt when Luke Jansen approached, a huge grin pasted to his face. Jansen was tall, the same age as Jake, but already with a thinning scalp and thickening waist. They'd all gone to school together years ago, and Luke had played football with Jake and the boys.

"Christ, Edwards." Luke stuck out a hand and shook Jake's vigorously. "Good to see you." His smiled widened as he glanced down at Raine, though he took a moment and she saw the concern there. The questions.

For a second, she panicked, her chest tight, her breath caught in her throat. The pressure was too tight and she looked away, exhaling slowly as she tried to stay calm. Shit, why had she ever thought it would be a good idea to come to this with Jake?

Because she was so happy to see the back of Lily St. Clare's head that she invited Jake on a whim, and he surprised her by accepting.

"Raine, how have you been?"

She swallowed and met Luke's eyes, pasting another fake smile to her face. "Good."

His gaze lingered a little too long. His eyes were a little too intense.

God, it was hot in here.

Raine tugged at her soft pink turtleneck and glanced at Jake—which was the wrong thing to do, because he was looking between the two of them, and she could see him mind working. He knew something was up.

"I'm glad," Luke replied, but when he opened his mouth to continue, Raine didn't give him a chance.

"So, you're here to turkey bowl?" Her voice was overly bright and she was well aware that Jake was looking at her strangely. The panic in her gut spread out and she started to babble.

"Wow, what a crowd. The committee must be really happy.

"Shoot, isn't that your girlfriend over there?

"No? Oh, sorry, I didn't know you guys broke up.

"So, you're here to bowl?"

Luke glanced from Raine to Jake and he slowly nodded. "Uh, yeah, Backhouse cornered me into it, but we're looking for a third member for our team."

"Backhouse?" That got Jake's attention, thank God, and he turned to look over her shoulder at the ice.

"Yep." Luke nodded and then paused, a slow smile spreading across his face. "Why don't you join us, Edwards? We're up next."

Jake started to shake his head, but then Matt Backhouse sidled up alongside the ice and grinned at them through the glass. "Hey, Raine."

"Hi." Her mind went blank until Jake coughed sharply and she thought he said…

Skirt.

She glared at Jake.

"Matt," she continued. A good-looking guy, he was of average build, with curly blond hair and blue eyes the color of a robin's egg. But Jake was right. He was entirely too nice. He was the kind of guy who always opened the door, said please and thank you, and didn't know how to swear properly.

Everyone knew that *feck* wasn't a swearword.

Skirt.

He was boring.

Skirt.

And hell-bent on pleasing.

Skirt.

And he always agreed. Hell, *Yes* was his middle name.

Skirt. Skirt. And skirt.

No wonder his wife had left him. What kind of relationship thrived when there was no friction?

"Raine, do you want to be our third?" Matt grinned from ear to ear. "We're up next, but Kenny Davidson isn't here yet."

Jake grabbed a beer offered to him by Luke and stepped forward. "That's all right, Backhouse. I'm in."

Raine frowned as Jake smiled down at her. "Unless you want to play?" he asked silkily.

"No," she answered hastily. The last place she wanted to be was out there on the ice, under the scrutiny of all those eyes. Everyone would be wondering how the young widow was doing, and they'd be commenting on her weight or how pale she was, or maybe—she touched the jagged ends of her hair—the state of her last haircut.

"Don't worry," Jake said, "I'll play this one game and then we're outta here."

Chapter 13

EXCEPT THAT ONE GAME TURNED INTO FOUR, BECAUSE they kept winning, and by the time they were well into the championship round, it was nearly midnight. Raine was running on fumes. She was tired and cold and tense and pissed off.

She couldn't relax if her life depended on it, and Jake? Well, Mr. Jake Edwards was half in the bag and tossing his turkey as if he were playing in some life-or-death tournament. A permasmile had taken up residence on his face, and he was the life of the party.

What. The. Hell.

He was supposed to be as dark and twisty as she was.

Her fingers clutched a large hot chocolate and she slowly sipped, avoiding eye contact with anyone who crossed her perimeter, because she wasn't feeling social at all. She watched Jake line up his shot, his muscles well defined by the plain, long-sleeve henley shirt he wore.

She watched him pause as several women shouted encouragement from the sidelines, including Melinda from the Coach House and Lori from A Cut Above—even though her new squeeze, Brad Kitchen, stood by her side. Melinda, however, had poured her *assets* into skintight jeans, a cute black top that hugged her considerable curves, and shoes that were totally inappropriate for an ice rink. She tossed her hair back—okay, what was with all the hair tossing?—and inched her way closer to Jake.

"Win this one and I'll buy you another drink!" she shouted.

Over my dead body.

If Raine was surprised at her possessive thoughts, she paid them no mind. Jake had had too much to drink, and even though he seemed happy, jovial even, she knew it wasn't real.

He *was* as dark and twisty as she was, dammit.

Jake flashed a smile at Melinda, though his dark eyes settled on Raine briefly before he accepted a fifteen-pound frozen turkey from Luke, took aim, and whipped it down the ice. He obliterated the row of soda bottles, scored a strike, and Raine tossed her hot chocolate into the bin beside her.

She strode forward, inching through the crowd that surrounded him, and honestly, it was as if he'd just scored a touchdown in the freaking Super Bowl. She glared at Melinda. The woman hung off Jake like a bad rash, her arms on his shoulders as she laughed up at him. If she pressed her boobs into him any harder, he'd end up with two very large and very round imprints across his chest.

It's a turkey bowl, you idiot. He's not saving the world.

"Jake, it's time to go."

Jake whipped his head around, and though he still smiled widely, she saw the shadows that clung to the corners. The ones that filled in the lines around his eyes.

"Raine, you were our good-luck charm!" Matt Backhouse slid alongside her, his face flushed from the effects of one too many beers. Or three or four.

"I don't think so." She shook her head and smiled politely, jostled forward by a raucous bunch of teens. "You guys won that all on your own."

Matt slid his arm around her shoulders, his weight heavy as he leaned into her, and she wrinkled her nose. He smelled like beer and sweat, and she wished he would take his hands off her.

"I think you and I should maybe do something sometime."

"Something?" Raine tried to push away from Matt, but he was more than a little drunk and his fingers now clutched at her, tight along her elbow.

"Yeah." He nodded, a sloppy grin claiming his mouth. "Maybe a movie or something."

She shook her head. "No, I don't think so, Matt. But thanks for asking."

She was hit from behind again and stumbled forward, with both of Matt's hands on her now as he helped to steady her. She was inches from his face, helpless to stop him as he leaned forward, his intention obvious.

"Matt, what are you doing?" she said carefully, trying to push away. His audacity took her by surprise, but she supposed when you were a lightweight and downed as many beers as he had, anything was possible. But Matt Backhouse was harmless.

He was, as Jake said, a skirt. She could handle him.

"I think I wanna kiss my good-luck charm."

Her stomach rolled. Oh God, the stale beer.

"Hands off, Backhouse."

He was yanked from behind, and the only reason he didn't fall on his ass was because Jake held him by the scruff of his neck.

Jake released Matt and he rounded, fists ready, only to fall limply to his side when he gazed up at the dark, intense, and pissed-off Jake. The good humor and easy camaraderie fled as Luke slid between the two men.

"Hey, now," Luke said, hands up. "Let's calm down, boys."

Melinda shoved her chest out and licked her lips. "Jake why don't we get out of here?"

Jake turned to Melinda, and Raine was suddenly too damn hot and too damn bothered to pay attention. If Jake Edwards wanted to dip his wick into someone like Melinda, then who was she to stand in the way?

At least Melinda wasn't some platinum-blond trust-fund baby. Nope, she was a good old small-town girl who could show Jake a good time, and she wouldn't break his heart in the process. Maybe she was what he needed. Someone normal. Someone who kinda sorta understood where he came from.

Raine's gaze passed over Jake, who was bent down listening intently to whatever the hell was coming out of Melinda's mouth.

Why did she care who he slept with? Was she that selfish? Did she want him to suffer the way she did?

Raine turned on her heel and shoved through the thinning crowd. She said good-byes to those who shouted at her and made her way off the ice and out into the lobby. Out here the crowd was thinner, though the booze had flowed steadily and the majority of those left behind were going to be nursing some pretty serious hangovers the next day.

Good to see that turkey, beer, and whiskey could raise a crap ton of money for the community center.

Outside the air was crisp, and with one deep breath she banished the stale beer and sweat from inside. For a second she paused, her face lifted upward. The snow fell gently, tickling her nose as the huge, fluffy flakes drifted all around her. Colored lights were strung up across the top of the arena, the reds, blues, yellows, and greens twinkling around her like a fantastical light show. Off to the right, just outside the front doors, was a massive Santa Claus—she wasn't sure how she'd missed him on the way in—the jovial face frozen in perpetual glee.

Christmas was less than four weeks away, and just the thought of it was enough to make her throat swell with emotion. Time marched on, it seemed, with no regard for those who preferred to be left behind.

There was a time when Christmas had been her favorite time of year. A season of parties and goodwill. Of snowmobiling in the bush and bonfires until the morning hours. It had never been about presents for Raine. It had been about family and love. Of belonging to someone.

And sadly, even though Marnie and Steven tried their best, she just didn't feel like she belonged to anyone anymore. She thought of the damn empty chair at Thanksgiving. Did she really want to go through that again?

Raine started forward, shrugging off the melancholy as she trudged through the snow in search of her car. She thought briefly of Gloria and wondered if she was going to be around for the holidays. By chance, she'd talked to her mother briefly at the grocery store. If not for Mrs. Lancaster's presence, she would gladly have slipped down another aisle and ignored her mother altogether.

But Mrs. Lancaster was hard to avoid, and the woman had eyes in the back of her head. How many times had Raine been busted for reading Sweet Valley High books in church?

She spied her Volkswagen near the center of the parking lot, an overgrown pile of white, buried beneath at least a foot of snow. Grabbing her keys from her pocket, she was about to unlock the trunk and grab her snow brush when Jake appeared so suddenly, she dropped them.

"Jesus Christ, Jake. What the hell?" Irritated, she searched through the snow at her feet, retrieved her keys, and glared at him. "Aren't you going somewhere with Melinda?"

His dark eyes narrowed a bit, and though he seemed steady on his feet, he'd consumed enough alcohol to fell most men she knew. "Are you serious?" he said.

She shrugged. His tone was sharp, and she really didn't want to get into it with him right now. She unlocked her trunk and lifted it up, cursing as snow fell over her hands.

"She was offering, and that's something most guys wouldn't turn down."

"I'm not most guys," he said roughly, grabbing the snow brush from inside and moving to the front of the vehicle. "You going to warm this thing up, or what?"

"Am I driving you home?" she retorted, opening the driver-side door.

"Do I look like I can drive?" He swooshed a large chunk of snow off her windshield, and she squealed as a good amount of it ended up in the car. In her lap. And in her face.

She didn't say anything else. She just watched him through the glass as he methodically cleaned her entire car. Snow glistened in his hair, which he hadn't cut since he was home, and it was now officially—as Mr. Edmonds, their high school football coach, used to say—girlie man. Though with his strong features, large athletic build, and five o'clock shadow, there wasn't anything remotely girlie about Jake.

There never had been.

When he was done, he tossed the brush back into the trunk and hopped into the passenger seat, his large frame filling up the space in a way that made her nervous.

"Shit," he exclaimed as he searched for the seat belt, "this thing is a hell of a lot smaller than I remember." His knee banged against the dash as he twisted, seat belt in hand, trying to find the buckle. He bumped the dash again, swore, grunted, and then laughed.

"Oh my God, Jake. Could you be any more of a loser?"

Raine reached over and grabbed the belt off him, her fingers nimbly shoving it into the buckle. She waited for the click and then slowly glanced up at him, a scowl in place, but one that melted away like sand through an hourglass.

Snowflakes glistened in his hair like diamonds, reflecting from the security light just to the right of the car. One perfect flake nestled on the edge of his eyelash and she held her breath, afraid to breathe.

Afraid to move.

How long did they stare at each other with nothing but the wind in their ears?

No clue.

But it was long enough that the snowflake began to

melt, and for no reason—other than insanity—Raine's hand crept upward to carefully brush it from his face. Her eyes followed her fingers, and for the longest time she just stared at him. At her paleness against his tanned and masculine cheek, and then his jaw.

She felt the rough stubble from his beard, the heat from his body, and she smelled the musky spice that was all Jake.

His eyes were hooded, his long lashes downcast, but she heard the catch in his throat and something inside her woke up. Something hot and heavy and so exquisite, it was painful.

Christ, but the Edwards brothers were attractive. Even though Jesse had been the serious twin, he'd been lighter in coloring, more like pretty boy Mackenzie Draper. But Jake…God, there was nothing gentle, or soft, or pretty about him.

And as she watched him in silence….as his hooded gaze widened and stared back at her from beneath lowered lids…she found herself feeling something she hadn't felt in a very long time. Want. Need.

Desire.

God, it was so hot.

Which was insane, because it was still frosty inside her car, and their hot breath made small puffs that evaporated into nothing as they stared at each other through the heavy silence.

He moved slightly and she noticed for the first time how glassy his eyes were. Whether from fatigue or… The smell of whiskey hit her.

"You're drunk," she whispered.

His generous mouth curved into a frown. "I'm not

drunk enough," he answered roughly. "Because if I was as drunk as I should be, I'd be passed out cold. I'd be sitting here like a zombie, and we'd be on our way home, where you would dump my ass at my parents' place, and hopefully I'd stay drunk until tomorrow morning, maybe even sleep." A heartbeat passed; his voice was husky. "Instead…"

She leaned forward a bit more, barely able to hear him.

"Instead," she repeated softly.

Jake exhaled and grabbed her hand, rolling it along his skin until it rested near his mouth. The air between them was charged with something tangible. Something fierce and hard.

Something scary.

"Instead, I'm thinking about things I shouldn't be thinking about." His hand crept to her chin, his touch gentle, though his fingertips were rough. Maybe his fingers trembled—she couldn't tell, because all of a sudden things seemed wonky, as if reality were out of sync.

No longer hot, she was cold as hell and shivered violently, her mind crying out, though the scream was buried inside her head, where no one could hear.

Such longing rushed through her, such an intense need to be touched—to matter to someone—that she whimpered and closed her eyes. She moved her head slightly, her mouth parted, and she was afraid that her heart would beat out of her chest. Blood rushed through her veins, senses long dead erupted, leaving her breathless. Aching.

Her breasts swelled. His fingers splayed across her jaw now, not as gentle as before, and yet she wanted more. She wanted…

"Jake," she whispered, her body warring with her mind. On what planet was this okay? To be here like this with her husband's brother?

Yet she leaned into him instead of pulling away. She didn't want his warmth to leave her, because she was afraid that she would never get warm again.

"Please," she whispered.

And then his mouth was on her hers, his lips hot and hungry. She opened for him and it was neither a gentle nor a coaxing kiss, but rather a clashing of emotion. It was want and need and anger and guilt.

But that didn't stop the surge of desire that rolled through Raine, and she whimpered as she moved and tried to get closer to him.

His hands were on her chin, holding her steady, and she felt him stiffen—felt him withdraw.

And when he pulled away from her, she was more confused than ever.

"What are we doing, Raine?" Jake's voice was ragged. "What the hell are we doing?"

She heard his pain and the hole inside her expanded. It twisted and twisted until she could barely breathe.

"We're trying to survive," she whispered through tears. *I'm trying to stay alive.*

"We can't, not like this. Not again."

Jake pushed her away and leaned back. "Not again," he repeated, and closed his eyes. "Christ, I feel like shit. Just get me to a bed."

He settled back into his seat, head turned toward the window, away from her.

For a few seconds Raine was too stunned to do anything. What had she just done? Eventually she became aware of doors slamming shut and engines roaring to life. The truck next to her pulled away, and she watched its taillights fade away to nothing. It would seem that the turkey roll was officially over.

Her fingers gripped the steering wheel, and after a while she flipped the radio on, reversed out of her parking spot, and headed into the night.

Chapter 14

DAWN CAME LATE THIS TIME OF THE YEAR AND IT WAS usually cold, dark, and nasty. Jake rolled out of bed, his mood black before he'd even given it a chance to improve. He was still in the clothes he'd worn the night before and hadn't bothered to change, which meant that now his bedroom smelled like a damn brewery.

He glanced in the mirror and groaned at the sight of his bloodshot eyes and rumpled T-shirt and jeans.

Coffee was the order of the day and something he needed in the worst way possible. The rest—like a shower and a change of clothes—would have to wait.

Noiselessly he made his way downstairs, but the smell of a freshly brewed pot greeted him, and he knew someone was already up. He hoped it wasn't his mother, because God knew she deserved a hell of a lot better than his sorry ass first thing in the morning.

God, he felt like shit.

But that's what Canadian whiskey will do to you, if you let it.

With a groan he entered the kitchen and winced at the bright lighting. His father was at the kitchen table, Saturday paper in hand and two steaming cups of coffee in front of him.

"I heard you up and poured you some java," his father said.

"Thanks."

Steven peered over the paper at him and shook his head. "Hitting it a little hard last night, were you?"

"Appears so."

Jake grabbed his coffee, leaned against the table, and glanced at the clock. It was barely five in the morning, pitch dark, and the wind that howled along the lake was something fierce.

"Mom still in bed?" Jake savored the warmth of his cup and studied his father.

Steven nodded, folded the paper, and grabbed his mug before settling back in his chair. His thick hair, white as the snow outside, was kept short, and though his color was better than it had been, he was still pale. He was still thin. Still heartbroken.

Would any of them ever be whole again?

"How's Wyndham coming along?" Steven asked. "Sorry I haven't been out this week, but the new development on the other side of the lake is keeping me busy."

Jake smiled wryly. "It's coming…I guess."

"You sure you don't want any help? I could spare a few men."

"Nah, I'm good. I've got Weasel coming to look at the electrical on Monday morning to get that mess sorted out, and I plan on framing and drywalling the two load-bearing walls that some jackass decided to move by the end of the week. The roofers are coming Wednesday, and the windows should all be replaced by next week as well."

His father nodded in approval. "Sounds like you've got everything under control."

Jake shrugged. "I don't know about that, but once the main stuff is done, I've got a hell of a lot of work to do inside. The place has gone to shit, and most of the woodwork needs to be redone, walls replastered, floors leveled." He rubbed the back of his neck. "And that's just the beginning."

"You're working real hard."

Something in his father's tone, a note of concern, caught Jake's attention. He took a sip of his hot coffee and shrugged. "It feels good."

For a few seconds nothing was said, and then his father spoke so gently that Jake had to strain to hear him. "You're working too hard, son."

Jake's heart skipped a beat, heavy at the sadness in his father's voice, and he glanced away. How could he make any of them understand that he needed to push himself? He needed the mental and physical exhaustion, because sometimes—hell, most of the time—it was the only way he could forget. The only way he could function.

"I hear you at night," Steven said hoarsely.

Jake's head whipped up. "What was that?"

Steven's eyes were misty and he cleared his throat. "I hear you at night, Jake. You don't sleep. You're up pacing your room, or down in the gym, killing the equipment, or off for a run."

For a moment Jake could only stare at his father helplessly. Now would be the time to open his damn mouth and get everything out into the open. Now would be the time to spill the dark secrets he'd kept. Could he seek salvation?

Was he strong enough to ask for forgiveness?

Yet his throat was so tight that he was barely able to breathe, and the demons he'd been running from for the last year and a half were suddenly here, with him, right beside him, laughing their fucking asses off.

We got you.

We've always had you.

He closed his eyes, his heart beating crazily as the pressure inside him built steadily. White noise erupted in his ears so loud that he winced, and he groaned, hanging his head in his hands in an effort to get a grip. He couldn't lose his shit. Not here. Not at home in front of his father.

And yet he could taste the desert in his mouth. Feel the heat of the sun, the stinging sand in his eyes. He could hear the steady ping, ping, ping *of the sniper shots, the hoarse shouts of his men. The cries of rage and retribution.*

Civilians screaming in pain, children running mad. A dog named Len, the mangy critter his unit had adopted.

And he saw Jesse, striding through it all as if he wore a death wish around his neck, like the crazy fuck from Platoon.

The blackness inside Jake was so big he felt like he was coming apart. His eyes flew open, but he was still back there. Back in hell. And for a moment he was confused. Something fell at his feet. Something shattered.

His coffee mug.

And then two arms were around him, holding him tight, not letting go even as he struggled to break free.

Eventually everything fell away as it always did, and he was left trembling, drowning in cold sweat.

"Jesus, Dad, I'm sorry."

His father's gripped his shoulders tightly, and when he had enough balls to look Steven in the eye, Jake's world tilted a little. His throat was so tight, his jaw clenched in an iron grip and there was nothing more that he could share.

Not now anyway.

Steven's eyes were wet, and Jake was startled to realize his stung as well.

"I don't want to know, Jake...what happened over there." Steven gazed at him, his right hand gripping Jake behind his head to keep him steady. Just as he used to do when Jake was ten, and it was the bottom of the ninth, winning run on base, and Jake was up to bat. Steven would always look him in the eye and calm him down.

"I don't need to know how Jesse died. What I need, as a father, is for you to let go and come back to us, because this family won't survive another blow. We just... we just won't."

Jake carefully pulled away from his father. He bent down and picked up the pieces of his mug and then grabbed a cloth from the sink to wipe up the mess. When he was done, he shoved his hands in his pockets and hunched his shoulders forward. He was freezing.

Outside, it was still pitch dark, though a frosty December moon shimmered along the top of the still-unfrozen water. Snow was falling, nothing more than a light dusting really, and the wind was all but gone. Crystal Lake was as smooth as glass.

In another lifetime he might have gone back to bed. He might have tried to get some rest, but in this life that he was left with, that wasn't an option. Even though he was bone tired, he knew that hard, physical labor was the only thing that settled him.

He should go.

"I'm sorry," he said quietly, not knowing what else to say.

"Jake, I need you to get better," his father said quietly, and it was that quiet strength that got to him. Jake blew out a hot breath and took a moment to compose himself. He wasn't a child, for Christ's sake, but sometimes the thought of launching himself into his father's arms was more than he could bear.

"I'm trying," he managed to say.

"Not good enough." Gone was the warmth. "You need to try harder for the people who love you. For your mother and me…and for Raine. She needs you more than you know, and I'm pretty damn sure she's not going to make it through unless she has you in her corner."

Jake blinked, his chest beating hard. But what could he say? He'd failed them all, Jesse the most. If they knew the truth, would they still be so damn gung ho to keep him around?

"You get that, right?" Steven ground out. "We need you, Jake. This family needs you."

Jake stared at his father for a long time, and when he finally spoke, his voice was subdued. "I don't know if I'll ever get back to good. After—" His voice hitched and he cleared his throat. "After what happened over there, I don't know if it's possible." He paused. "But Dad, you have to know I'm trying. I'm trying my best, and right now that's all I got."

For several long moments the two men stared at each other, and then Steven nodded. "Okay then."

—⁘—

Less than an hour later, Jake pulled up to Wyndham Place and parked near the new refuse bin that had been dropped off sometime last night. It was empty, and if he wanted to make a dent in the pile of crap out front, he'd best get started.

The sun was now up, and with the temperature hovering around the freezing mark, it wasn't all that cold. With only a few weeks until Christmas, he was damn lucky to have escaped any real major snowstorms, but one was on the way.

Jake exited his Jeep and glanced up at the sky. It was filled with dark gray clouds and he figured they were in for one hell of a snowfall in the next twenty-four hours. A thought crossed his mind and he made a mental note to dig around his father's garage for his snowmobile.

Maybe a ride would help clear his head later, but in the meantime—he glanced at the pile of crap again—he had other things to occupy him.

He took two steps and noticed tire tracks leading to the stone cottage. The overgrown cedar hedge didn't let him see shit, but the tracks were fresh, and there was only one set going in. What the hell?

He took off, thinking it was most likely a teenage couple using the place for what most of them had done through the years—getting lucky. But it was time to let them know that a new owner had taken up residence and the cottage was off limits, and anyone thinking to use it for a quick lay was trespassing.

He followed the tracks down the path, and when he rounded the corner, he tripped over something that tied up his feet but good. With a curse Jake tried to keep his balance but instead fell backward onto his ass.

"Jesus!"

Jake landed in mud and wet snow and was immediately attacked by a bundle of fur that came with a wet, sloppy tongue and the unmistakable odor of puppy breath.

Gibson.

The little bastard strained against Jake's hands, trying to get to his face, but damned if he was going to let Raine's puppy lick him as if he were a piece of candy. Everyone knew dogs spent half their time licking their junk. He shoved the puppy off him. No way was he getting close to that.

"Gibson," he growled. "Stop."

But the dog just yipped happily and jumped toward him, his tongue aimed for Jake's mouth again. Firmly, Jake grabbed Gibson by the scruff and tucked him into his embrace. He got to his feet, spying Raine's rust bucket a few feet away. He also noticed for the first time that the lights were on inside, which surprised him. He had assumed the electricity didn't work out here.

Carrying the squirming puppy, he marched toward the house. His ass was wet and his black mood had just got blacker. What the hell was Raine doing out here anyway? He wasn't ready to see her again.

Not after last night. Not after he'd come so close to taking something that didn't belong to him.

He opened the front door and strode into the cottage, his eyes finding Raine almost immediately. She was in the kitchen area, hunched over the sink, scrubbing away and humming along to whatever was playing on her iPod.

Her hair was clipped to the top of her head, though straggly pieces hung around her ears and neck. Dressed in a gray sweatshirt two sizes too big and a pair of jeans that were well worn and threadbare in the ass, she looked no older than a college kid. Her pale skin shone like alabaster in the muted light as her head bobbed to a beat that only she could hear.

For that one moment, she looked young, carefree and—as she smiled and sang, "So, call me maybe"— like the most beautiful thing in the world.

His eyes and his heart drank her in as if he was dying of thirst, and he took a step back, hiding in the shadows near the door. It had been so long since he'd seen her like this. Dancing, singing, *living*.

She wiggled her hips and took a step to the right and her voice rose, trying to reach a note that he knew she wasn't able to reach, but he knew she was going for it anyway. One thing about Raine: she couldn't carry a tune to save her life, and she totally didn't give a shit. She sang it out and he winced—it was particularly bad— but then she bent over, head bopping, hips swaying, and his mouth went dry as his gaze rested on the sweetest ass he'd ever laid eyes on.

With it thrust in the air like that, he supposed any red-blooded man would react the same way he did. His gut tightened. His heart rate increased. Blood pounded in his ears and rushed through his body. It rushed down and kept going. Down to where it had no business being, and he clenched his jaw tightly as his cock hardened, his erection instant and fierce.

Hot, consuming need rippled through him, and for a second he closed his eyes, because he was *that* close to the edge. He thought of the women he'd had in the past. The ones who'd assuaged that ache, even if it had only been for a brief time. But that was the thing. The ache never completely went away, and after last night he was pretty damn sure he was cursed to live with that hole inside him.

Gibson ran across the floor and attacked her feet, the tubby bundle of fur yipping and tugging on her sneakers. She laughed, scooped Gibson into her arms to scold him, and froze when she noticed Jake for the first time. The light in her eyes vanished immediately as she slowly removed her earbuds and stared at him in silence.

A silence that she was first to break.

"Jake, I…didn't think you'd be here today."

Her words snapped him out of his funk, or maybe it was just the sound of her voice. Whatever it was, something ugly sprang to life inside him. "Really? I kind of own this place, so I'm not sure what part of that you don't understand."

She opened her mouth, no doubt ready to curse him out, but then she closed it again, setting Gibson back onto the floor before leaning against the cracked countertop.

"Don't get your panties in a knot," she said slowly. "Last night you told Salvatore that you would help him with his Christmas float and"—she glanced at her watch—"he was expecting you about an hour ago."

Jake frowned. *Shit*.

He remembered Salvatore bugging him about something, but the man had been buzzing in his ear at the same time Matt Backhouse had been all over Raine. Jake was good at a lot of things, but fielding questions fired at him by Sal while at the same time trying to listen to whatever the hell Matt was saying to Raine wasn't one of them.

"Christ." He ran his hand over the two-day-old stubble along his chin and shook his head. "I don't have time
for that crap. I've got my own pile to deal with."

"Call him and tell him you can't go."

He thought of the list he'd made—the one that was
miles long—and he knew he'd have to call and cancel.
Maybe he could help Salvatore out during the week, but
right now he needed to get the garbage off his driveway
and into the refuse bin before the storm hit. And he had
a few things to get ready for the electrician when he
came Monday.

"I hope you don't mind," Raine said softly, "but
I thought I would work on the cottage for you." She
glanced around and smiled. "It's actually not in bad
shape. I think the last Wyndham rented it out about ten
years ago. The water runs and the power's on too. It just
needs to be cleaned really well, because you don't even
want to know what I've found inside the cupboards."

"Why are you here?" He sounded like a dick, but
couldn't seem to help himself. She'd really thrown him
for a loop. The look in her eyes last night? The sexual
signals she'd thrown at him? What the hell was up with
that? Didn't she know what he wanted to do to her?

Didn't she know how weak he was?

Another thought struck him and his fists clenched so
hard, they ached, while the muscles along his shoulders
tightened painfully.

Raine was a young woman, and she was no different
than any guy he knew. No different than himself. She
had needs. Everyone had needs. If she'd sent those same
signals out to any other guy, they would have been all
over her. Even Matt Backhouse, fucking skirt that he

was, would have taken what Raine was offering. The thought of anyone touching her made him sick.

And that was a problem, because Raine Edwards could do whatever the hell she wanted with whoever the hell she wanted to do it with. She was a grown woman.

A grown woman with needs.

God, he needed time and space to think so that he could get his head screwed on right. He needed her to be gone from here.

"Why are you here, Raine?" he asked again, his emotions so ragged he was sure he sounded like a lunatic.

Raine glanced away but not so fast that he didn't catch the hurt in her eyes. It was a look he'd seen before. A look he'd been the cause of before. And a look he would surely see again.

It's what he did to her, bastard that he was.

His heart squeezed tight, and it took everything in him not to cross the floor and crush her to his chest. He hated that he was the cause of her pain, but he felt helpless to do anything about it.

For several moments there was only the sound of Gibson poking around beneath the sink, and then Raine looked back at Jake, her blue eyes shiny like they were full of tears.

She grabbed the sponge that she'd held and shrugged. "I have nowhere else to be."

And then she put in her earbuds, turned back to the sink, and proceeded to scrub the hell out of it.

Chapter 15

JAKE HAD JUST FINISHED SWEEPING UP THE MESS IN THE foyer when his cell rang. He grabbed the phone from his pocket and glanced down. It was Lily. *Again*.

Shit. His gut twisted as he held the cell and stared down at it. This was either going to be a high-maintenance thing to deal with or bad news. And after the morning he'd had, he didn't know if he was up for either one.

He felt like an absolute shit for the way he had treated Raine earlier, and having Lily ream him out would be the frosting on the cake.

He cursed and looked outside. It was nearly three in the afternoon and was already getting dark—though considering the low, mean clouds in the sky, it shouldn't have been surprising. They were rain heavy, and a steady drizzle had fallen for the last few hours. As another wave of water hit the window hard, he noticed the pings weren't soft anymore. They were sharp, and that meant freezing rain.

He crossed over and looked out the front window, his eyes on the cedar hedge and the warm light that spilled into the gloom. Already the driveway looked like a sheet of ice.

His cell vibrated and chirped again, and with a sigh he held it to his ear.

"Yeah," he said distractedly.

"Jesus, Jake, if you don't want to talk, why the hell did you answer your cell?"

"Because I wanted to piss you off," he retorted sharply. Jake wiped a dirty hand across his forehead and took a second. "What's up?"

"What's up?"

Jake winced. She sounded pissed.

"I've been texting you all day, and this is the tenth time that I've actually called, so I guess I should be grateful that you care enough to pick up? And when you do, all you got is *What's up*?" She made the same throaty sound she did when she was annoyed. "Hmm, let me see." She'd moved from annoyed to sarcastic. "Shit, Jake, thanks for asking, but not much. What the hell is up with you?"

Okay, she was more than just a little pissed, but this was Lily. She would get over it.

"I've been working my ass off here, you?" He decided to overlook her mean streak and get on with it.

"Me? Well hell, I've just had about the best day ever. It involved a pedicure, a manicure, and a massage by some big guy named Lars."

"Lars," he said drily. Lily's mind worked differently than most people's, and when she went off on a bullshit tangent, he knew things weren't great.

"Yep, Lars…or maybe it was Gabriel. I don't know. The point is, this man had magic fingers, and I could have stayed on his table all day, but since I had a date with the king of England, I had to pass up an afternoon with Lars."

"You mean Gabriel," he deadpanned.

"Or Gabriel. But shit, Jake…the king of fucking England."

He supposed he could point out that there was in fact no king at the moment, just a queen, but he decided to let it go. He wasn't in the mood to fuel her fire. Jake gazed out the window toward the cedar hedge that hid the stone cottage.

He couldn't believe Raine was still out there. Christ, she had to be freezing. He at least had a propane heater.

"Earth to Jake, are you still there?"

"Yep."

"So anyway, turns out he's a huge fan of my reality show and—"

"Who?"

Lily made that noise again. "The king of England, who else?"

"How's Blake?" He turned away from the window.

A few seconds passed and then she spoke, her voice subdued and small. "Not good."

"Ah, Christ," Jake whispered. He rubbed his hand along his forehead as a muscle worked its way along his jaw. "How bad?"

"On top of everything else, he's fighting pneumonia."

"Shit," he rasped, fighting to keep some sort of control. His chest was so tight, it was difficult to breathe, and Jake paced the foyer, cell against his ear, struggling to keep the dark memories at bay. Blake had been a stand-up, no-bullshit kind of guy, and it made him crazy to think of him so weak and wrecked in that damn hospital bed.

"I'll be there as soon as I can." Why the hell hadn't he picked up earlier? Lily would be alone, because her family was a bunch of self-absorbed assholes that were as screwed up as she was.

Her father was too removed from life to care anymore—too busy with his latest trophy wife and pack of kids that were legitimate. Her sister Eve, a party girl who spent all her time in LA or New York, didn't give a shit about a younger brother who was the result of an affair with one of the hired help.

Their father had deigned to give Blake his last name, and Jake suspected it was because at the time, there were no males in the family. He'd soon grown to regret it, of course, mostly because Blake hadn't turned out to be a cookie-cutter version of his dad. St. Clares didn't enlist and become Rangers. They cultivated a place in office and made the decisions that grunts like Rangers or SEALs obeyed.

"No," Lily said quickly. "Don't. You have enough to worry about. I'll be fine."

"I can be there"—he glanced out the window again and frowned—"tomorrow some time. The weather is crap, or I'd leave right now."

"So how's your situation?' Lily asked.

She'd always been good at deflecting.

"My situation?"

"Yes, your situation with that annoying little orphan girl."

"She's not an orphan girl, and it's what it's always been. Complicated."

"I see." There was a noise in the background. "Shit, Jake, I have to run."

It was a voice, a male voice, and he shook his head. "Lily, you need to keep it together and don't do anything stupid. Where are you?"

"Don't be such a douche, Jake. I'm close to the hospital."

He tried to think of someone he could call to go get her but at the moment drew a blank. "What bar?"

"I don't remember."

Jesus Christ, he didn't have time for this. "Lily, I'll see you tomorrow."

"No, Jake, seriously don't. I just wanted to hear your voice, and I wanted to tell you…"

He waited for a few seconds but there was nothing. "Tell me what?"

She sighed into the phone. "You have a second chance Jake. Don't blow it."

"Lily…" He ran his hands through his hair. God, if she was spouting this kind of sap, she wasn't doing as well as she wanted him to believe.

"I really have to run. But I'll call you tomorrow and let you know how Blake is doing. He might get through this, Jake. He just might make it."

And then she was gone.

Jake stood in the darkened foyer for a long time, staring at the cell in his hands. Fighting the images in his head. By the time he got his shit together, it was so dark in the house, he could barely see his hand in front of his face. Outside the wind howled and the steady driving rain was hard against the window.

He grabbed his jacket and headed outside, swearing as the sharp, frozen pellets hit him in the face.

A quick glance over to his Jeep told him that he wasn't going anywhere, anytime soon. A thick sheet of ice coated the entire vehicle, and the roads would be no better. Only a fool would get behind the wheel.

He hunched his shoulders and carefully picked his way across the driveway, finding a bit of relief from the elements when he reached the cedar hedge. He rounded the corner, and a few seconds later, his hands were on the door.

And then he was inside, hit by a wall of heat and two eyes that regarded him warily.

He took a moment and glanced around, running his hands through his hair and shaking the excess moisture off. It was wet from the sleet and ice, and he impatiently pushed it out of his eyes.

The place looked immaculate. The entire room had been scrubbed, top to bottom. There wasn't one ounce of debris or garbage anywhere, and from where he stood, the kitchen gleamed.

Sure, the details were tired and worn—the linoleum, the countertops, the cupboards, and the walls—but they were clean. And it was warm. Toasty warm. Almost comfy.

"I thought you'd left," Raine said haltingly.

"I just finished up inside." Jake shrugged out of his jacket and looked around for a place to put it.

"Here, let me." Raine took his jacket and he watched her cross the room and hang it from a prong screwed into the wall near the back door.

Gibson was asleep in front of the fireplace, which wasn't surprising, since a fire burned on the hearth and that would account for the toasty air. Jake frowned, his hand on his chin as he took two steps forward.

"Shoes off, mister," Raine said, an eyebrow arched and one hand on her hip. "I didn't spend all day cleaning this place so you could dirty it up."

Jake stepped out of his boots and padded toward the fireplace. "I haven't had this one cleaned out yet, so I'm thinking this isn't a good idea."

"Already done," Raine said quickly. "I called Hearths R Us and they were here at eight this morning."

"Huh," Jake replied.

"I also booked them to come and do the ones at the main house, so he'll be back, Tuesday at the latest." She cocked her head to the side and raised her chin. "You're welcome, by the way."

"Thanks," he said absently.

Jake's gaze moved past her, toward the kitchen, and he noticed food on the table, or rather takeout—from the looks of it, Chinese from Yin's. A bottle of wine was open, with one half-filled glass beside it. On the floor next to the sofa—a sofa that now had a bright pink cover on it—was a bag.

If he were going to take a guess, he'd have said an overnight bag.

"What's going on, Raine?"

She moved toward the kitchen, her bare toes skipping over the worn—yet gleaming—hardwood, and cleared her throat as she reached for her wine. She took her time answering, and that grabbed his attention.

"Are you hungry? I've got lots left over. My eyes were bigger than my stomach."

Jake followed her and leaned his hip against the countertop. He folded his arms over his chest and glanced around the place. It looked amazing. He couldn't believe she'd done all this.

"I thought I'd stay here tonight," Raine said carefully.

He reached over to the table and grabbed an egg roll. "Why would you want to stay here?" He thought of her perfectly cute little cottage. Of the modern kitchen with all the fancy upgrades. He thought of the new floors and the flat-screen television. Sure, her cupboards were probably bare, but hell, she was at least into Chinese these days.

Raine picked at the rice and shrugged, her eyes downcast. "I just…" She sighed. "I don't know, I just really like it here."

He finished the egg roll and grabbed another one, his stomach grumbling with hunger. "When did you get this?"

"They delivered an hour ago."

Jake paused before taking another bite. "You do know that the roads aren't fit to be driving on, right?"

She nodded. "Yes, Christopher told me I was his last delivery and they were closing early. We're supposed to get freezing rain all night." She pointed toward the bags on the counter. "He brought extra, just in case I got stranded."

"That was real nice of him."

She looked at him warily. "Wasn't it."

"So no one is going anywhere."

Again she nodded, her eyes huge, her perfect mouth so soft and pink, it made his insides ache. He was stranded here. With Raine.

"Could be for a good long while," he said carefully.

"Could be," she retorted and gestured toward the table. "Do you want some wine? Though the only glass I have is an old coffee mug. It's tin, not even ceramic."

Jake grabbed the wine and filled the mug to the brim before taking a long sip. He let the smooth cabernet sauvignon rest on his tongue before he swallowed as he watched Raine move back to the living area. She darted a look back at him, a quick sort of glance that seemed somehow…off.

"Are you sure you don't want to sit down?" She patted the sofa before settling on the edge. "It's really comfy." She licked her lips nervously and Jake's eyes narrowed thoughtfully. Something was definitely up. He'd expected her to be pissed at him—and she should have been, after he'd nearly bitten her head off this morning—but instead she was accommodating.

Too accommodating.

"I know it's pink and everything, but…"

Her eyes nearly popped out of her head when he reached for the last egg roll, and at first he thought it was because he was being a pig. He held it up. "You want it?"

She shook her head and bit her bottom lip. She chewed at it so carefully that his freaking "Raine radar" erupted and he glanced around the room. She was hiding something from him. She always did that damn biting thing when she was nervous about something.

He spied a thick book on the counter, and she groaned so loudly that he knew he'd just scored, but what?

He glanced back at Raine, a grin creeping across his face as he grabbed it and flipped it over so that he could read the back copy.

"Jake, really, that's a woman's book. Not something you'd want to read."

"How do you know what I like to"—his eyes skimmed the copy—*Hello*—"read."

What the hell? He flipped the book back over. Shit, the cover had a set of handcuffs on it.

He glanced at her in surprise.

"That's not…" Her chest heaved, and the color in her cheeks was so damn cute he couldn't take his eyes off her. "That's not a book that would interest you," she said haltingly.

Jake ignored her and flipped it open, his eyes skimming the words and widening as he read a few paragraphs. Jesus. He'd heard of this book. Heck, half the guys on base had read it the year before or had benefited from their wives or girlfriends reading it.

"Damn, woman," he said, a grin splitting his face wide open. "I had no idea, Raine."

She was across the room in an instant. "Give it to me."

Jake easily held it above her head. "Holy hell, sweet cheeks, this is the filthiest thing I've ever read."

"Jake! Give it back," she yelped, jumping for his arms.

"And it was only two freaking paragraphs."

"Jake! I'm going to…"

He held the book inches above her head. "Gonna what?" He laughed, his eyes resting on her mouth for several long moments. The laughter dried up in his throat and he was suddenly aware of many things. The length of her lashes. The smell of peaches. The way her pink tongue rested on the edge of her teeth, and the sound of her breath catching in the back of her throat.

His body tightened, his heart rocketed out of his chest, and the blood pounding in his veins was so strong, it hurt.

"What are you going to do, Raine?" His voice was husky.

She stared up at him, those big eyes of hers like glass, and when she swallowed, his eyes fell to the delicate area at the base of her neck, the one that dipped into the hollow of her collarbone. She'd shed the old, worn sweatshirt and wore a tight, baby-blue T-shirt with a deep V, one that showed the tops of her small breasts.

Her bra strap peeked from beneath—her black bra strap—and the sight was so incredibly erotic to him that his groin tightened even more.

He was hard, achingly hard, and weak enough not to be able to do anything about it.

The air between them was charged with something fierce, something electric and alive, and for the first time in ages, he felt exhilarated. Reckless.

Aroused.

The book fell from his fingers onto the floor, and neither one of them looked away from the other.

She licked her mouth again.

He exhaled a long, shaky breath.

A heartbeat passed between them. And then another. The world slowed down, and for that one moment there was nothing but Raine. Nothing but her sweet face, her exquisite eyes, and a mouth that begged to be kissed.

Years of want and need and pain and anguish rolled through him. He was weak from the enormity of it all and for a second saw nothing but darkness. But she was there—right there in front of him—and the look in her eyes gave him strength. It gave him hope, even though he knew it didn't belong to him.

He inhaled her scent and closed his eyes, wanting to find the strength he knew he needed to stay away from her.

But when her heat slipped over his skin, when she slid up his chest and her mouth touched his, a tentative, soft caress, he did nothing to stop her. He let his body control what his mind knew was wrong, and his arms slipped around her waist. He felt her shudder and he pulled her in hard, so that she was crushed against him and he felt every single inch of her.

"Jake," she breathed into him.

He opened his mouth beneath hers and let her tongue slide inside. She tasted like heaven, just as she had so many years ago, and when she moaned into him, when her soft sigh fell into his mouth…

He gave up any pretense of fighting the one thing he'd wanted his entire life, it seemed. Wrong or right didn't matter anymore, not when he'd been lost for so long and finally, *finally* felt as if he'd found himself.

In that moment, Jake Edwards said to hell with the consequences and ignored the voice in the back of his mind.

The one that told him he'd be damn lucky to survive it.

Chapter 16

RAINE REVELED IN THE WANT AND THE NEED AND THE pleasure she felt in Jake's arms.

As his hands moved down her back and settled at the base of her spine, there just above her butt, she realized that she'd been heading toward this ever since Jake came home.

Maybe even longer.

She'd been asleep for so long, her body and mind dormant, that she'd all but given up hope of ever feeling anything again. Jake had always been that spark, the one to light her up, and now he was the only person who made her feel alive.

Sure, she was still pissed at him. So pissed and hurt at the way he'd abandoned her last year. For not being there for her when she was at her lowest point ever. But still, as his large palms gripped her ass and held her in place against him—against the evidence of his own needs and passion—she was willing to forget all that.

For this one moment she would forget. If only to feel alive once more with someone she trusted.

With Jake.

"Raine," he breathed into her, his voice husky and full of need.

They kissed forever, it seemed. Tongues entwined, lips giving and taking, their bodies crushed to each other, held together by burgeoning desire.

Her hands sank into his thick hair, and she wondered at the silkiness of it. For so long he'd kept it trimmed in the standard military cut, and as her fingers slid through the glossy waves, she relished the feel of it, the feel of *him*. She groaned as his tongue licked her bottom lip before suckling her there.

But then suddenly, he was gone, swearing like a fiend as he pulled back and took two steps away.

Raine's fingers fell to her swollen lips, her gaze avoiding his eyes as she hungrily took in every inch of him. His T-shirt was askew and a fair bit of his skin was visible above the low-slung, faded jeans he wore.

Her mouth went dry as she focused on the thin dusting of hair there, the arrow that pointed and disappeared beneath the waistband. His erection strained against his jeans, an unmistakable hint as to the depths of his need, and she licked her lips at the sight of it, an answering ache heavy between the folds of her sex.

"Jesus Christ, Raine, don't do this," he said raggedly. "We can't do this again."

"Why not?" she whispered. "Why the hell not?"

Her eyes flew back to his, and she took a step forward but stopped when she saw the pain reflected in his gaze.

His chest rose and fell rapidly, and when he rolled his shoulders and rested his hands behind his head, she knew how conflicted he was. How aroused he was. And as he held her gaze, his beautiful dark eyes heavy with emotion, she knew he wanted her as much as she wanted him.

And for once in her life, Raine was done playing it safe. She was done being afraid. Done thinking of others and putting herself last. Her hand fell to her mouth, and her fingers ran over her swollen lips—lips that were swollen from Jake's mouth. That was the point of this, wasn't it?

She didn't want to think past her needs. Past what she wanted. She didn't want to think past the one thing that maybe, just maybe, could force the demons away and fill the hole inside her.

Raine sank her forefinger into her hot, wet mouth and took another step toward Jake, watching the way his eyes, now hooded, glittered in the firelight, as he focused on her lips.

"I want you," she said simply.

Jake shook his head and swore again. "You don't know what you're saying." He nodded toward the table. "You've had too much wine, and now you're just… you're just…" He looked at her helplessly, and if she were a bigger person, she might even have felt sorry for him. He was conflicted, fighting his own inner demons, and she wasn't helping him at all.

But she'd done this dance with him before and had been the bigger person. She had let him push her away, but now? Now she would take what she wanted, because she was done living in the shadows. Done feeling only half-alive—if that.

"I haven't had too much wine, Jake. My head is clear and you need to know something. You need to listen to me."

His dark eyes rested on her—tortured, yes, but hungry for a connection.

"I needed you once before, and maybe sex wasn't the answer then, but at least it made me *feel* something, but now…now it's not the need so much. It's the want, and

I'm not going to apologize for it. I want you. I want to make love with you. Right now. Do you know what kind of gift that is to me?"

Jake Edwards, one of her oldest and best friends, had returned home weeks ago, and she'd been slowly coming alive ever since. But she wanted more.

Her eyes rested on the bulge between his legs again. Hell yes, she wanted more.

Jake groaned, his hands now clenched into fists at his side, his dark gaze settled onto her with an intensity that struck a chord inside her.

She swallowed and took another step toward him.

"Raine, we can't." Jake shook his head, his mouth tight, a frown between his brows. "We just…"

"Why not?" She took another step, stalking him like a leopard after her prey, and now she was so close to him, she could feel how hot he was. His body heat was off the charts, and a thin film of sweat coated his skin like a sheet.

"Because…" he started roughly. "Because it's wrong."

"Why don't you say what you really mean, Jake?" Raine inched closer and reached for him, resting her palms against his chest and feeling the strength of his heart beating inside.

"Because you're Jesse's wife, and you belong to him, and I never should have touched you. That night should never have happened."

Raine took a moment to let his words roll around inside her brain. She blew out one long breath and gazed up at him.

"Jesse is dead."

"What the hell kind of thing is that to say? You think

I don't know that?" he replied angrily. "God, you have no idea…you don't know…"

"Jesse is dead," she interrupted, her voice soft, "and it's awful and painful and wrong. But he wouldn't want me to stop living, and he wouldn't want you stuck in this dark place that you're in."

Jake looked away.

"He wouldn't want that." Her breath caught. "I don't want that. I've been living like the dead for way too long and—" She had to stop because her throat closed up, choked with emotion. "I don't want to anymore."

Her hand was on his cheek, and a tremulous smile crept over her face at the feel of his rough, day-old stubble beneath her fingers as he turned back to her.

Several moments passed as the two of them stared at each other in silence. And then she pressed her body against his, leaned up, and pulled his head down toward her. Her mouth rested just below his ear, and she kissed him lightly there, loving the way he shuddered against her.

"I don't belong to anyone but me, Jake. I can give myself to someone, but that doesn't mean they own me. Jesse didn't own me. You can't *own* a person."

"That's not what I meant," he said stubbornly.

"But it's what you said. Jesse and I shared a moment in time, but that moment is gone and nothing we can do will bring it back."

Jake jerked his head at her words, an angry sound gurgling in his throat, but she ignored it and whispered. "He's not coming back, and that doesn't mean I'm going to forget about him, or that I didn't love him. He'll always live in my heart, but I need to move on. I *have* to move on."

A heartbeat passed between them.

"I want to give myself to you, but I want to do it for me. Do you understand what I'm saying?"

His breathing changed, the rhythm faster, but he remained silent, his dark eyes glistening in the candlelight.

Raine pressed her mouth to the base of his neck and kissed the pulse that beat there. She inhaled his earthy scent and leaned into him as her insides liquefied, leaving her so weak that if not for Jake, surely she would have melted into a puddle of hot, churning need.

"I don't just want you, Jake." She licked her lips and tilted her head up so that she could see his face. She put it out there, three simple words that said so much more. "I need you."

His eyes regarded her intently as his hands slowly crept to her shoulders, and she knew how conflicted he was. This was Jake—a man of honor. Was she asking too much of him? Was it selfish for her to want him as much as she did? Would he run away again?

Then another thought crossed her mind, and Raine's fingers flew to her mouth in horror. Her cheeks heated with shame and she looked at the floor, suddenly defeated and ashamed and…so sad. So incredibly sad.

Maybe she'd read this all wrong. Maybe he didn't want her the way she wanted him. Maybe he…

"Oh no, Jake. I'm sorry. I thought you…I thought you wanted me." She shuddered and took a step back. Or she would have, but his hands were still on her shoulders, and he cupped her chin gently, forcing her to look up at him.

"Raine."

She shook her head, not wanting to look up at him.

Hot tears stung the corners of her eyes, and she wouldn't cry in front of Jake.

"Raine," he said again, and something in his voice pulled her gaze upward.

His brown eyes looked almost black, and for a moment something so fierce and raw reflected in their depths that her mouth went dry and she gasped. His right hand slid into her hair, cupping the back of her head, while the other slipped to her jaw.

She couldn't have moved if she'd wanted to.

Her heart took off, nearly beating out of her chest, and her nipples, already hardened, strained against her thin T-shirt.

He leaned down, his mouth only a whisper from hers, and spoke. "I want you."

Something burst inside her. Something hot. Something that ached and throbbed and spread throughout her body.

Someone whimpered. Was that her? Was she that pathetic? That starved for touch?

Raine closed her eyes, but that was the wrong thing to do. Images danced there. Erotic pictures of Jake. Of his hands traveling over her body and his mouth gliding across her stomach, her breasts, and her...

"If we do this, everything changes. It won't be like before, because I'm not going anywhere." His voice was hoarse, rough like sandpaper. "Do you understand what I'm trying to say? Things could get complicated."

"I don't care," she whispered.

He wanted her.

"Because I need someone strong enough to go the full nine yards with me. I need you to bring me back to life."

"You're fucking killing me," Jake said roughly, his mouth creeping over to her neck and nuzzling her there.

"Sorry. Now kiss me."

She was on fire. Her body, long dormant, now raged with hormones and pheromones and whatever the hell else kind of *mones* were out there.

Outside, a blast of wind threw ice pellets against the window, shaking the glass and filling the cottage with the sound of winter. Yet it did nothing but fan the flames inside the small house. For a moment it was the only noise they heard, and then with a growl, Jake's hands slid down her body.

Raine couldn't take her eyes off him, and when his head dipped low and his mouth slid over hers again, a teasing pass that spread fire everywhere, her legs gave out. His large palms cupped her butt, and he lifted her as if she weighed nothing. Raine wrapped her legs around his waist and sank her hands into his hair.

Jake's mouth hovered over hers for a second, and then he said something unintelligible and took what she offered. His kiss was an aggressive exploration, and she accepted it wholeheartedly, her hands kneading his scalp, her body pressed against him intimately. He tasted her, his mouth and tongue stroking and nipping and sucking, each motion tugging a response, and her hips began to move of their own accord.

His hands cupped her as she slowly gyrated against him, gasping into him when her jeans rubbed against the place where she ached to be touched the most.

Raine had no idea how long they strained against each other, her legs wrapped around him tightly, her breasts crushed to his chest as he continued to assault her mouth with the most intense, rough kisses she'd ever had.

Nothing about Jake was soft or gentle. He was an alpha, and at the moment, exactly what she needed.

Except she needed more.

With a strangled noise, Raine jerked in his grasp as his mouth slid from hers and traveled a wicked path down her neck, down to the base, where her pulse pounded crazily. He suckled her skin, his tongue leaving her weak as he slowly made his way across her collarbone to the sensitive area just below her ear.

And when his tongue stroked in a small circle there, she couldn't help the gasp of raw need that escaped her lips.

"I want more," she managed to say, squirming in his arms until he was forced to let her go.

"Shit, what about birth control? I don't have anything on me," he said roughly, sounding as if he was in pain.

His words stopped her cold and she swallowed hard. God, she was out of practice. Of course. Of course he'd be worried about something like that.

"I'm on the pill, Jake, for other reasons, so you don't have to worry, and I've…" She blew out hot air. "I haven't been with anyone since…" The lump in her throat was so thick she couldn't speak, and she glanced away.

"Hey," Jake said softly as he kissed the corner of her mouth. "I'm clean, so there's no worries there, but you have to be sure about this, Raine." He blew out a long jagged breath. "Are you sure?"

Raine's answer was to slide down his body, her hands seeking his skin, desperate to touch him. Nimble fingers tugged on the edge of his shirt, yet she couldn't seem to get it past his abs. With a groan Jake pushed her back, ripping it off and tossing it to the ground.

Holy hell.

Her eyes slid over ripped abs, defined pecs, and—Lord have mercy—the indent above his jeans, the one that made any woman weak with want. Jake had a few tattoos: one that was identical to Jesse's, a Gemini—the sign of the twins, and another down his right side. It was new; she'd never seen it before, and it added an air of danger to his already-badass physique.

"You're beautiful," she said. Her hands greedily covered every bit of flesh she could reach, and when she felt him tremble beneath her fingertips, she smiled and glanced up at him.

Jake's mouth was open slightly, his even, white teeth barely visible. Several inches taller than her, he stared down at her with hooded eyes and an almost painful expression on his face.

She licked her lips and he groaned, and when she opened her mouth and then closed it over a turgid nipple, he swore.

"Jesus."

His hands, however, held her in place so she couldn't leave even if she'd wanted to. She twirled her tongue over him, loving the taste of his skin, loving the feel of a large, strong man in her grasp.

He bent lower and she surged upward, meeting his mouth and deepening their kiss as her hands fell to the waistband of his jeans.

And when her fingers tugged on the snap, when she yanked on the zipper and slid her hand just inside and felt his flat skin there, he froze for a moment and then pushed her away, a ragged breath exhaled as he ran his hands through his messy hair.

Jake's chest heaved and a chill ran over her as she stared up into his pained eyes. Eyes that were also dark with desire—desire for her—desire that she wanted to wrap herself in.

Slowly her eyes ran down his wide chest, past the rock-hard abs and past the low-slung, and now-open, jeans. Hello, the man was commando.

She licked her lips at the sight of the bulge that was barely hidden, and her fingers crept to her swollen mouth as she tried to hide the whimper of need in her throat.

The heat from the fire enveloped her already-hot skin and she held Jake's gaze, watching as his eyes widened when she reached for the edge of her shirt and yanked it up past her rib cage and then over her head. With a toss, she sent it flying to the ground beside his.

"Raine, I don't…I don't know if…" His words ended on a strangled gasp as she cupped her breasts, slowly rubbing her aching nipples through the soft material of her bra. And then she undid the snap and it joined her top on the floor.

His teeth were bared like an animal's as his gaze rested on her exposed breasts. Her fingers lingered, teasing the nipples, and she swelled beneath his hunger, smiling wantonly as he took a step toward her.

"Touch me, Jake."

Oh, God, did I just say that?

And yet, as his hungry gaze was riveted to her aching, swollen breasts, she grew more bold.

Raine cupped her breasts and offered them up like

offerings to a god. "Touch me," she breathed, her thumbs caressing her nipples.

"Since when did you become such a fucking tease," Jake growled, taking a step toward her.

"Since I decided I was going to take what I wanted, and to hell with everything else."

A slow grin tugged the corners of his mouth. "And when was that exactly?"

He was now inches from her.

"About ten minutes ago," she whispered.

Before she could say another word, Jake's large palms covered her breasts and held them as he bent low and took one turgid nipple deep into his mouth.

Everything fell away except Jake.

And his hands.

And his mouth.

And his incredible body.

Raine's senses filled until she was dizzy with the heaviness of it, her head spinning at each pass of his tongue across her nipple. When he tugged and gently began to suck, she yelped and ground her hips against him, frantic to feel him everywhere.

Her hands reached for his jeans again, and for one split second she froze, wondering if she was in fact doing something she would regret.

But then he blew on her wet, aching nipples, and all thought flew out of her head except one.

Jake.

Chapter 17

Jake had a moment, one pristine and clear moment, where he could have put the brakes on and stopped things cold.

Halfway between the taste of her in his mouth and the low moan that hung in her throat—right in that sweet spot—he could have taken a step back.

But he didn't.

How could he? The one thing he'd wanted his entire life was right here, right in front of him, and she was his for the taking. He wasn't going to think about it as a temporary thing. He wasn't going to go there. Because there, back where all the pain and shit was—that was a place that had no room in here.

Not in here, in this warm haven that Raine had created—a cocoon that existed only for them. And for once in his sorry-ass life, he was not going to do the right thing. He was sick and tired of the right thing. He wasn't going to step aside and consider the big picture.

He held Raine prisoner, his lips worshipping her mouth, his tongue staking a claim as he tasted her forever, it seemed. When she groaned into him, the sound fired him up and left him weak in the knees. The thought that she wanted him as badly as he wanted her did crazy things to his head.

And this wasn't the alcohol talking. Or the anger.

It fueled all sorts of fantasies, which he pushed

away, because the only fantasy he wanted to deal with at the moment was getting her the hell out of the rest of her clothes.

Impatiently he scooped her into his arms, striding toward the fireplace, and grabbed the bubblegum-colored blanket off the sofa along the way. He tossed it on the floor and broke their kiss, aware that her fingers were still tangled in his open fly.

Raine stared up at him, her mouth wet and swollen from his, and such a wave of desire and—he had to be honest—possession rolled over him that for a moment, he could do nothing but breathe hard and stare right back at her. He wondered if she knew how close he was to losing it completely. If she knew how many nights he'd thought of her and how many nights he'd gone to sleep, aching with the need to have her.

His eyes dropped to her small, perfect breasts—to their pebbled, rosy nipples—and his hand clamped over them. His cock swelled even more at the sound of her breath hitching in the back of her throat, and he gently rotated his palm, first over one and then over the other, excited at the sight of her pink tongue flicking out over her bottom lip.

She was wrong and he knew it. None of this was right, but he didn't care.

Tonight was about the two of them, and the rest of the world could go to hell. Tonight there was nothing but Raine.

Gently he put her down and took a step back. She wavered slightly, her hair a crazy, sexy mess in her eyes, and her mouth—that plump, delicious mouth—parted as she struggled to breathe. He had done this to her.

Jake was no choirboy, and in the past he'd made many a woman hot and bothered, which for a guy was as much of an ego kick as anything else. But none of those women had ever made him feel the way he did right now, as if he'd just climbed Mount Fucking Everest. As the guy on the *Titanic* had said, he felt as if he were the king of the world.

Raine dragged in another long breath and pushed her hair away, licking her lips as her eyes zeroed in on his jeans. Right there, where his erection strained so painfully full that it was all he could do to not relieve the pressure immediately.

But that would be wrong.

He arched an eyebrow and smiled. Totally wrong, because tonight it was ladies first.

"Come here," he said, his voice low yet controlled.

Raine didn't hesitate. She took two steps until she was so close to him that he could count her eyelashes. He bent low and took her breast into his mouth, his tongue circling her nipple. But it was a quick, gentle tug and he smiled when she moaned her displeasure as he let it go.

"Jake, I'm dying here," she said throatily.

"Really," he murmured against her skin, his mouth now between her breasts and moving downward.

He sank to his knees and slipped his hands into her jeans as he did so, yanking on her zipper and loosening her snap. He tugged the material down over her hips while she lifted first one leg and then the other so that he could take them off completely.

Another piece of clothing to add to their growing pile.

Jake leaned back on his haunches. He winced at the

exquisite pain between his legs. And he took a few moments to drink in the sight of her half-naked body.

She stood there, legs parted, her butt barely covered by the sexiest pair of black undies he'd ever seen. They rode her hips low and left half of her ass cheeks hanging out. And though Raine had lost some weight lately, she still had curves where curves should be.

"Jake," she said again.

He leaned forward and kissed her bellybutton, his tongue swirling around it in a gentle motion. Her skin trembled beneath his lips and his fingers hooked into her panties, pulling them down slowly as he gazed up into her stormy blue eyes.

Her lips were open slightly, that damn little pink tongue peeking out just a bit—enough to drive him even more crazy—and when she stepped out of her underwear, he had to close his eyes and concentrate. His cock was so hard, he was afraid that if he moved he would blow early, and there was no way he could let that happen.

He rested his forehead on her belly, felt her hands sink into his hair, and when she made that sound again—the one in the back of her throat that sounded as if it were a cross between pleasure and pain—he nearly lost it.

His eyes flew open and he inhaled her woman's scent, the one that told him she was aroused and ready. He grasped her hip with his right hand and dared to look below, down at the thin strip of fine hair. Down at the place he ached to be.

"Jesus Christ, Jake, if you don't touch me—"

Her words ended on whimper, followed by a gasp as he slipped two fingers between the folds of her sex.

Without hesitation, her hips began to gyrate and he needed to hold her still, his right hand gripping her hard as his left slowly ran up and down her opening, sliding through the slickness, teasing her swollen clit with a gentle pass.

Once.

Twice.

She smelled like heaven, and she was so damn wet that Jake knew she was close to the edge.

Three times he passed his forefinger over her, until she pushed against him so hard that he glanced up and smiled.

"You a little anxious, Delgotto?"

A soft smile curved her lips, and he didn't realize he'd used her maiden name—something he'd called her when they were younger—until her hand caressed his cheek.

"I've been waiting a long time, Edwards," she said hoarsely, her fingers digging into his skin as she squirmed against him.

"Well, then, I'd better get my ass in gear, though I gotta warn you—" He barely got the words out; his jaw was clenched so tight, his need so raw, it hurt. "This is going to take a while," he managed to say before plunging both fingers deep inside her. "Because I'm just getting started."

Whatever her reply was, it got swallowed in a groan as he carefully rotated his fingers. Almost immediately she began to shudder, her whole body reacting to his touch in a way that he hadn't anticipated.

With total abandon.

Jake had never seen anything as hot as Raine writhing,

gyrating, beneath his touch. And Christ, but she was wet and tight. The woman was every man's fantasy.

Her hands fell to his shoulders, her fingers digging in deep as he continued to play with her.

"Do you like this?" he whispered hoarsely, his cock aching as she moaned and pushed against him.

"Well," she replied breathily, "I'm not sure."

His thumb rotated against her clitoris while he massaged her from the inside.

"That is, you should keep…"

He leaned forward and replaced his thumb with his mouth.

"Oh, sweet Jesus, Jake, don't stop."

She tasted exactly as he'd imagined. Full-on woman, and so ready for him that it was insane. Raine jerked beneath his tongue, and with each pass, her fingers dug in harder. With each tug, she groaned. With each suckle, she whimpered.

Jake stroked her, reacting to the way she responded to his touch—a gentle pass here, an aggressive stroke there—and when she broke, when her body shuddered against him, he couldn't put into words the power it gave him, knowing he had given her such pleasure.

For several moments, Raine leaned on him, her small body heaving as she struggled to breathe in the aftershocks of her orgasm. Gently he withdrew his fingers. He kissed her belly and then looked up into her eyes.

"That was…" She licked her lips and blew out a long, hot breath. "That was…" She shook her head, her beautiful eyes as big as saucers.

"I know," Jake answered, loving the blush that slowly crept into her cheeks when she realized his face was still so intimately close to her. He stood, his hands running up her body, and he slid his mouth across hers in a searing kiss that left them both breathless.

When they finally separated, his hands went to the waistband of his jeans and he finally released his cock.

"Like I said before…" His mouth was dry at the look in her eyes as she stared down at him. "I'm just getting started."

He stood there for a second, legs spread, cock jutting out, and aching for her in a way he hadn't thought was possible.

And then she nearly undid him. She nearly sent him over the edge without even trying.

Tentatively, Raine reached for him, her fingers soft as they touched his flat stomach. Her fingers bold as she slid down and wrapped her hands around the straining length of him. A smile was on her face—one of power—as he groaned and clenched his hands at his side when she touched ever fucking inch of him.

"You're beautiful," she murmured.

"Keep that up," Jake managed as she cupped his balls and sank to her knees, "and I'm not going to—" His teeth clamped down painfully and he could no longer speak. Muscles strained and control was thin.

Holy hell, she wasn't going to…

But she did. She wrapped her sweet mouth around the edge of his cock, and immediately he jerked into her.

"Ah, fuck." He stared down, his insides twisting almost painfully at the sight of Raine between his legs, her wet, plump lips wrapped around his cock. Her tongue slid along the length of him in slow, precise movements.

He closed his eyes, trying his best to wipe out the

erotic picture, because he knew if he didn't keep it to-gether, he would ruin things. He would come way too fucking early, and there was no way he was going to allow that to happen.

She suckled him hard, and for a moment he saw noth-ing but blackness and stars. He felt nothing but the heat of her mouth and the agility of her tongue. She stroked him with her hand and licked and suckled until he was so close to the edge, he couldn't see straight.

"Jesus Christ, Raine, you gotta stop." His hands were in her hair, and gently he pulled her away from him, his control thin at best. Their bodies were covered in sweat, a thin sheen of desire that coated them and made the flickering light from the fire dance across their skin.

Jake pushed her back until she was on that god-awful pink blanket. Until she lay back, with her legs spread, with the most vulnerable part of her exposed to him. He stood over her and stared down at the woman who would break him.

Because that's exactly what was going to happen, and Jake was no more able to stop that from happening than he'd been able to stop everything else that had happened to him over the last few years.

Including the last time he'd been with Raine. But he wouldn't think about that now.

He fell to his knees, his hands on her stomach.

He'd been heading here—he positioned himself between her legs—right here, forever, it seemed, and right now in this moment, he didn't want to think about the consequences.

Jake bent over and gently kissed her, his tongue tast-ing her mouth, his lips cajoling a response. Her hips jerked up toward him and she pleaded into his mouth, "Please, Jake."

He leaned close to her, one hand on her hip to hold her steady as the head of his cock slid into her wet sheath. "There's no going back now, Raine."

He was at the edge, poised and ready, when her hands slid into his hair and she yanked him so that she was able to look into her eyes.

"I want this, Jake."

Moisture glimmered in the corners.

"I want you," she whispered.

And then her mouth was on him and he was buried deep inside.

For a second he stilled. He let her body adjust to his size and length, and he reveled in the tight, hot wetness that surrounded him.

Slowly he began to move, smiling when she would have hurried things along.

"Not so fast, Delgotto."

She made a noise in the back of her throat. "Edwards," she gasped as he thrust into her again. "I can't take this much longer."

He rested most of his weight on his elbows so that he could look down as he rocked into her. So that he could watch the play of emotion across her face and anticipate her reaction as he carefully controlled their pace.

"Jake," she cried out, her eyes dark and wet and so hauntingly beautiful, he was sure he'd see this in his dreams.

He captured her mouth as he increased his rhythm, his large body sliding in and out of hers, his tongue doing the same. When he knew she was there on the edge with him, when her body began to shudder and the walls of her vagina clenched so tight around him that he couldn't hold back, he groaned into her.

He worshipped her with his mouth, with his tongue and his hands, and with one last hard, intense thrust, he came.

Jake had no idea how long they stayed that way, with him buried deep inside her. All he knew was that he didn't want to lose this connection. He was afraid that if he withdrew, it would be gone forever. He caressed her face and stared down into eyes that he would never forget. Ever. Not as long as he lived.

And eventually, when he couldn't stay that way any longer, he rolled to the side, grabbing the pink blanket and Raine in one motion. He carried her over to the sofa and tucked her into his arms.

There were no words. There was only the cocoon they had built around themselves, and Jake didn't want to think about the aftermath of their actions. For the moment he was content to hold and cherish the woman he loved.

He held her, listened to her breathing and her heartbeat. He gazed into the fire as outside the storm continued to rage, and eventually his eyes closed, and Jake Edwards fell into a dreamless sleep.

And that was something he hadn't done in years.

Chapter 18

THEY SAY THAT ALL GOOD THINGS COME TO AN END, but for Raine, this "end" wasn't something she wanted to face. If she had her way, she and Jake would disappear inside this paradise they'd found and maybe, somewhere in the near future, they'd venture out. But for now? Right now in this moment, *here* was good. *Here* was where she wanted to be.

Here was everything she thought she'd never find again.

The storm had raged for two entire days and nights, pounding Crystal Lake with a torrent of freezing rain, and when that had finished, several feet of blowing, drifting snow had been unleashed. It was the first real snowstorm of the season, and for some, it wasn't exactly appreciated or convenient. Roads weren't safe for travel, businesses were closed, and appointments were missed.

But here, nestled inside this stone cottage, she and Jake had survived on leftover Chinese food, chips, beer, and sex.

She'd supplied the Chinese—thank God Yin's had left extra. Jake had grabbed a stash of chips and beer from the main house.

And the sex. Oh God, the sex. It had been incredible. No, it had been mind-blowing and intense…and heartbreakingly tender.

Raine lifted her head from Jake's shoulder and glanced out the window, blinking rapidly at the bright play of sunlight that fell into the room. She had never in her life felt this sated. This complete.

Should she feel guilty? Guilty that deep down inside her soul, where she'd been broken, she was finally at peace? How could this feeling be wrong? She thought of Jesse and of the life they had shared. She thought of their love.

This was different. It didn't in any way negate what she'd had with her husband, and it certainly wasn't just about the sex—though that was nothing to complain about. It was about all the other stuff. The quiet looks, the tender touches. The way Jake anticipated her mind and body without even knowing. And now…now she wasn't sure where to go or how to react.

Where *did* you go from this place? This place of contentment and aching muscles and warm flesh.

Jake moved slightly, burrowing deeper into the comforter he'd taken from his truck—the one they'd been using as their bed. The last of the firewood had been put on a few hours ago, and the flames flickered, dancing warmly. The shadows they cast provided an endless amount of amusement for Gibson, and she smiled as the puppy jumped up the wall in an effort to catch one.

Raine relaxed and settled into his shoulder once more, moving her hips slightly as she did so. Her lower half was tucked between his legs and—she smiled—his erection was already saying hello.

Jake's eyes were still closed, and judging by the long, even breaths, she thought that he was still asleep. After the night they'd had, he should be. She took the moment to enjoy watching him unobserved—a bittersweet sort of thing—because being with him like this, lying so close that his heartbeat seemed to be a part of her, reminded Raine of a past that she'd tried so hard to forget.

And yet for the first time since Jesse died, Raine felt as if she could grab hold of some of those memories without pain. Or regret.

For as long as she could remember, the Edwards boys had been a part of her life, and she had loved them so much that it sometimes hurt. Her love for Jesse had been solid and reliable…and safe. But Jake, he'd always touched something wild inside her—he *got* her, while Jesse took care of her.

She was starting to figure out a few things, and it was those things that scared the crap out of her. Jake Edwards touched her deeply—maybe more deeply than any other human being. Ever.

Including Jesse.

The thought fell into her head and she froze, her stomach rolling as a wave of guilt washed over her. How could she even think such a thing? Jesse had been her world for years. He'd been her rock-solid base, the one she could always count on. In some ways, he'd been the mother she'd never had, and for that she'd been grateful. In a world where stability meant everything to her, Jesse was her safe harbor. He'd allowed her to truly belong to something she'd always wanted.

A family.

A family that included his best friend and twin, Jake. She thought of her teen years and that brief moment when she'd been so infatuated with Jake. Man, he'd broken her heart when she was fifteen and she'd caught him with Rebecca Stringer.

"You were mine," she whispered.

Heart pounding, Raine let out a long, labored breath as her fingers traced a path from Jake's forehead and lingered next to his mouth. Slowly she reached for him and pressed her lips to his, moving languidly over him.

Maybe it was never an infatuation. Maybe she'd been in love with Jake her entire life as well.

Her eyes widened at the thought. *Was it possible?* Could she have been in love with both Jesse and Jake?

How screwed up was that?

"Hey."

She realized Jake was awake, his warm brown eyes now open, their depths clear and staring at her with concern. "Everything all right?"

No.

She nodded yes.

Her eyes drifted back toward the window and she sighed. "The storm is over and I'm not sure I want to leave yet."

Jake slipped his hands around her and buried his head in her hair. "Unfortunately, there's this pesky thing called life and responsibility."

His hands slid to her breasts and she smiled.

"There is that," she murmured, her hands now buried in his thick waves as he moved and tossed the blanket off them.

For several moments she stared into his eyes, trying to read him, but couldn't. Something had changed. She felt it. Just the thought of the outside world was enough to crack their delicate environment.

And that was something she wasn't ready to give up, not yet anyway. Cool air rolled over her skin, but she didn't feel it. She felt nothing but a need and desire to connect to Jake. To keep whatever it was they had alive as long as she could.

She reached for him and with a groan slid her mouth across his cheek as his hands cupped her hips and moved her between his legs. His erection was heavy, thick and full, and she ached at the thought of him inside her.

"Jake," she breathed, her voice shaky with emotion.

"I know," he answered, and she kissed him as if she were dying. As if there were nothing in the world except Jake. As if the connection between them were the only thing that mattered. His hands caressed her skin, lingering here and pressing there, finding her pleasure points and toying with her until she was mad with desire.

In the space of a few short days, Jake had learned exactly what she needed, what she wanted and craved, and he played her with everything he had.

There were no more words. No soft sighs of contentment or whispers of need. There were only straining bodies, slick wet skin, and moans of pleasure. They made love with an urgency that fed on an undercurrent of desperation or maybe sadness. Raine felt it, but she was too weak to fight it. She was too weak to do anything but take what Jake was giving, and for Raine, it was life.

He'd brought her back to life. Not just with his body, but with his mind and spirit. Here in this cocoon they'd built over the last few days, she'd laughed and cried and laughed some more. They'd argued the way they always had, from politics to music to last Monday's football game. Her soul was no longer asleep. It was awake and hungry and full of need.

When Jake thrust into her that last time, his body

shuddering in release, Raine held him close, listened to his frantic heart, and was more afraid than she'd ever been.

"Jake," she whispered into his neck.

His cell went off and he swore, the ringtone a blues riff. "Shit, hold on."

He slipped from her arms and padded across to the kitchen, her eyes following in his wake. His tall, muscular frame was something else—holy hell, was it ever—but her eyes lingered on the scars near the small of his back. Scars that were a testament to the fact that this man was, or rather had been, a soldier. A soldier who'd given a hell of a lot for his country and a soldier who had lost so much.

The ringtone told her it was his mother calling, and just thinking about her mother-in-law was enough to kill the buzz that she'd been floating in. It made it think of her own mother, and of the twenty or so text messages Gloria had sent over the last week or so. Marnie and Gloria meant reality, and reality meant…

At this point, Raine wasn't sure what it meant anymore, other than complicated.

"Christ, you've got to be kidding me."

Her head snapped up and she watched him. Jake's shoulders were hunched forward, and he rubbed the back of his neck slowly while listening to his mother. She heard him swear again before he turned and caught her watching.

The look in his eyes was fierce, and she swallowed thickly, turning her eyes away and settling on Gibson instead.

"Ma, I'm not…there's no way in hell… I can't…I just can't."

The rest of his words were lost as he walked over to the kitchen window, obviously wanting some privacy. She was dying to know what had him upset, but it wasn't her place to ask, so she remained silent.

He tossed his cell onto the table and stared down at it, brooding. Everything about his posture screamed tension and anger. It was so far away from where he'd just been.

She had a bad feeling about this.

"Everything okay?" she asked hesitantly.

"Yep." His answer was brisk, and the bad feeling in her stomach tripled.

Jake pulled on his jeans, stretched out his shoulders, and rolled his neck. When he turned to her, no longer were his eyes filled with mischief and desire; they were curiously devoid of emotion.

God, had her world changed already? Had complication dared to infiltrate her space?

She pulled the blanket up to her chin. "What did your mother want?" she asked, hating that she wanted to know so badly.

Jake's jaw clenched, and for one second something so bleak and painful crossed his face that she sat up and pushed her hair from her eyes, suddenly more than just a little concerned. "Jake? Is everything all right?"

"Yeah," he answered, "I'm good. Everything's good."

But it wasn't. No way in hell was it.

"The roads are open, so I'm going start chipping away at the ice out there. It's going to take a bit to get the vehicles clear."

He put on his shirt and yanked his boots over his feet. Gibson nipped at his hands, and after a tussle with the puppy—which basically meant Gibson rolled onto his back and Jake scratched his belly real good—he rose and crossed the room to stand by the sofa.

Suddenly everything about their situation seemed awkward, and Raine couldn't help the blush that stained her cheeks. In the harsh light of day, she felt like she was doing the walk of shame, and that was ridiculous.

"I'll let you know when your car is done so you can go home."

She nodded but didn't answer. She didn't trust the lump in her throat.

I don't want to go home.

His hand caressed her cheek, lingering near her mouth. "You look beautiful, like this."

She cleared her throat. "Like this? You mean all crazy hair and no makeup and in bad need of a shower?"

"No," he said softly. "Like a woman who's been loved. A woman with swollen lips"—his finger slid inside and he cocked his head to the side—"and a hickey on her neck."

"What?" She wriggled away. "Are you serious? I have to help out the youth meeting on Wednesday night. Oh my God, I don't even know if I own a freaking turtleneck. I—"

His grin told her he was bullshitting, and she punched him in the arm, then settled back to watch him head for the door, calling for Gibson to follow him out. He'd just yanked the door open when panic hit and she grabbed the blanket around her and flew over the wooden floor, her bare feet making no sound.

"Jake!"

He turned and she shivered at the gust of cold air that slipped into the cottage.

"You planning on helping me in that?" he asked, a hint of a smile on his face.

"Are we going to be all right?"

The light in his eyes dimmed a bit, and her teeth chattered as her body began to shiver uncontrollably. Whether it was from the cold was anyone's guess, but she stood there like an idiot as Jake hiked the comforter up just under her chin.

He kissed her forehead and stepped out into the brightly lit morning without saying another word.

Raine didn't know how long she stood there, staring at the door. But it was long enough that her vision began to blur, and angrily she wiped the wetness from the corners and set about getting dressed.

Luckily, she'd brought an overnight bag, and even though her overnight had turned into a few extra days, always the practical girl, she had clean undies and socks. Once she was dressed in a plain gray sweatshirt and matching yoga pants, she threw her hair up into a clip—she didn't need to look in a mirror to know how awful it was—and tidied up the living area.

A steady stream of yipping sounded from outside—good to know Gibson was having a blast—and once she was satisfied with the way things looked, she grabbed her coat and bag, slipped into her boots, and headed out into the sunlight.

Her car was running, and Jake was just finishing up chipping the ice off the back window. She tossed her bag into the back, grateful to feel the heat, because even though the sun was shining at about a thousand watts, it was freaking cold.

"So," she said, her breath floating in the air, small puffs that evaporated instantly.

"So," Jake answered.

Gibson jumped at her and she scooped him into her arms, laughing as the puppy tried in vain to lick her entire face. In the end she was forced to throw him into the backseat, and even then he pushed his nose against the window, yelping happily, searching for a way back out.

So many thoughts whirled in her head, but one stood out.

"Am I going to see you later?" she asked, watching him closely.

Jake hesitated, and the disappointment and hurt that rolled through her was instant.

"Not that I expect you to, you know, spend all your time with me or come over, or…"

"Hey," he said softly, taking a step toward her until his tall frame blocked all the sunlight. "You need to know that these last few days have been amazing." His lips swept across hers and he pulled her into his embrace, resting his head on top of hers.

"Why does it sound like you're about to say good-bye?"

The wind picked up then, and she shivered against him, not liking the silence.

"Jake?"

A hint of sorrow touched his eyes and then was gone in an instant.

"I have to go to Boston for a few days."

"Boston."

He nodded.

"Boston, as in Barbie doll?"

He frowned. "Lily is in Boston, yes."

Something hot and furious rushed through Raine.

He'd just spent the last two days and nights with her. Loving her. And now he was off to see Lily St. Clare?

"Wow," she said and reached for the door handle. "I must suck at this whole sex thing, you know, if the minute you leave my bed you're headed for Barbie."

"Raine, it's not like that." The guarded tone should have been a warning, but it was one she ignored.

She arched an eyebrow, suddenly raw inside. "What's it like then? We've never had that conversation. The one about Lily. So, what's her story?"

Jake shoved his hands into his front pockets and studied her for a few moments. "Babe, I don't know where this is coming from. Lily is a good friend...a close friend, and she's got some really bad shit going down right now. Her brother is dying, okay? Her brother, a guy who served with me, is dying, and she has no one else who gets what it's like."

When had the warmth fled? The intimacy? Guilt slithered through Raine and nestled under her skin because she knew she should feel something more than anger toward a woman who was about to lose her brother. But she couldn't help the way she felt, and at the moment it felt as if Jake was choosing Lily.

Right or wrong, there it was.

"Okay, I get that. I do. But what is she to you? What's Lily and Jake's story? Have you fucked her?"

If he was shocked at her language, he didn't show it, but he was angry. *That* she could tell clear as day. He got that look in his eyes, the blank one. The one she hated.

"Christ, I don't have time for this." He ran his hands through his hair in agitation. "Lily was there for me when I needed someone. When I thought I was at the end of my rope. I can't explain how or why or… She saved me from myself."

The hurt inside Raine exploded. It was red-hot and it filled her vision until all she could see was darkness.

"*She* saved you." Hot tears burned the back of her eyes.

What about me? She raged inside. *What about what I gave you? What about what I lost?*

"Good for Lily." She yanked on the door. "Good for you." Raine slipped inside her car. "I'm glad you had someone, Jake. I really am."

Don't cry. Don't cry. Don't cry.

"Shit, Raine, don't—"

"Was she there the night I called you? The night I needed someone so badly, it felt like I was dying? Was *she* the woman who answered your cell?"

"What are you talking about?" he asked harshly, his face white.

"You don't even know, do you?" she shouted. "I called you because I needed you. Because I was dying without you."

"When?"

"Does it matter when? What day? What month? You were with someone else, going on with your life, while I was stuck in hell. You weren't there for me, Jake." A tear slipped down her cheek and she wiped it away angrily. "No one was."

Gibson barked once and then stopped, sensing the distress and anger.

Raine stared straight ahead, her voice shaky as she wrapped her hands around the steering wheel. One big fat tear slipped from her eye. "Don't get me wrong. I'm glad that you had someone, I really am."

She put her car into gear. "But I wish it had been me. I wish you had never left, because then maybe I wouldn't have gone through hell by myself. Maybe then I wouldn't have lost…"

"Lost what?"

But she flinched and refused to answer.

For a moment there was silence, and then Raine cleared her throat and whispered, "I'm sorry for her, I am, but I can't help the way I feel. Maybe that's selfish, but it's all I got."

Raine slowly backed out of the driveway, ignoring the man who stared after her. Ignoring the pain in his eyes and the pain in her heart.

Once she was on the road, the tears came and she made no effort to stop them. The pain was intense and she let it flow through her. She let it touch every cell in her body until she thrummed with anger and pain and loss.

By the time she reached the bend in the road, she had to pull over, her hands were shaking so hard. She wasn't sure how long she was there, crying like an idiot, but eventually the tears subsided and she felt strangely calm.

"Damn," she whispered as she pulled back onto the road and drove through a winter wonderland. "Coming back to life sucks."

Chapter 19

"JAKE, WHERE HAVE YOU BEEN?"

His mother's voice was more than a little concerned, and he paused in the foyer, his only thought a hot shower, hopefully one that would help clear his head.

"I was holed up at Wyndham, I told you that."

Marnie crossed the foyer and paused a few inches away. Free of makeup, with her hair clipped back off her face, she looked delicate. The lines around her eyes and mouth didn't look as sharp, and he thought that maybe she looked halfway relaxed.

"I know that, mister," she said affectionately, "but I called you nearly six hours ago. Didn't you check your messages? We need to leave for Texas, for your medal ceremony. I've already checked, and the flights—"

"I'm not going to Texas, Mom."

Shocked silence followed his words, and the guilt inside him, so raw and heavy, pressed into his chest. He swore underneath his breath and looked away, not able to deal with his mother's pain in addition to his own. Or Raine's.

God, he'd screwed up. He'd screwed up huge, and at the moment, he had no idea how to fix things.

"Jake? We just thought…well, we thought you might want us there. Your friend Mr. Baker invited us and…" Her voice broke. "He said he served with you and Jesse."

Damn. Leave it to Baker. The guy had never had his

timing down. Never. It's why his nickname was Trigger.
As in fast. But that wasn't always a good thing.

"Look, there's no ceremony. I'm not a Ranger anymore. There's just Baker, holding a medal for me that I
don't deserve."

He closed his eyes, hating the tension that sat across
his shoulders. Hating the memories embedded in his
brain. The ones that told him he sure as hell didn't
deserve a fucking Bronze Star, especially one with the
word *valor* attached to it.

If he were the hero they all thought he was, Jesse
would still be alive. He would be here with Raine where
he belonged, not buried six feet under.

Things were so screwed up. Beyond screwed up.
Where the hell did he go from here?

"Jake."

Something in his mother's tone grabbed him hard and
he whipped his head up, his blood running cold at the
look in her eyes. Shit. Could he do this? His father had
joined his mother, linking his hand inside hers.

"Jake, what happened to you?"

"Marnie," Steven cautioned.

"No," she said sharply. "This has gone on long
enough. Jake, what is going on with you? Can't you
share some of your pain with us? We gave you space
when you wanted it. When you disappeared and cut us
off. We let you, because we thought that's what you
needed, what you wanted."

"Mom—"

"No, let me finish." She shook her head. "I don't
know how to help you, but clearly, being away from
your family hasn't accomplished anything. It hasn't

helped at all. You need to explain things to us. You need to help us understand."

Marnie glanced up at her husband, exhaled slowly, and spoke. "We've never asked you what happened over there. What happened the day Jesse died. But I think it's time that you told us." Her voice trembled slightly and she let Steven's hand go, so that she could cross over to where Jake was. She placed her hand on his chest and he ached at familiar warmth of her touch. God, he was so cold.

He was sick inside.

"I think you need to tell us what happened. I think that you need to tell me why you can't sleep and what those nightmares mean." Marnie slipped her arms around him and laid her head against his chest. "I think you need to do this, not only for us, but for yourself, Jake, because I can't stand seeing you hurt like this. I already lost one son, and I'm terrified that I'm going to lose you too."

Jake's arms slowly pulled his mother as close as he could. His eyes stung and his lungs hurt to breathe because the lump in his throat was so huge, he was afraid he'd choke. He cleared his throat and glanced over to his father.

"Okay," he said, knowing he'd reached the end. He just hoped when they heard the facts, they wouldn't hate him as much as he hated himself.

His mother grabbed his hand and pulled him into the family room. She sat in her chair, the one that had always been there, the one he and Jesse used to squeeze into when she got out their favorite book, *The Black Stallion*. She used to read them one chapter every night before bed, and God, he'd loved that time with her. With Jesse.

His father passed by and clasped his shoulder before moving behind his wife.

Jake sighed and glanced out the window, across the snow-and-ice-covered lake, and an image popped into his mind. One he hadn't thought of in a long, long time.

"Do you remember when Jesse and I decided to go ice fishing? I think we were ten? Eleven?"

His mother nodded slowly. "You'd asked for days to go out there, because Cain and Mackenzie wanted to go."

"Yeah, we did, and you told us that it was too danger-ous. That the lake was too deep and that the ice wasn't thick enough. Of course we didn't listen. That Saturday we waited for you guys to leave." A frown creased his brow. "I think you guys were bowling or…"

"It was the church bazaar," his father murmured.

Jake nodded. "That's right, and we were supposed to help, but I convinced Jesse to pretend to be sick so we could stay home. So that we could go ice fishing while you guys were gone."

He turned back to the lake and closed his eyes, mem-ories washing over him as if it were yesterday.

"It was cold. The kind of cold that freezes the hair inside your nose. I remember the sun was so bright, we had to wear sunglasses, and that Jesse wore his new ski jacket. The red one with black sleeves. He liked it be-cause it was the Detroit Red Wings colors."

"You had the blue and black one," Steven said, a soft smile on his face.

"It took us a while to find the perfect spot, mainly

because I wanted to go out farther, near Old Man Jenkins's place. That's where the sweet spot was, along the north shore. It didn't take us long to cut through the ice either. I guess that should have been our first clue that we didn't know shit. That the ice wasn't thick enough." He glanced at his mother. "I should have known it was dangerous."

Marnie shook her head. "There were two of you out there, Jake. It wasn't just you."

He ignored her comment. "I think we'd been sitting in our chairs for maybe twenty minutes when I got a bite. Man, we thought we'd scored huge. I jumped up and down and he yelled at me, told me to stop being an idiot. I think I flipped him the bird and pounded the ice once more before sitting back down in my chair so I could reel in my catch. But then the ice cracked and heaved, nearly dumping me into the water because I was so damn close."

He shoved his hands back into the front pockets of his jeans. "Jesse let his rod go and tried to grab me. He tried to push me out of the way but ended up sliding through the hole. I remember how awful I felt, like was I was going puke. It was panic and fear. God, it was so thick and hot that for a moment, I was frozen. I couldn't move."

"You were a ten-year-old boy, Jake." Marnie turned to her husband and grabbed Steven's hand.

"I fell onto my stomach and slid forward, yelling because I couldn't see Jesse at first, and I was so scared that he'd get trapped under the ice and then I'd never be able to get to him. It was getting dark, too, and it was so cold."

Silence followed his words, filling the room, but only for a moment.

"And then I saw his hand and I grabbed it. I don't know how in hell I didn't fall in with him." He shook his head, "I don't know. But I got hold of him and pulled him out." He blew out a long breath. "His lips were already blue, and there was a moment when I thought he was dead. I remember it clear as day. The fear slipped away, and for that one moment, I was empty. But then his eyes flew open and he slammed his fist into my face.

"Bastard broke my nose." Jake took a moment. "That was the first time I had a broken nose. The first time I nearly lost Jesse, but over there…"

He shook his head and looked at his parents. "In Afghanistan, there aren't any second chances, and when the shit hits, someone gets injured or dies. The thing is—" His voice broke as the wall of emotion he'd been pushing away for months slammed into his chest with all the fury and strength of a freight train.

"Just like that day on the lake, Jesse should never have been there. He shouldn't have gone out with us. I shouldn't have let him."

"What are you saying?" Marnie's voice shook, and though he wanted to look away, he wanted to be anywhere other than where he was, he couldn't. He owed his parents the truth.

"Afghanistan broke Jesse. It took his soul and crushed it. I knew it. But he didn't. It was like he was out on the lake, walking across thin ice, and he didn't give a shit. He just didn't care. I don't know what happened, what event or place or person broke him, but he wasn't right. He wasn't strong enough to be safe. He became cocky, and fear didn't even factor into anything. He thought he could walk on water." Jake closed his eyes. "He thought he could walk across the ice."

"Oh, Jake." His mother's soft voice nearly did him in.

"He was careful, never a danger to the rest of the men in our unit, but when it came to his own personal safety? It was like he had a death wish. When I threatened to go to our commander, he laughed in my face. He pulled me close and told me I was paranoid and no one would believe me."

Jake shrugged. "He was right. None of the guys knew him the way I did. What they saw as bravery, or damn American strength, was him falling through the ice all over again. I knew the only way I could keep him safe was to stick by his side. To just stay there and not leave. But that morning…"

"It's okay, son. We don't need to hear any more." Steven's rough voice cut through the haze in Jake's mind, but the pain inside him was too intense. It was rolling through him, and he didn't think he could stop if he wanted to.

"That morning we had orders to retrieve two targets being held by insurgents. Our intel was confirmed and it was a go, but everything about it felt wrong. The location was off, it was full of civilians. Families." He paused. "Kids."

He sighed and rubbed the back of his neck, his mind still back there, his nose full of desert, and sand, and the burning stench of human flesh.

"We went in just before dawn and cleared the perimeter before slipping inside the compound. Jesse was on point and I was following up the rear, Blake—Lily's brother—and Headsy making up the rest of our team. This mangy animal, a dog, wandered into the building we'd just cleared. I remember it looked at me for what seemed to be a really long time. I remember thinking the shit is gonna hit. I felt it." He paused. "I tasted it. And then all hell broke loose. Mortars were going off, rounds firing into the air, and I could hear the other teams from our unit outside returning fire. We joined them, and the firefight lit up the night like the Fourth of July."

Jake shook his head and grimaced. "Jesse walked into that hell with his head up like he was walking down a sidewalk in Crystal Lake. I couldn't believe it, and I wanted to knock him down so badly that I started toward him. I had every intention of taking him out myself, except Blake took a hit and went down, and I knew it was bad. By the time I got to Blake and pulled him to some sort of safety, Jesse was already out of sight."

"Oh, my sweet boy," Marnie moaned, clutching Steven as she stared at her son.

"I was pinned down. There was nothing I could do, and when I found him, it was too late. He'd taken out several insurgents, but he was down, and it's a miracle I wasn't killed trying to get to him. I think it was my anger that got me through, and when I finally made it to his side and pulled him back out of harm's way, it was too late."

The well inside Jake burst, and his body shuddered so violently that when his mother's arms wrapped around him, she shook as badly as he did. When Steven grabbed them both and held them tight to his chest, Jake finally let loose everything he'd been holding inside.

For the longest time, the three of them stood there,

huddled together in the family room, three bodies melted into one.

"I tried to save him, Mom. I did everything I could, but it wasn't enough," Jake managed to say. "His wounds were…they were fatal, but the thing was, he didn't want it. He didn't want to come back from Afghanistan, and I hate him for it."

For a moment there was silence, and then Jake gently disengaged himself from his parents. He wiped the wetness from his eyes. "I don't know how he could do that to Raine or you guys. I can't forgive him for that, and there's no way in hell I can accept a medal because someone thought I was brave that day." He shook his head. "I wasn't brave. I was running scared, trying to get across the ice before he fell through, because I knew I was too late."

He took a moment and gathered his thoughts while his parents absorbed his words. When enough time had passed, he spoke softly.

"I have another reason for not going to Texas. Lily called and Blake's in a bad way. He was transferred to Boston last week and I promised her I'd be there for her."

"Oh God," Marnie said, "her brother?"

Jake nodded. "He'll be lucky to survive the night."

He thought of Lily and the phone call he'd got this morning just after he walked outside the cottage into the cold Michigan morning. The scent of Raine was still in his nostrils and the feel of her was still on his skin.

Damn, but it had been so easy being with her, loving her the way a man should love a woman, and Lord knows he wanted more. He wanted a hell of a lot more.

But easy and Jake weren't going to be friends anytime soon, and he knew deep down that until he dealt with his past, there was no future with Raine.

He just didn't know if he was man enough to do it. Even for her.

Chapter 20

Snow was falling, big fat flakes that melted almost as soon as they touched skin. Raine tugged her hat down a little more, and she wiped away a particularly large flake that teetered on the edge of her eyelash.

She was parked downtown near the square, across from Mrs. Avery's flower shop, where Mr. Avery and her son were trying their best to keep the sidewalk clean. The temperature was mild and the fluffy white stuff plentiful. It covered the ground, filling up the cleared spaces almost as fast as those hardy souls could get it shoveled.

She took another step away from her parked car and paused. Definitely packing snow, every kid's winter dream.

It was nearly four in the afternoon, and evening was fast approaching. With only a few days until Christmas, downtown Crystal Lake was a hive of activity. She'd just come from the grocery store, having stocked up on a bunch of essentials: milk, eggs, bread, and chocolate—an entire bag of chocolate-covered almonds, to be exact. The cashier had raised an eyebrow, and Raine had given her a "don't judge me" look before tossing in two bags of potato chips as well.

With this one last stop under her belt, she'd hit the hardware store for some more Christmas lights and be on her way back home.

Or rather, the place she'd been calling home, anyway.

Her cell phone vibrated against her waist, and with

her heart suddenly pounding, she tugged it from the pocket of her pea-green jacket. Was it Jake?

He'd called several times over the last few days, but not to her cell—he'd left messages at her house, and since she hadn't been staying there, she'd missed his call every time. The last message had been left two days ago, and he had told her that he was going to be home today, not sure what time, and that he missed her and needed to talk.

Of course she had called him back, but both times his cell was off.

God, she felt like an absolute shit.

Marnie had filled her in on why he'd flown back to Boston—Lily's brother had passed away. A lump formed at the back of her throat at the thought, and as much as she felt awful for the woman, she couldn't help the thread of jealousy that ran through her. Jake cared enough about Lily to be there for something as awful as the death of her sibling, and yet—as much as she tried—she couldn't forget that he hadn't been there for Raine when she needed him the most.

And it was unfair of her. He had no idea what she'd gone through, and Lord knows he was going through just as much, but still.

But still, it would have been nice.

She glanced at the number and sighed. It was her mother.

Raine wandered over to the massive display of Christmas trees, searching for a balsam fir, or a Fraser, if there wasn't one left. She supposed it wasn't the most environmentally friendly thing to do, but for Raine, a fake tree didn't signify Christmas. She had one at the carriage house, but this year it wouldn't do.

"Gloria," she said as she cocked her head and studied several candidates. Picking a Christmas tree was tricky. It had to be right. The right shape and size.

"Raine, where are you?"

She leaned closer and inhaled deeply, a smile on her face when she stood back. The right Christmas tree also had to have the right smell. It needed to be sharp and fragrant. It needed to smell like Christmas.

"I'm at Kris Kringle Trees, why?"

She tried to keep the sharp tone from her voice, but it was hard. The woman had played at being an absentee parent for as long as she could remember, so now, having her here in Crystal Lake, butting in where she wasn't exactly wanted, was hard to deal with.

Though if she was honest, Raine would have to admit that Gloria Delgotto had managed to be a bit of a distraction this past week—even if Raine didn't always appreciate it.

"I'm just wondering if you're still coming to the candlelight service at the church?"

Friday. Christmas Eve.

Four whole days away.

"Uh, I don't know. I might be busy."

I'll take this one, she mouthed to the bored-looking teenager who was assisting the jovial Kris Kringle.

"Seventy-five bucks," the kid said, pushing his orange knit cap farther back on his head. His pinched nose was red from the cold, and the long hair that hung down to his neck was jet-black. He sported a nose ring and attitude that could fill the entire square.

"Are you kidding me? That's freaking robbery."

"Raine? Who are you talking to?" her mother asked.

She ignored Gloria, her focus on the teen, who chewed a wad of gum as if it were the most precious thing in the world. The kid glanced toward his boss, but Kris Kringle was busy with another couple.

"I'll give you fifty bucks, and you're going to tie this sucker to the top of my car, and I won't tell the fat jolly man over there that you just tried to rip me off and pocket twenty-five bucks for yourself."

The kid scowled, muttered, "Whatever," and went about securing the tree.

"Raine, are you still there?"

"Yeah, I'm still here. I'm trying to buy a damn Christmas tree, but I'm still here."

"Oh, do you need help setting it up?" The hopeful tone in her mother's voice was too much. She needed to cut things off before Gloria got too comfortable.

"No, I'm fine."

"I can come out to the house, I don't mind."

"I've got this handled. It's a Christmas tree."

Silence filled the phone, and for a moment Raine felt a tingle of something. Guilt, maybe?

"Look, I just want to do this on my own. Okay? You don't need to get all bent out of shape."

A sigh sounded in her ear. "All right. But please try to make it out to the candlelight service on Friday night."

Yeah, Raine thought. *Like that's going to happen.* She hadn't been inside a church since Jesse died and had no plans to start now.

"Look, I gotta run."

"What are you doing Christmas Day?"

"I don't know."

"I could make a turkey, or we could do ham, or—"

Okay, she really needed to nip this in the bud.

"Mom, it's not going to happen. You need to stop pushing so hard. Have dinner with your church friends or your missionary buddies or whoever the hell you've spent every single freaking Christmas with for the last ten years. You can't just expect us to bond and be like *Gilmore Girls* or something. That's not the way life works." She paused and inspected the tree, now hoisted and secured on top of her car. "It's not the way I work."

"I'm not going anywhere, Raine. I'm here to stay."

"I've heard that before."

"But this time I mean it."

For a moment, Raine didn't say anything. What was there to say? She'd heard that line before too.

"I have hope, because as much as you pretend not to care, you do. I know you do."

Raine rolled her eyes and frowned.

"You just called me Mom, instead of Gloria."

She had nothing to say to that, so she remained silent.

"I hope to see you Friday night, Raine, but if not…" Her mother's voice wavered a bit, and dammit, hot tears suddenly sprang from the corner of Raine's eyes. Angrily, she wiped them away and yanked on her car door.

"If not," her mother continued, "I wish you a merry Christmas and I hope that you find some kind of peace."

Raine sniffled. She blew out a long, hot breath. And then she pocketed her cell phone, carefully maneuvered her car out of its parking spot, and drove to the hardware store.

She made it in and out in under an hour, her arms laden with purchases—new decorations for the tree and cottage. She also managed to get to her car without dropping anything, but once there, she stared down at the locked door and swore. Crap. Her keys were in her front pocket, but there was no way she could reach them without dropping her bags and—

"Raine, what a surprise."

Marnie and Steven stopped a few inches away, hand in hand, warm smiles on their faces.

"Oh my God, your timing is perfect. Can you help me out?"

Steven grabbed her bags so that she could retrieve her keys, and once she had everything loaded inside, she turned to her in-laws.

"Last-minute shopping?" she asked brightly, not asking the one question she really wanted to ask.

What time is Jake coming home?

"It's so nice out tonight, we thought we'd walk to the park and see the light display. Do you want to come along? They're serving hot apple cider and hot chocolate too," Marnie said hopefully.

"Oh, thanks for the invite, but I have a date with a tree and boxes and boxes of decorations."

Marnie glanced up at the large balsam on top of her small car and frowned. "I thought you had that lovely prelit tree."

"Oh, I did, but wanted the real deal this year." Her in-laws had no clue that she had basically moved into the stone cottage at Wyndham, and for the moment she preferred to keep it that way. If they knew, it would lead to questions, and at the moment Raine wasn't even sure what the answers to those questions would be.

All she did know was that everything was finally

starting to feel right. Wyndham felt right. Her new balsam fir felt right.

Marnie took a step closer and cradled Raine's cheeks between her gloved hands. "It's so wonderful to see you out. You look lovely, honey."

Raine lowered her gaze and leaned into her mother-in-law's touch. "I feel…I feel as if I'm waking up, you know, and…" She paused, unable to stop herself. "Have you heard from Jake?"

Marnie gave her a quick kiss and smiled. "He called us from the airport. He and Lily will be home soon. As long as the roads are good, within the next few hours."

"Oh," Raine replied, her heart sinking. "Lily's spending Christmas with us?"

"Jake invited her, and of course we couldn't refuse. That poor girl, she needs us. She needs real family." Marnie's eyes narrowed thoughtfully. "I wonder if our original plan might still work."

"Plan?" Raine said dully.

"Jake and Lily. He swears up and down that she's just a friend but…I'm not sure I believe him."

"Marnie," Steven said softly, "let the young ones work things out on their own."

She laughed. "I suppose I should keep my nose out of it. He is a big boy now." She shrugged. "But it's Christmas, and one never knows what kind of miracles can happen."

"One never knows," Raine replied, moving toward her car. "All right, I'll see the two of you Christmas Eve?"

Marnie nodded. "Yes, we plan on attending candlelight service, and then we'll be home by nine."

"Good, see you then."

Raine slipped into her car and watched Marnie and Steven meander down the sidewalk, holding hands, their bodies touching whenever they could—shoulders, elbows, cheeks.

She couldn't help but wonder what it would feel like to have that kind of love. A love that grows with you. A love that is accepting and nurturing and forgiving.

She thought of Jake, and that familiar heaviness twisted insider her chest. It was a sensation she'd grown accustomed to, one she'd had a lot over the last few days. She thought about their past and the secrets she'd kept from Jake. And for the first time in forever, it seemed, she thought about a future.

And God help her, when she was alone, wrapped in the blanket they'd made love in only days ago—as she'd inhaled his scent and kept him close—she'd dreamed of a future with Jake.

A car horn erupted into the night and pulled her from her thoughts, which was for the best. What was the point in wondering about a future with Jake, when Barbie doll was back in the picture?

Twenty minutes later she pulled into the main driveway at Wyndham Place, which was in darkness, and followed it around to the cottage. Warm light flooded from the windows, and a feeling of lightness overcame her as she gazed at the simple stone structure.

What was it about this place that made her feel so settled? So at peace?

Her mother knew she'd been staying here and probably thought she was going through some sort of weird grieving stage, and who knows, maybe she was, but she didn't care. At the moment all she cared about was that it felt right to be here. She would get the place up to muster and ready for Jake, and then she'd…well, then she would leave. It wasn't as if this was a permanent sort of thing.

"Whatever," she muttered as she slipped from the car. She wouldn't think about it now. She'd leave all that stuff for another day. At least she had tonight, and even if it meant she only had one more perfect evening here, then so be it. If this was to be her doll house to dress up, then she was going to make the most of it.

It took nearly half an hour for Raine to empty her car of the groceries and decorations she'd bought. A new fridge and stove had been delivered a few days ago. At the time, she told herself she was doing it for Jake, making him a home to stay in while he worked on Wyndham Place.

But that was a lie. She'd only been back to her house for clothes and a few essentials. She'd spent every night here, on the blanket by the fire, with Gibson for company. She'd cleaned the loft upstairs and had her old bed brought over from her mother's. The main level was spotless—the floors gleamed, the walls shined—and now, as she placed a huge wooden nutcracker near the hearth, it was perfect.

Gibson nipped at her toes, a bone in his mouth as he tried to get her to play fetch, but she was thinking of the tree.

"How the hell am I going to get it in here without making a huge mess?"

Gibson barked and she scratched him behind his ears, trudging back outside once more. She approached the car and decided the only way to get it done was to get it done.

And so she did, totally unaware of the eyes that watched from the shadows. If she had been paying attention to the dog, she might have noticed that Gibson was sniffing around suspiciously. She might even have noticed a soft *ssshhh*. But as it was, Raine was much too focused on the tree. And after she cut the bindings and it fell over the side of the car, taking her out with it, she swore a mean streak, heaving the prickly balsam to the side as she scrambled to her feet.

"Wow," the male voice shot at her from the dark, and Raine froze. Her heart did that weird twisting thing and her stomach rolled.

There go those damn butterflies again.

"I haven't heard you swear like that since the Pennyback wedding." Jake strode into the light and she melted. Right there. Melted into a puddle of need.

"The Pennyback wedding," she managed to reply, her eyes hungrily taking him in.

And then he was inches from her, his dark hair glistening from melted snowflakes, his handsome face half in shadow. He wore his leather jacket and a dark turtleneck, jeans, and boots. He was all male, all man, and her mouth went dry at the look in his eyes.

"Yep." He nodded. "The Pennyback wedding. Don't you remember?"

Vaguely.

"Uh, sure."

"You were pissed because Paula Pennyback got married a week before you did, and she apparently stole your bridesmaid dresses or something stupid like that."

"Right." She nodded slowly, flooded with the memory. She'd stormed out of the church, because as much

as Raine wasn't religious in any sense of the word, she
could not swear in church. She'd barely made it outside
when she let loose, and both Jake and Jesse had followed her out, watching in amazement as she marched
up and down the sidewalk in front of St. Paul's, cursing
Paula Pennyback and every single member of her family, including her mother *and* her great-grandmother.

For a moment she lost herself in Jake's dark eyes, and
then he reached for her, his hand wiping a snowflake
from her cheek. She resisted the urge to lean into his
touch and instead attempted a smile, but failed miserably.

"What are you doing here, Raine?"

A heartbeat passed. Then another.

"I'm moving in."

Jake glanced at the house and then back to her, his
dark eyes glistening, the look inside them intense.
"Moving in," he repeated slowly.

"Yes," she said softly and then nodded toward the
Christmas tree. "You want to help?"

Chapter 21

THEY SET THE TREE UP JUST TO THE RIGHT OF THE FIRE-place. And it wasn't the easiest thing to accomplish. Not with Gibson jumping and whining for Jake's attention.

Raine shook her head as she straightened and watched the puppy try his hardest to take Jake down. Gibson tugged on his jeans and nipped at his boots. He growled and tossed his bone. He licked Jake's hands, his face, and then licked some more.

"Jesus, Gibs, you'd think I never touch you."

Jake smiled. "He's something else, that's for sure."

Raine nodded and slipped out of her jacket and her boots. She padded in her sock feet to the kitchen and grabbed a rag, intent on wiping up the floor—wet from the snow tracked in off their boots.

"No." Jake grabbed it from her. "Let me."

While he cleaned up, she put away the rest of her groceries, suddenly nervous and unsure about the whole situation. What *was* she doing? Was she really moving in here? Into this stone cottage that belonged to Jake? She had a home, a beautiful home with the best of every-thing, and yet...

She sighed. It hadn't felt that way in a long, long time.

So why did she think she was going to find that here? Or maybe it had nothing to do with that at all. Maybe sub-consciously, she was angling to stick as close to Jake as she could. Was she pathetic? Or just plain old confused?

Jake leaned against the kitchen counter, a wine bottle in his hand, his eyebrows raised questioningly.

Raine nodded and grabbed two glasses for him, and while he poured their wine, she threw some wood into the fireplace and knelt down so that she could get it going properly. Jake joined her and she accepted her glass, taking a sip and hoping it would help to calm her nerves.

Of course that didn't happen, and the silence between them grew so heavy that she could barely keep her merlot down.

Jake was so close to her that she felt his body heat, yet it felt as if he were on the other side of the room. It felt like the space between them, that polite, awful space, were larger than she could manage.

It was the damn elephant in the room.

"I was sorry to hear about Lily's brother," she whispered, her eyes on the flames as she drew her knees up and rested her chin on them. She took another sip of wine, but when she nearly choked, she set her glass aside and stared into the fire.

"Yeah," Jake answered. "It was rough. A long time coming, but still hard as shit to deal with."

"He was in your unit."

Jake didn't answer, but he nodded.

"He knew Jesse."

"Yeah, Blake knew Jesse. He knew Jesse real good."

"Was he hurt in the attack that…"

"He was injured in the attack that took Jesse." Jake's voice trailed off, and Raine glanced up at him. He looked so tired. So tired and just…done.

"Jake," she said slowly, her hand reaching for his cheek.

"Christ, I didn't want to get into this right now."

"We don't have to," she said softly, her heart turning over when he glanced her way. "Not now."

"There are things you don't know. Things we need to talk about."

"I don't…" she began, her voice wavering. "I don't want to talk about Jesse right now."

She closed her eyes, felt the heat from the fire against her skin, but inside she was cold. So cold and scared.

And it was the fear that held her tongue. It sneaked up on her, fueled the parasites playing in her mind. The ones that told her not to talk. The ones that whispered she was crazy to discuss anything that might lead to questions. Because those questions would lead to an expectation of answers, and there were some answers she wasn't willing to give just yet.

It was best to avoid questions at any cost for the moment.

Except one.

"Are you in love with Lily St. Clare?"

"Where the hell is that coming from?" He muttered something under his breath and ran his hand across the stubble on his chin.

To say he sounded surprised would be an understatement.

"I just need to know, Jake."

"I don't believe this." He set his wineglass down and moved until she was forced to look into his eyes, and what she saw there was anger.

"Are you kidding me?"

Okay, so maybe it wasn't plain old anger. His eyes flashed and a muscle worked its way along his jaw. He was way beyond anger.

"What kind of man do you think I am?"

"Jake." She returned his gaze as steadily as she could. "We've never really talked about that kind of stuff, and it's obvious she means something to you."

He looked like he wanted to strangle her. "Of course she does. She means a hell of a lot to me, but that doesn't mean I'm in love with her. And you can be damn sure that if I was, I wouldn't have spent two days and nights making love to you."

Oh God, she was making a mess of things, and the damn elephant was still smiling at her.

"Jake, I didn't mean to upset you. I just...I don't know where we go from where we've been."

He was still angry, and when he leaned closer, when his hands crept into her hair and cradled the back of her skull, the look in his eyes scared her even more. Because it was a look she couldn't crack. She had no idea what was coming next, and that scared her more than anything, because...

I love him.

"We have a lot to talk about. *A lot.*" Jake's voice was hoarse, the way it got when he was dealing with too many emotions. He cleared his throat while her eyes fixated on the pulse that beat at the base of his neck.

I love him. Her brain was frozen, because it wasn't just a thought anymore. It was real—just as real as the elephant in the room. The elephant that really was nothing more than a manifestation of her fear. The fear that when he found out the truth about the secrets she'd kept, it would all go away.

Jake's fingers slid to her chin and he forced her head

up so that she had nowhere to look other than directly into his eyes.

"I can't lose you."

Mortified, she realized that she had spoken out loud, like an angst-ridden, overly dramatic teenager. Her cheeks flushed hot, and when she tried to yank her head away, he wouldn't let her.

"You won't lose me."

Jake's breathing changed, but then her heart was beating so rapidly, she felt faint. Every bone in her body had liquefied, and it was all she could do to not melt into a pathetic puddle at his feet.

He moved so that his knees touched hers, so that they faced each other dead on.

So that she had nowhere to run or to hide.

Trembling, Raine let him hold her up, her throat tight with emotion, her eyes filled with tears.

"I love you, Raine."

Her eyes widened and her breath caught as his gaze followed the path of one lone tear that slowly made its way down her cheek. He bent forward, his tongue warm against her skin as he licked it away.

When he spoke again, his words caressed her cheek; they vibrated and made her shiver. "I *think* I've been in love with you since we were kids."

"That's a long time," she whispered.

"Yeah," he said haltingly. "But the thing is, I *know* I've been in love with you since…"

Another tear slid down her cheek as she nudged him with her nose. She glanced up at him and saw her heart reflected in his eyes.

"Since when?"

"This is so screwed up." He shook his head. "You were Jesse's, and I…" He exhaled as she moved her hands up to rest against his chest. "I couldn't seem to help myself." The last words spoken were more to himself, and for a few moments he said nothing.

"You remember your wedding day? You remember how it rained?"

She nodded. "Your mom told me it meant good luck."

Her mind rolled backward and she squeezed her eyes shut. Images from the past slid through her brain. She saw Jesse. Her serious, steady Jesse. She saw him watching her with amusement in his eyes.

Amusement, because she'd just come in from the rain, where she'd spent the last half hour dancing up a storm with Jake. The hem of her wedding gown was in tatters, the entire skirt mud splattered and soaked.

She remembered feeling invincible, as if she'd found the things she had been searching for her entire life. Love. Stability. Family.

"I knew then," he said hoarsely. "You are the only woman I know who wouldn't think twice about dancing in the rain in your bare feet."

"With you," she whispered. Then more urgently. "With you, Jake."

Rising up to her knees, Raine cupped Jake's face between her hands and kissed his forehead. Gently she trailed soft kisses down the side of his face, pausing, making time to whisper, "Only with you."

She reached his mouth, her breathing as heavy as Jake's, and rested her forehead against his. "I loved Jesse, but I loved you, too."

He wrenched away and gazed into her eyes.

"Don't mess with me, Raine. I don't think I…"

"I'm not." Gently she kissed his mouth, her lips moving against him as she settled into his lap. Slowly she coaxed his mouth open and slid her tongue inside, touching him hesitantly until he groaned into her and kissed her back with such urgent, sweet need that it made her ache.

She broke the kiss, barely able to breathe. "I need you to know this." She stared straight into his eyes so he could see the truth in hers. "I love you, Jake Edwards. I've always loved you. It doesn't lessen what I felt for your brother or cheapen the time I had with him. Nothing can take that from me." She shuddered and exhaled slowly, trying her best to keep it together. "But right now, in this lifetime, in this moment…it's different. It's raw and it's hungry, and I don't think that I can live without you."

He opened his mouth, but her finger was there to keep him silent.

"The other day I told you that I didn't belong to anyone, but that was a lie. I belong to you, Jake. I always have." She grinned through her tears and shrugged. "One way or another, I guess."

His hand rose to wipe away the tears that lay in the corners of her eyes. "I love you, Jake. So much. And I don't want to think about a tomorrow without you."

"You love me," he said as if he didn't believe her. "And you don't think that's screwed up?"

She shook her head. "We don't choose who we love, Jake. It just happens. And sometimes, if you're really lucky, you get a second chance at it. I love you. It's different than what I had with Jesse, but it's just as real

and it's strong. I don't care what anyone else thinks."
She reached for the edge of her top and pulled it over her
head. "All I care about is you."

She pushed him so forcefully that he had no choice
but to fall backward until he was flat out on his back.

Raine straddled his hips, gazed down at the man
she loved, and bent over until her bare breasts were
crushed to his chest. She felt his erection between her
legs and nuzzled his neck...there, where she knew he
liked it.

"I'm going to make love to you right now, if that's
all right?" A hint of tease colored her words, and she
grinned when he shifted beneath her and groaned.

"Good," she whispered. Her hand reached between
her legs so that she could cup him through his jeans.
"This feels good."

Slowly she teased him through the fabric of his jeans
until she knew it was too much, and then she kissed
him again, pouring every ounce of her love into that
one perfect kiss. Tongues danced, lips cajoled and then
commanded. He tasted like every piece of decadent
chocolate she'd ever had, and when she finally dragged
her mouth away, they were both breathing so raggedly
that Gibson whined a few feet away, his tail at half-mast,
his large eyes full of concern.

Gently, Jake pushed her off and rolled over to get to
his feet. He grabbed Gibson's bone, and when the puppy
erupted into a fit of barks and yips, Jake tossed it into
the kitchen.

Within seconds they were both naked, and Raine
licked her lips as she grabbed the blanket off the sofa
and tossed it in front of the fireplace. Jake was behind

her, his arms around her waist as he kissed the back of her neck and ground his erection into her backside.

One hand snaked over her hips, moving lower, past her belly. Raine spread her legs in anticipation. She leaned back into him as two fingers slid between her wet folds and plunged inside her body.

"You feel so good," he said huskily, moving his fingers as her body twitched in response. "So damn good."

Raine's hands rose over her head and she touched his face, gyrating her hips as his other hand fondled her breasts and his mouth tortured her sensitive neck. She felt the spiraling heat burst inside and then spread rapidly as she moved against him, his hand buried between her legs, his fingers stroking and pressing and rubbing.

The pressure built until she knew she couldn't hold it in any longer, and when she came, when she shuddered against him, Jake was there to hold her. To make sure she didn't fall.

"That was pretty intense." Raine turned and slid her arms behind his neck as she rose on her tiptoes, her mouth seeking his, relishing the hard feel of him against her softness. She kissed him long and languidly, her tongue teasing, the heat already building inside her as his hands cupped her ass to hold her in place.

She broke the kiss and grinned mischievously. "But I'm still feeling a little…"

Jake bent low and with his tongue, slowly circled her turgid nipple.

"I'm feeling a little…"

"Uh-huh," he said and then opened wide, his hot, wet mouth sucking, tugging, and licking her breast, each movement—each tug and pull—hitting her low, between her legs, where she ached.

"Oh God," she breathed, head thrown back as he moved from one breast to the other. She let him love her, let him play with her, and when she was nearly to the edge again, he paused.

"You were saying?" His dark eyes were hooded as he gazed down at her.

Raine nipped his chin. "I want you inside me."

She wriggled out of his grasp and pulled him along behind her until they stood in the middle of the pink blanket. His erection jutted out bold and ready, and Raine didn't hesitate. She pushed him, had him on his back within seconds, and then stood over him, her legs spread, her skin glowing from the heat of the fire.

"Oh damn, but you're killing me," Jake growled, his eyes set on the apex of her legs.

"That's not very nice of me, now, is it?"

Raine tweaked her nipples and her hands drifted over her belly, lingering near her belly button.

"I love how you watch me," she said softly.

"Babe, what else would I be doing right now?" Sweat beaded his forehead while pieces of hair clung to his neck.

Her fingers slid inside her body and she opened her lips so that he could see what she was doing.

He groaned.

She smiled seductively.

Never had Raine felt this powerful. In control.

"I could think of a lot of things," she murmured, placing her heel on his chest when he would have grabbed her.

"I can't hold back much longer," he managed to say. Veins on the side of his neck stood out, and she knew how hard it was for him to just lie there beneath her, unable to take what he wanted.

Carefully she lowered herself, positioning her body just so, and she kept her eyes on him as she sank onto his cock.

His hands were on her hips and he held her still, which was good—she needed a moment to adjust to his size.

"Jesus Christ, Raine."

She began to move, her breasts swaying above him, her body controlling their rhythm. She'd never felt this complete and was well on her way to being utterly sated. She bent over and kissed him. Then, as she increased the rhythm, as the orgasm built inside of her, she leaned closer and whispered, "Jesus has nothing to do with it, my friend."

Chapter 22

RAINE WOKE UP WITH A START. ONE MINUTE SHE WAS snuggled, warm in Jake's embrace, and the next she'd rolled out of the blanket and was on her knees, shivering in the cold. The fire was low and the heat it threw weak.

She took a moment to stretch, her limbs heavy—but it was a good kind of heavy, a satisfied kind of heavy—and glanced back at Jake, who was just beginning to stir, his long frame barely covered by the shocking-pink blanket. For a few seconds, she let her eyes rest on him and just enjoyed the moment. And why not? The man was beautiful. Her gaze lowered to where the blanket nudged his "cut," that indent low on the hips that made her mouth water, and she was just about to taste him there when she stilled.

Something wasn't right.

Gibson barked. He growled a bit and then barked again. Rubbing her eyes, she shot to her feet, realizing the reason she'd woken in the first place.

There was someone at the door. Knocking. Softly at first, and now banging much louder.

Balls! Who the hell would be poking around Wyndham? Or rather, who in hell would be poking around the stone cottage at Wyndham? It's not as if anyone knew she was here.

Gloria!

Raine swore softly and grabbed her yoga pants and

T-shirt off the floor, and after nearly falling on her ass while trying to wiggle into them, she crept across the floor, feeling slightly foolish and more than a little irritated.

If her mother was out there, she was going to let her have it.

Raine peeked outside from the window, and her stomach rolled over. *Shit!*

She whirled around just as Jake rose to his feet—all six feet, four inches of his hard, naked self on display.

"Oh my God, Jake. You've got to get upstairs."

He frowned. "What? Why, what's—"

Another round of banging rumbled from outside, and this time a voice cut through. "Raine? Honey, are you all right? We're starting to get a little worried out here."

Raine's eyes widened to comical proportions, and a sliver of irritation ran through her as a slow grin spread across Jake's face. He scratched the stubble under his chin. "That sounds a lot like—"

"Yes!" she whispered hoarsely. "It's Mrs. Lancaster, and she's not alone. Pastor Lancaster is out there with her." Raine jumped over the sofa and grabbed the pink blanket. "Now get your ass upstairs, and don't you dare come down until they're gone."

His grin widened. "I distinctly remember you saying at some point last night…maybe after you did that amazing move with your—"

She growled like an animal and slapped him on the chest. "Get going."

Jake grabbed the blanket and saluted her. "I'm just saying that you were all gung ho about not giving a damn what anyone thought about our…" He dipped low as the banging continued and kissed the corner of her mouth. His tongue slid up near her ear, and she shivered violently as he murmured, "…about our situation."

"Yeah, that's true, but I don't feel like explaining to our pastor and his wife that we've just spent the night having all sorts of kinky sex just yet, thank you very much." She sniffed the air and alarm bells rang. "Oh my God, what if they can smell it?"

Jake laughed and trotted to the stairs leading to the loft as Mrs. Lancaster bellowed, "Raine, are you in there?"

He paused at the top of the stairs, his smile breaking her heart all over again. God, she loved him.

"I wouldn't get too bent out of shape, sweet cheeks. Mr. and Mrs. Lancaster have seven kids. So, you know, they've done it at least seven—"

She scowled and cut him off. "Well I don't need them to know we did it seven times last night."

"Seven?" His grin widened. "I thought it was at least eight."

She turned in a huff and smoothed her hair as she ran to the door and opened it.

"Mrs. Lancaster." She nodded to the woman and smiled at her husband. "Pastor."

Mrs. Lancaster was bundled in a red and black checkered wool coat with knitted purple hat, pink scarf, and knee-high black patent-leather boots. The woman was either color-blind or didn't give a rat's ass about fashion. Raine had always believed it was the latter.

"Oh, thank goodness," Mrs. Lancaster said, her concerned face relaxing as she took in Raine, her eyes moving from the top of her head to the tips of her toes. "My dear, you look wonderful."

Uh, really?

Raine's hands automatically went to her hair, smoothing the ends a bit before she crossed her arms over her chest as the early morning chill attacked her skin. She knew she looked like she'd just rolled out of bed, but hey, she'd take the compliment.

"Oh, thanks. I got a good night's sleep—"

Was that a snort?

She kept her smile in place but moved a bit so that she blocked any view of inside as she continued. "Despite the fact that there was a lot of snoring."

"Snoring?"

Another snort.

"Yep." She smiled and shrugged. "Gibson."

"Oh." Mrs. Lancaster smiled. "Your puppy."

"Who else?" she replied, smiling warmly at Pastor Lancaster. "I'm looking forward to Christmas. You guys must be busy."

"Oh, good," Mrs. Lancaster said as she moved slightly and tried to peer inside the cottage. "Your mother told me you were spending some time out here, and from what I can see, you've done a lovely job for Jake."

"Ah, yes. I did this all for Jake."

Another snort.

"You know, he needs a place to stay while he's restoring the Wyndham house."

Mr. Lancaster nodded and glanced behind him. "A wonderful idea. I was very pleased when I heard the property had fallen into local hands. Jake will do a wonderful job with it."

Raine nodded. "Um, was there a reason you stopped by?"

Mrs. Lancaster was still trying to see inside, and Raine

knew it was rude of her not to ask the woman and her husband in, but how could she? That's all she needed—the pastor and his wife to be overcome by all the sex fumes. Wouldn't that just ruin everybody's Christmas.

Her cheeks darkened as she thought of the night before and of all the things she and Jake had done. *Hello. Who knew if you bent this way and he did that with his...*

"Raine?"

"Yes?" She shook the image from her mind and concentrated on the couple before her, though it was hard, because even though she was hot as hell, she was shivering and her teeth began to chatter.

"You're going to catch a death of a cold if you don't go inside," Mrs. Lancaster said.

"Oh, yes." She glanced down at her bare feet.

Mrs. Lancaster must have realized she wasn't going to be invited in. She cleared her throat—pointedly—and gazed into Raine's eyes with a look Raine remembered well from Sunday school. The woman wanted something, and she wasn't going to take no for an answer.

Good. At this point Raine was willing to agree to anything so that the woman and her husband would just leave. Not very Christian of her, but there it was.

"I was making the list of floats for the parade tonight and noticed that the youth home you work at isn't entered this year. I called but couldn't get a straight answer from anyone, so I thought I'd check with you."

"Oh." Raine exhaled and looked away. "I, uh, haven't been working there for a while now, so I'm not really sure what's going on, but I can call Marie if you'd like. I'm sure it's an oversight. The kids love getting a float ready."

"Oh." Mrs. Lancaster seemed a bit surprised and she glanced at her husband. "That would be wonderful." Her eyes narrowed thoughtfully. "I wasn't aware that you no longer worked there."

Raine shrugged, holding herself tighter as a blast of wind hit her in the face. "They needed someone more reliable. I—" She licked her lips and glanced away. "I missed some shifts and for a while wasn't good for anyone, let alone counseling and helping troubled teens."

"Well you look like you're finally on the mend, and it's wonderful to see."

"Thanks," Raine replied. "Was there anything else?"

"I was wondering if you knew where Jake was." Pastor Lancaster stepped forward.

"No," Raine answered hastily—maybe too hastily, judging from the look Mrs. Lancaster shot her way. "I mean, I haven't seen him."

"Oh." Pastor Lancaster rubbed his chin and glanced behind him. "His truck is parked in front of the main house."

Balls!

Raine shrugged. "He's probably inside working on something?"

"We knocked, but there was no answer."

"Hmm." Her teeth were now rattling against each other so badly that Raine had to take a moment and force herself to speak. "He's probably got his iPod on and can't hear you. I can give him a message when I see him later, if you like."

"No, that's fine, dear." Pastor Lancaster smiled. "I just wanted to say hello and ask him what his plans for the house are. Just an old man being nosy."

"I'm sorry I can't help you there."

"We'd best leave you then. See you at the parade tonight?" Mrs. Lancaster said hopefully.

"For sure, I wouldn't miss it."

Just then Gibson began to bark up a storm, and Raine moved out of the way so the little monster could get outside, no doubt needing to make a nature run. The puppy flew past and skidded to a halt at Pastor Lancaster's feet, his joy at finding a new set of leather boots to nip and bark at making the puppy so excited, his tail erupted in a blur of wagging, and he dropped something on the ground, right next to the Pastor's feet.

Something blue. And cotton.

Raine's face turned as red as Santa's suit when she realized what it was.

"Sorry, let me," she said and would have walked across fire to retrieve the item, except Mrs. Lancaster bent over and grabbed it. She gazed down at it for a few moments and then turned to Raine, the blue cotton garment in her hands, a slight smile on her face.

"These must belong to you?"

Raine gazed down at Jake's boxers and wanted to die. She wanted a hole to open up beneath her and to fall all the way to China. She was pretty sure the sight of Mrs. Lancaster in all her red and black checkered glory holding up Jake's boxers was going to be a funny memory someday. Maybe.

But right now? She was horrified and hoped like hell they weren't soaked in the sex fumes that were surely pouring out of the house and choking them both.

"Thanks, yes, they're…" she mumbled. "They're like a new style of…"

"It's okay, my dear." Mrs. Lancaster couldn't hide her giggles anymore. "I'm sure they look wonderful on you."

She turned abruptly and nudged her husband. "We should go, Frank."

The pastor nodded and stepped back. "I look forward to seeing you tonight, Raine."

Raine nodded and watched as they made their way down the path. She heard Pastor Lancaster tell his wife they should try the main house again—that maybe this time Jake would hear them.

And she cringed when she heard Mrs. Lancaster laugh softly and answer, "I don't think he's at the main house, but we can try if you want to."

Oh God.

She closed the door behind her, scowling when she spied Jake a few feet away. He had pulled his jeans on, though the snap was undone and the zipper…

Abruptly, she glanced up, irritated at the laughter in his eyes. "What's so damn funny? It wasn't you out there trying to make small talk with the woman who taught your Sunday school class."

His grin widened. "Got me there."

"I know!" she exclaimed. "And I swear she's got X-ray vision. She knew you were inside."

"Don't forget her super sense of smell."

She made an irritated noise but couldn't look away as he strode across the room and reached for her. He slipped his arms around her and murmured into her hair, "You're freezing."

She let him scoop her into his arms, and she snuggled against his chest as they flopped onto the sofa. For a long time, Raine rested on him, listening to his heartbeat and loving the feel of his arms around her.

She could stay like this forever. But reality was only inches away, on the other side of the door. And though she knew that things had changed for the two of them—dramatically—she wasn't entirely sure how to proceed. She knew what she wanted—a future with Jake—she just didn't know how to get there without dealing with the crap that was still unexposed. Still hidden away.

"So," she began hesitantly, her eyes closed as he slowly stroked her hair. "The Christmas light-up parade is tonight."

"Yep."

She decided to jump off the cliff and put it all out there. It was one thing to be here with him, like this, together—but another thing entirely if they chose to venture out in public.

"I want to go."

"I got that."

She looked at him quizzically and cocked her head. Jake smiled down at her and shrugged. "Well, it's what you told Mrs. Lancaster."

She moistened her lips. "I want to go with you."

She held her breath as Jake shifted, and what she saw in his eyes made her heart skip. With his five o'clock shadow, wild crazy hair, and lazy brown eyes, he was sexy as all hell without even trying.

And he loved her.

"Good to know," he said, and reached for her, his mouth closing over hers. Jake kissed her slowly, with great care, as if she were the most precious thing in the world. Their bodies melted into each other, and when they came up for air, he leaned his forehead against her and wrapped his arms around her possessively as he held her close.

"So you want to go together," he said slowly.

She nodded, and kept her eyes lowered. "Is that going to be weird for you?"

"No," Jake said carefully. "I was planning on going anyway," he said, and something in the tone of his voice got her attention. Raine squirmed until she could see his face.

"You were," she said.

He nodded and couldn't hide the grin. "Yep, I need to hook up with the Lancasters and get my boxers back."

"What?" Raine popped up out of his arms and glanced around, her hands on her cheeks when she realized that, in fact, Mrs. Lancaster had left with Jake's boxers. She groaned and whirled around. "You think this is funny, don't you?"

He was on his feet, the look in his eyes changing and making her all hot and bothered in seconds.

"I don't think this is funny at all," he replied. "In fact, that's not where my head is at the moment." His voice was husky, hitting a tone that sent shivers rolling across her skin.

"My head is as far away from funny as you can get." His hands went for his jeans and he slid them over his hips in one motion. "My head is thinking of naughty things."

Her mouth went dry as he strode across the room. "Naughty, wicked things that would make Mrs. Lancaster's head spin."

"Really," Raine managed to say.

"Yeah." He was in front her now, his dark eyes intense. "Really."

Jake Edwards spent the rest of the morning showing Raine exactly what he was thinking and feeling, and it was in fact naughty.

And more than a little wicked.

Chapter 23

It was nearly six in the evening, darkness had long fallen over the lake, and with the lights twinkling from the many homes that lined its shore, the view was postcard perfect. Snow fell, but the flakes were huge and fluffy, the kind that signaled a return to milder temperatures.

Jake leaned against his mother's chair, a beer in hand, as he gazed out across the still-unfrozen water that he'd spent so many hours on as a kid. He and Jesse and Cain and Mac.

He smiled a bittersweet kind of smile. It seemed like a lifetime ago. The Bad Boys, they'd been called, which was not really the case. They hadn't been bad so much as—what had his mother called them? Rambunctious. Spirited.

He snorted and took a long drink. Who was he kidding? They'd raised hell Monday to Saturday and gone to church on Sunday. If not for an overabundance of charm and bravado, they would have landed in a heck of a lot more hot water than they did. Christ, Jesse could talk his way out of most anything, and Mac? All he had to do was bat those long lashes, and every woman within miles would melt.

God, to be able to recapture some of that ease. Some of that youth.

"Hey."

He turned, spied Lily, and motioned for her to join him.

With her hair thrown up in a messy ponytail, and dressed in old jeans, a sweatshirt, and a pair of fluffy rabbit-ear slippers, she looked like a kid.

"Where is everyone?" she asked as she joined him near the window.

He shrugged. "Mom left a note. She and Dad are running some errands in town but should be home soon."

Lily grabbed the beer from his hand, took a long drink, and then handed it back to him, wiping her mouth with the back of her hand. She stretched and sighed.

"I don't know what it is about your parents' place, but I sleep like a baby when I'm here." She gazed out across the lake. "It's been a long time since I've slept like that."

"Huh," he said slowly, taking another sip, thinking that he was feeling pretty damn good too.

"So," Lily said coyly.

Shit. Here we go.

"You look well rested."

"Yeah, I feel good."

"So"—she smiled—"you slept good too."

Sure, when I wasn't having the best sex of my life.

"Yep."

"But you didn't sleep here."

"Nope."

"So where were you?"

"Out," he replied.

"Out, as in out with your buddies, whooping it up at that hole-in-the-wall you all like to drink at? Or out, as in you spent the night with Raine?"

He tipped his beer and scowled when he realized it was empty. She wasn't going to let this go. He knew

Lily too well, and he knew that he may as well just get it over with and spill, because she'd keep nagging until he did anyway.

"I was with Raine."

The screech that erupted from her mouth was enough to give any man a heart attack, and when she threw herself into his arms, he had no choice but to grab hold of her or the two of them would have landed on their asses.

"About time," she said.

He hugged her tightly, this woman who had come to mean so much to him. And when she grabbed his face and held it between her hands, he couldn't help but grin at the look in her eyes. It had been too long since he'd seen that kind of joy inside her, and to think it was there because of him—because she wanted him to be happy. *That* was really humbling.

His throat tightened as he gazed down at her.

Lily pushed away and shook her head. "Don't go getting all emotional on me, Edwards. I'm not used to you being such a damn pussy." She paused and glanced around. "Where is she?"

"In the basement."

"What's she doing down there?"

He shrugged, smiling slightly as he thought of the mischievous look in Raine's eye just before she'd disappeared downstairs. That was well over ten minutes ago, and he had no clue what she was up to. She'd mumbled something about Christmas, and that was it.

"Oh God, Jake. Please tell me you're not going to turn into one of *those* guys."

"Those guys?"

"Yes, you know the ones. They get all emotional and

pathetic every time they think about the girl they're in love with." Her eyes widened, as they tended to do when she was about to stir shit. "The girl they're having *sex* with."

"Lily," he warned.

"So, is it good?"

"What?"

Why the hell was he playing along?

"The wild, hot monkey sex, you dumbass, which reminds me…" She was grinning widely now.

"Can we dial it down a bit, Lily?"

"When are you going to tell your parents that you and Raine are sleeping together?"

A strangled noise was his first inkling that he and Lily were no longer alone. His head shot up and he glanced toward the kitchen, where he spied Raine, one foot on the step leading into the family room, the other still in the kitchen.

Her eyes were huge, her face stricken, and that's when he noticed his parents just behind her.

Oh Christ, this wasn't the way he had wanted this to go.

He shot a dark look toward Lily, who at least looked contrite and more than a little embarrassed. She wrung her hands and mouthed *I'm sorry* before nodding in the general direction of his parents and disappearing back from wherever she'd come from. That was Lily to a T: stir up shit—whether she meant to or not—and clear the hell out.

Steven carefully set his jacket across the back of a chair, while Marnie made a big deal of doing the same. Snow clung to their hair and color was high on Steven's cheeks, which any other time Jake would have been happy to see, but now? Now it meant something else entirely. The man was uncomfortable.

He groaned inwardly and thought that he was definitely going to strangle Lily the first chance he got.

His dad cleared his throat again, and his mother looked at Jake with an expression that was unreadable, which only made matters worse. He had no clue where her head was at. Hell, as far as he knew, she was still cooking up the insane idea of him and Lily together.

Her eyes glistened, reflecting the twinkling lights on the massive Christmas tree in the corner, as an uncomfortable silence fell between them all.

Jake hazarded another look at Raine and his heart twisted. Sure, they'd agreed to talk to his parents tonight and ease them into the idea of the two of them together. They wanted to start things out slowly. But now—he swore under his breath—now, thanks to Lily, that plan had been blown to shit.

He strode to Raine's side and glanced down at her. "Hey," he said gently, "are you all right?"

"I think so." Her eyes were wide and she exhaled slowly. He could tell she was nervous and more than a little scared. Hell, he felt the same. What if his parents didn't understand? What would he do if they didn't support him and Raine?

"Jake," his mother said softly.

His eyes never left Raine and he held his hand out. When Raine slipped her smaller one inside, some of the tension inside eased a bit. He stared down at her hand in his and thought that he could pretty much face anything, with her at his side.

They both turned to face his parents, who'd stepped down into the family room. Steven's hands were in his front pockets, while Marnie's were clasped in front of her.

"Mom, I can explain..." he began, and then stopped when he realized he didn't quite know how to start. How did he explain what was in his heart, what had always been in his heart, without making it look like he'd betrayed his brother?

"Marnie," Raine said hesitantly, and then she too stopped, looking up at him for guidance, but he had nothing. Big fat zilch.

His mother's eyes glistened like diamonds now, and his heart turned over when he realized they were full of tears. Every negative thought he'd had over the last few days—every reason why he thought this would never work—was suddenly amplified, and he gritted his teeth, unsure how to proceed.

"Jake," his mom said again, her voice trembling.

She crossed the room until she was inches from him and Raine, and shit, when the dam broke and her tears overflowed, he felt like the biggest asshole on the planet. He gripped Raine's hand so tightly, he was surprised she didn't yelp.

Not that he'd let go even if she did, because right now he needed her more than anyone knew.

Marnie let out a long, shuddering breath and wiped away her tears, and when Jake chanced a look at Raine, he hated that she looked so sad and lost. He rubbed his thumb against her palm and faced his mother. He'd make his parents understand. He had to.

He glanced up at his father and grabbed what courage

he could from the nod of encouragement and warmth in Steven's eyes.

"Mom," he began, but stopped when she held up her hand.

"Are you sleeping through the night?" she whispered hoarsely.

What? He shot a look at his father, but the man was focused on his wife.

"I'm not sure what you mean," he said hesitantly.

Marnie, stepped forward and reached for him. She slid her hands along either side of his face, cupping him gently as she studied him intently. For several seconds she did nothing but stare into his eyes, and then she looked away, toward Raine, and spoke softly.

"Is he sleeping through the night?"

"I'm not sure I understand, Marnie." Raine glanced at him, obviously confused.

"His nightmares," Marnie said. "Are they gone?"

He felt something inside him shift and held his breath as Raine answered softly, her hand squeezing his.

"He doesn't have any nightmares. At least none that I've heard." She smiled tremulously and glanced up at him. "He sleeps…he sleeps all the way through."

"Oh, thank God," Marnie whispered, her eyes closed. And then again, as she gazed up at him, "Thank God."

Her arms enveloped him in a hug that damn near broke him. Raine stepped away, and he was vaguely aware that she was talking to his father. But it was his mother who had all his attention. She clung to him, her soft warmth and subtle scent so familiar it made his heart ache.

"I just wanted you back," she murmured before

slipping from his grasp. "I prayed every night that God would give you back to us, that he would heal you, and I had no clue that the answer was right in front of my eyes." She sniffled. "How could I have not known?"

He didn't know what to say to that, so he just hugged her tighter, and the two of them clung to each other for the longest time. Mother and son.

"It's so good to have you back, Jake."

Marnie pulled away from him and wiped at her eyes before turning to Raine. "You are a gift, do you know that?"

"I'm not sure what you mean," Raine said carefully.

Jake shoved his hands into the pockets of his jeans, exhaling as the wall of emotion and energy in him seeped out like air from a balloon. For the first time in forever, it seemed, he felt lighter.

He was…happy.

Marnie touched Raine's cheek. "I believe that people come into our lives for a reason. I don't believe that anything is random. And you…" She paused and wiped away another tear. "Raine, you are the glue that holds this family together. It was always you. Jesse knew that, and for a brief time you held him together. Do you remember the conversation we had a few weeks ago? You thought that maybe Jesse didn't want to come home to you."

Jake watched Raine carefully, his gut a mess at the play of emotion in her eyes. There was love there. Love and sadness.

"I remember," she answered softly.

"As much as it hurts to say this, I think I've finally realized that Jesse wasn't meant to come home, and it's foolish of us to even want to know the why of it. It just is. He wasn't meant to."

Raine closed her eyes, and Jake's heart damn near broke in two.

"But Raine…" Marnie's voice strengthened and Jake glanced at his father, who was busy staring at the ceiling, trying to control his emotions the way men do.

"Raine, you kept Steven and me alive when we both wanted to crawl into a cave and never come out. You were our reason to go on." She glanced at Jake, her eyes shiny. "When Jake was off fighting his own demons, you anchored him. I'm sure he didn't even know it, but it's why he came back to us, and I believe you saved him."

Marnie enveloped Raine into her arms.

"You saved this family. You've given your heart to each and every one of us, so how in the world can Steven and I not embrace what you and Jake have?" Her voice broke, but they all heard her whisper, "Because of you, he sleeps at night, and that's good enough for me."

Chapter 24

THE COACH HOUSE WAS FILLED TO CAPACITY WHEN Raine arrived later that evening with Jake and Lily. The three of them had made it to town in time to watch the Christmas parade of lights, and even though the only thing Raine wanted to do was escape back to the stone cottage with Jake, Mac was in town, and they'd agreed to meet him for a drink.

With Christmas Eve looming the next day, the town was full to bursting with holiday cheer, and it was hard not to get caught up in it. The parade was always a highlight of the season, and this year was no exception. Kids ran up and down the sidewalk, excitedly waiting for a glimpse of Santa Claus, while parents kept a close eye, sipping hot chocolate and catching up with friends.

Snowflakes fell from the night sky, illuminated like diamonds by the parade floats that moved down Main Street. It was perfect.

"I'll grab us something if you guys get a table." Jake pointed toward an unoccupied table in the far corner.

Raine nodded and slipped through the crowd, smiling and waving to several familiar faces. Lori was out with Brad Kitchen, and though the hairdresser did her best to hide it, her head swung like a pendulum as she looked from Raine to Jake and back to Raine. There had been a lot of similar looks cast her way as they stood along the parade route, Lily on one side of Jake, while she was on the other.

She was pretty sure the rumor mill was already chugging full steam ahead, but it wasn't as if she could hide the way she felt. Raine was in love. He'd held her hand off and on, and at one point she'd said something to make him laugh and he had surprised the crap out of her by planting a kiss on her lips.

The night would have been perfect except for the third wheel who had insisted on coming along for the evening. *Lily*.

Raine still wasn't entirely clear on Jake's relationship with the woman, though she trusted Jake when he said it was platonic. But still, the woman was gorgeous, a celebrity of sorts, and from what she'd seen, Lily totally had Jake's back.

Raine wasn't threatened, but the two of them together made her kind of crazy. Did that make Raine a bad person?

Marnie thought Raine had saved Jake, but Raine suspected Lily had had just as much to do with it, if not more. Lily knew things about Jake—things he hadn't shared with Raine—and that was a bridge she wasn't sure how to cross.

Raine shrugged out of her jacket and slipped into the closest chair, smiling politely at Lily as she did the same. The blonde had changed out of her old jeans and sweatshirt and was dressed like a million bucks in a deep blue sweater, the kind that clung to her generous curves, and indigo skinny jeans tucked into leather boots that probably cost more than the average weekly salary for most folks around these parts. Her hair hung down her right shoulder, a platinum braid that was arranged as artfully as her makeup.

Which was flawless.

She was the kind of woman you'd love to hate, yet Raine sensed that the woman didn't have her shit as together as she liked everyone to think.

A few moments of silence passed between them, broken only by a rousing shout of "Hell, yeah" when Springsteen's "Merry Christmas Baby" rolled over the crowd. The dance floor was full, and it was hard not to get caught up in the good vibes that were abundant and robust.

"I was sorry to hear about your brother," Raine said quietly, her eyes on Lily. This was the first that they'd been alone all evening.

"Thank you," she replied, a hint of waver in her voice, "but please don't say it was for the best, or I might have to hurt you."

"I didn't say that," Raine replied.

"No," Lily said grudgingly, "it's what everyone else said. I swear it was my father's mantra." Lily smoothed her braid. "He'd been in a coma for so long that everyone told me it was a blessing, that he's in a better place, but they're full of shit." Her eyes hardened. "His place was here, and it's not right that he's gone."

Raine nodded, because she understood how the woman felt. "He served with Jesse."

Lily glanced over to the bar before leaning closer. "Blake thought the world of Jesse and Jake. He talked about them all the time. He told me that Jesse was intense and that Jake was a bit of a hell-raiser."

Raine nodded and smiled. "That sounds about right."

"He said that both of them were the kind of guys you wanted at your back when the shit hit."

Something flickered in Lily's eyes and Raine swallowed thickly, suddenly feeling anxious and not knowing why. She shot a quick glance toward the bar, but the crowd was three deep, and Jake was nowhere near getting their drinks.

"Jake means a hell of a lot to me, you know that, right?" Lily's intense gaze touched something inside of Raine, and she was adult enough to acknowledge it and call it what it was. Jealousy.

"Yeah," she replied drily. "I got that."

"I love him."

Okay, the woman had balls. Raine cocked her head to the side. "Do you want to elaborate on that a little more?"

Raine got the feeling that Lily was enjoying herself.

"Sorry, that didn't exactly come out right," Lily said sweetly. "What I meant to say is that Jake was there for me when no one else was, and for that I'll always be grateful. For that I'd do anything for him."

The angry green monster inside Raine twisted again, and as she gazed across the table at one of the most famous women in tabloid land, she wanted to dislike her. She wanted to thank her very much for whatever it was she'd done for Jake and to tell her to go home.

But there was something in Lily's eyes, something that told Raine all was not what it seemed. So she held her tongue and said nothing.

"It means that I'll do something for him even if I know it will piss him off." She leaned forward. "Because I know he won't do it for himself."

"That's some kind of love," Raine said carefully.

"It is," Lily agreed. "I wish it was more. I wish it *could* be more, but I'm not holding out hope for myself at the moment, and…" She exhaled and stared at her fingers, which tapped out a staccato rhythm on the table top. "Jake's a one-woman kind of man, and he's had it bad for you forever." She glanced back up at Raine. "It killed him to love you the way he did, especially with the way things were left between the two of you after Jesse died."

Unease spread through Raine, and that hint of jealousy that hummed beneath the surface exploded inside her. It rushed through her veins, leaving green in its wake and a bitter taste in her mouth. Jake had told Lily about that night?

Before Lily could say anything else, she reached into her pocket and withdrew something. "You need to have this. You need to know what he did for his brother and what he did for mine and the rest of the men in his unit, because he doesn't get it yet."

Lily got to her feet and pushed the small package toward Raine.

Raine stared at a brown leather box. It was small and fit into the palm of her hand.

"What doesn't he get?" she asked softly, her fingers caressing the smooth texture of the box.

"He might think he's happy and that he's finally got the world by the balls, but he doesn't. Nothing will work out for the two of you until you both face your past."

Raine couldn't meet Lily's gaze, because there was too much truth in the woman's words.

"He saved a lot of lives that day, and the one thing he didn't think about was his own. He still doesn't."

Lily's words were bitter, and something in her tone struck a chord with Raine.

"What happened to you, Lily?"

For a second she thought the woman was going to confide the inner turmoil that was so obvious on the carefully made-up face. But then, just like that, her cold mask slipped back into place and she was once more the imperious trust-fund baby.

"There's a letter in there from a guy named Baker. He served with Jesse, Jake, and my brother. It explains everything. It tells the story. The real story. The one Jake doesn't believe in." She tucked a strand of hair behind her ear and moistened her lips, oblivious to the whistle that rang out behind her. "Read it, and when you think the time is right, you need to give him that." She pointed to the package in Raine's hands. "It belongs to Jake, and whether he knows it or not, he needs to own it. He needs to own his actions and he needs to realize that everyone else does too."

Lily paused and then whispered. "Even Jesse. Even the ones who are no longer here."

Without another word, Lily slipped through the crowd and left Raine staring after her, which was exactly how Jake found her several moments later.

"Hey, where's Lily? I wanted to introduce her to Mac."

Quickly, Raine slipped the package into her coat pocket and turned in her seat, her face spitting wide with a grin when she spied Mackenzie just behind Jake.

"She left already." She stood and was swept up into Mac's embrace, laughing when he faked a kiss and murmured into her ear, "About time you two got things figured out."

Raine kissed Mac on the cheek, but didn't reply. At this point she wasn't sure about a lot of things. She glanced back at Jake. The only thing she was sure of was that she loved him so hard that it hurt, and the thought of them not working out wasn't something she wanted to dwell on. Not right now anyway.

She knew that Lily was right, except it wasn't only Jake who needed to own up to his actions.

"Hey, what's up?" Jake's hand slid along the small of her back as he eased her back into her seat.

"Nothing, I'm good." She paused, startled at the level of intensity she felt as she gazed into Jake's eyes. She caressed his cheek and murmured, "I'm good."

"Shit, if this is the kind of crap I gotta put up with, then I don't know, maybe I'm better off sitting with—" Mackenzie cranked his head around and groaned. "Here comes Lori and…" He straightened. "It that Brad Kitchen she's with? What the hell happened to her husband? He's still the fire chief, right?"

"Long story," Raine replied, "but let's just say, her husband was putting out fires all over the county, if you know what I mean."

"No shit," Mackenzie replied. "Not that I blame him. That woman is high maintenance."

"Mac!" Raine scolded. "That's awful. There's no excuse for a husband to cheat. If you're not happy, then…."

"No one who is married is happy, trust me on that." Mackenzie shot a look her way. "Well, except for you." His gaze moved to Jake. "I mean, you were…you will be…" He ran his hands through the thick crop of blond hair at his forehead and sighed. "This is complicated, this thing with you two."

"Get over it," Jake said as he slid into the chair beside Raine.

"Oh, I will, but with Lori making a beeline for this table, you can bet your sweet ass that by tomorrow, everyone in Crystal Lake will know the two of you are sleeping together."

"Are you okay with this?" Jake pushed his chair slightly so that he faced her, his dark eyes intent, filled with concern. "We can move slow, if that's what you need."

She loved him for that. Jake was always looking out for everyone else and thinking of himself last.

"I can't hide the way I feel, Jake." Her hand crept to his face and she melted as he leaned into her touch. She thought of the package Lily had given her. Of what it meant. She also thought of the note from this Baker person.

Raine thought of the scars along Jake's lower back, and even though he hadn't talked about them, she knew they were from shrapnel, most likely from the attack that had taken Jesse.

There was still so much between them, so much noise and so many secrets.

"I love you, Jake," she whispered, though the intensity of the moment was broken when Mac groaned. Loudly.

"Seriously? This is what I have to look forward to? The two of you guys pawing each other in public?" He shook his head and scowled. "Thank God Cain and Maggie are coming home for New Year's Eve."

"What?" Raine whipped her head around. "I didn't know they were coming. The last I heard, Maggie wasn't sure, because she didn't know what Cain's schedule was going to be like over the holidays."

"Sucks to be out of the loop," Mac teased, and then he winked. "It's because she called your house, but you've been shacking up with Jake at Wyndham."

Raine made a face, and the heaviness of the moment passed as the three of them sat back and caught up. Just like old times.

Luke Jansen and a few others from their football days stopped by, and there was also a steady stream of every single unattached woman in the place, all of them anxious to say hello to two of the infamous Bad Boys. Jake ignored them, while Mackenzie relished every bit of feminine attention thrown his way. The guy was a natural charmer, and his dial seemed to be set to eleven.

But as Raine watched Mackenzie closely, she felt his loneliness. His pain. And the underlying anger that was always just below the surface. To the world, Mackenzie Draper appeared to have it all. Looks. Talent. Ambition. Prestige.

But she knew that deep down he was still the sad little boy whose father's love consisted of fists and beatings. The man was a bastard through and through, and no one understood why Mac's mother stayed with him. They say love is blind, but that kind of love was nothing but destructive.

"Hey, don't look so down." Mac smiled through glassy eyes—he'd skipped the parade and come straight to the Coach House, so he'd been into the booze for hours. He was well on his way to tying one on as he moved Rachel DeGroote off his lap. The woman tottered on heels that were four inches too high and giggled as she bent low over the table, her generous rack about to fall out and give them all a treat.

"You wanna come back to my place?" she asked saucily.

Mac tilted his head back as if he was considering the offer, and Jake groaned into Raine's ear. "Let's get him out of here before he causes more shit. Didn't she just split with her husband?"

Raine nodded, and whispered, "Yes, and he's a nasty son of a bitch."

"Okay, buddy. I'm going to get you home." Jake got to his feet.

Mac surprised them both by getting to his feet and nodding. "Sounds like a plan. I've been up for hours and need to crash." He swore. "That reminds me."

Raine buttoned her coat and knew where this was headed. "You need a place to stay."

"Yep. Ben is out of jail just in time for the holidays, and I'm not exactly welcome."

"It's okay." Raine tugged on Jake's hand. "You can stay at my place, you know, because I'm shacking up at the stone cottage with Jake."

"Perfect." Mac followed them out into the parking lot after they said good-bye to Salvatore. "Except I shouldn't get behind the wheel. I skipped the parade, remember? Had a head start."

"I'll drive you over," Jake said as he handed Raine his keys. "See you back at the cottage?"

She nodded, reached up to kiss him, and whispered, "I'll get the fire going."

When Jake's hand snaked around to her butt, Raine giggled and squirmed against him.

"Babe, it's already started."

"Just make sure it doesn't go out," she warned, and then pulled away. "The house key is—"

"I know where it's kept." Jake smiled, saluted, and then walked across the parking lot with Mackenzie. They were almost to Mac's car when she suddenly remembered something.

"Jake, grab Gibson's orange chew toy. It's the only one he has that doesn't squeak. I think it's in the living room."

He nodded and she watched them until they slid into Mac's rental, and then she climbed into Jake's Jeep.

It was cold, so she cranked the engine and waited a few minutes, her hand in her pocket fingering the package Lily had given her.

Without warning, tears stung the corners of her eyes, and she rested her forehead against the steering wheel. Why did she feel so damn unsettled? So damn scared?

But she knew why.

And as she pulled out of the parking lot, Raine Edwards tried to quell the panic that all of a sudden reared its ugly head. Her stomach turned over and it didn't settle. Not when she pulled out onto the road. Not even once she reached the stone cottage. She felt as if the devil was nipping at her heels and every single bit of happiness she'd felt tonight was threatened.

Cold sweat broke out along her forehead, and God, she was so hot.

She let herself into the house and doffed her jacket, barely avoiding the bundle of fur and wet sloppy tongue that raced toward her.

She frowned when she spied shredded newspaper and—her frown deepened—was that her slipper?

"Jesus, Gibs, couldn't wait for your chewie?"

Once she satisfied Gibson with several pats to the head and a cookie, she set about building the fire and then withdrew the leather box from her pocket, her fingers running over it nervously.

"Do I open it now?"

Gibson barked at the sound of her voice, and she sat down on the sofa, ignoring his mess as she stared down at her hands.

With a sigh she carefully opened it and felt her heart turn over. There, nestled inside the box was a medal. It was bronze, and there was a *V* fixed to the ribbon. She knew what this meant.

Valor.

Raine bit her lip and forced the lump in her throat away as she swept her fingers across the smooth surface. It was cold to the touch, and a shiver ran through her when she gingerly pulled out a folded note tucked into the seam of the box.

She held it for several moments, staring at the medal and trying to get hold of her emotions.

Valor. The word alone was powerful. Sacred.

And then carefully she unfolded the paper to stare down at words written by a hand she didn't recognize. Baker. A soldier who had served with Jesse and Jake. His penmanship was neat, controlled, and for a second the letters blurred together as her eyes filled with tears.

Slowly she wiped them away and focused. The past was suddenly staring her straight in the face, and maybe it was time to deal with it once and for all.

Chapter 25

JAKE DROVE THROUGH THE STILL NIGHT, NOT REALLY seeing the brightly lit homes that shone into the dark. Some were quite elaborate, with spotlights and colored lights adorning windows, doorways, and trees. Some were more humble, and the odd one had nothing festive at all.

He drove through a now-quiet downtown, past the town square and surrounding park whose Christmas displays and impressive nativity scene were still lit to the extreme. A few couples slowly meandered through the area hand in hand, enjoying a perfect winter's evening.

But his thoughts were on the woman who waited for him back at the cottage. *Raine*. And a goofy grin swept across his face as he thought of sliding into that stupid pink blanket she seemed to like so much and doing all sorts of things with her. Wicked things. Sexy things. Things that only a few short weeks ago hadn't seemed possible.

"Seriously, Edwards, I'm gonna puke if you keep that up."

Jake glanced at Mac and shrugged. "Can't help it, brother. I love her."

Mac straightened in his seat. "Yeah, I know. I've known it for years, but shit, you don't have to cross over to the dark side just because Raine has you by the balls."

Jake laughed. "Hey, I'm fine with Raine holding my balls."

Mac groaned. "That's just wrong. I don't need to know about that shit."

Jake turned onto Crystal Lake Road. "So what's going on in your New York world these days?"

Mac shrugged. "Same old. I made partner, but I think you already know that. Sold the condo I was in and bought a brownstone on the Lower East Side. It's a fixer-upper, but it gives me something to do."

"What about that woman—Tiffany I think was her name?"

"She did what they all do."

"And what's that, exactly?" Jake pulled into Raine's driveway and glanced up at the carriage house. The outside lights were on, but the house was in darkness.

"Got way too serious even after I laid out the ground rules. Too bad, because she was good in bed."

"You have ground rules?"

"You bet your ass I do, I need them. And even then, clearly they don't work. Hell, Tiff got pissed because I wouldn't spend the night at her apartment, but shit, why would I do that? I've got a perfectly fine king-size bed at my own place and complete silence in the morning. I can get up and work out, scratch my ass if I want to. I can have my coffee and read the paper in peace. No listening to her natter on about Gucci bags and Manolos. What the fuck is a Manolo, anyway?"

"You've got it rough." Jake knew his friend would never change. The guy was a commitmentphobe, but considering he grew up in a house with a father who used everyone in his family as punching bags, sadly, it wasn't surprising.

Mac opened the door and got out of the car. "I knew

when she started talking about the holidays and hint-
ing at spending it together in fucking Mexico or the
Bahamas, she needed to go."

"Yeah, because a vacation in paradise with a warm,
willing woman is so much crappier than spending the
holidays with your fucked-up family."

Mac shrugged and hopped up the steps onto Raine's
porch. "At least my fucked-up family is mine, and we
all know where we stand with each other." He grinned
and reached beneath the loose floorboard beside the
empty pot just under the window and grabbed the key.
"Besides, what's a holiday without a dustup at the
Draper place?"

Jake followed Mac inside and paused. The place
hadn't been lived in for days, and he felt it. There were
no Christmas decorations, no cards, no tree…there
was nothing. But that was because the one person who
made everything seem alive wasn't here. She was waiting for him at the cottage and it was enough to kick
him in the ass.

Okay, where was the damn chew toy?

"Are you going to tuck me into bed too?"

"What?" Jake doffed his boots and trudged into the
family room. "No, Raine wants Gibson's toy."

"Gibson?"

"The dog."

"Oh, forgot about him. All right, I'm gonna crash
in the back bedroom. See you tomorrow night?" Mac
tugged at his leather jacket and ran his fingers through
the mess of blond hair at his temple. His buddy looked
tired and more than a little lost.

Jake nodded. "Yep, after church, my parents' place."

"Wouldn't miss it for the world," Mac replied as he headed down the hall. "Besides, you promised an introduction to some hot blonde?"

"She's off-limits, my friend," Jake shot back as he entered the family room.

"Whatever," Mac shouted back.

Jake shook his head and grinned. Mac would never change. He saw every woman he met as a challenge, and once he conquered them, he was done.

First off, Lily wasn't the type to be conquered, and second, the two of them together would never work. They were too similar, too damaged and too broken, and the last thing he needed was to have two of his best friends at each other's throat.

Jake spied the chew toy almost immediately, tucked between the sofa and a magazine basket in the corner. He grabbed it and was about to leave, anxious to get back to Raine, when he heard Mac swear, followed by a loud crash and then more swearing.

What the hell?

He strode down the hall toward the sliver of light that fell from the spare bedroom—just past Raine's—and pushed the door all the way open.

Mac stood in the middle of the room, his jacket on the floor as he cursed and rubbed his knee. The cursing stopped almost as soon as Jake entered.

"Jake, what is all this?"

He shook his head—his mind reeling as he slowly took in the contents of the room. He saw a crib. A teddy bear. He saw a knitted blanket—half-finished—folded on top of a table. A rocking horse was in the corner, a couple of framed prints leaning against the wall, the satchel he had brought back from Texas beside them.

As if in a dream, Jake crossed over to the table, his fingers reaching for the blanket, when he saw something that nearly stopped his heart. Carefully he withdrew a black-and-white sonogram picture from beneath it, and as he stared down at the grainy image, at the name across the bottom, *Raine Edwards*, he thought he was going to puke.

"Jake?"

"I don't know," he managed to say, "but you can bet I'm going to find out."

Twenty minutes later, he pulled up the driveway and parked Mac's rental behind his Jeep. He cut the engine and stared at the stone cottage in silence. It was late, nearly two in the morning, and the night was thick, like black velvet. Warm light fell out of the window, pooling against the snow, and he stared at the spot for a long time. So long that the cold seeped into the car and he shivered as the brisk air rolled over him.

Eventually, when he knew it was either freeze his ass off or get the hell out of the car, he opened the door and stepped outside, the snow crunchy underfoot. Twin pipes of hot air blew out of his nostrils as he bent over and grabbed the satchel that lay on the passenger seat— the satchel he'd brought back from Texas. The satchel that still had the travel tags from Afghanistan intact.

Anger burned him, and he had to take a moment to push it away. But he couldn't help but wonder why the hell she hadn't looked inside? He thought of the room, of the picture, and his anger doubled. Hell, it tripled, because not only was he angry but he was scared as hell.

He tossed the satchel over his shoulder and carefully made his way up the path that led to the house. Jake paused in front of the door, his hand on the knob. He needed to get hold of his anger and the underlying confusion.

He was about to take a step back, wanting more time—needing more time—but then the door flew open and Raine was there. For a moment, he was blinded by the light from inside, and when his vision cleared, he saw the fire in the hearth, the pink blanket thrown on the floor in front of it. He saw the Christmas tree, decorated to the nines, the large nutcracker near the fireplace, and the puppy rolling around on the floor, a cookie in his mouth.

It was a scene straight out of a Rockwell painting.

And it was all wrong.

Maybe if he'd paid more attention, he would have noticed the tearstained face that looked up at him. Maybe he would have known that her heart was in his hands, and in that moment he was about to break it.

Maybe if he were a psychic, he might have known. But he wasn't. He was a brother. A soldier. A lover.

And at the moment, more confused and pissed off than he ever remembered being.

Jake pushed past Raine and threw the satchel onto the sofa where he'd made love to her only hours earlier. Where he'd held her close and listened to her heart beating against his.

"Jake?"

Raine sounded scared, but he fought the urge to grab her up into his arms.

God, this was so wrong.

"Jake," she said again, her voice trembling as she closed the door and walked over to the sofa.

He said nothing and just watched as she reached for the satchel, her long, delicate fingers running over the worn leather.

The fire crackled, a log popping loudly, and Gibson jumped up onto the sofa, whining as he pushed against Raine.

"Why haven't you opened this?" he said harshly, hating the way she winced at the sound of his voice.

"I don't know," she said so softly he barely heard her.

"You don't know," he said, feeling the well of anger inside him burst open and hit him hard in the chest.

He took two steps forward until he was inches from Raine. "Don't you think you owe it to Jesse to see what's in there?"

"I don't know," she said again, her face averted, her voice weak.

His hands bunched at his side. "Okay, you don't know. I get that. I get that maybe you're confused, when it comes to what you felt for Jesse."

Her head whipped up at that and she pushed him in the chest. Hard. So hard that he took a step back and nearly stumbled over the damn dog. Gibson had jumped off the sofa and was tangled up near his feet.

"Don't you tell me that I don't know what I felt for Jesse." She pointed to the satchel. "And don't give me attitude about not opening a bag that belonged to your brother. What do you care? It doesn't belong to you."

Something ugly twisted inside him, there, where he'd been dead before. Like a sleeping giant, the darkness in him erupted.

He watched her closely. "You're right. It doesn't belong to me, and neither did you. And now Jesse is gone, and I've got his wife and everything else he ever wanted. How fucking fair is that?"

Raine pushed a wild curl from her eyes, wiping at them angrily as the sheen of tears threatened to fall. "Life isn't fair, Jake. It throws shit at us all the time. It's how we deal with that shit that decides whether we're going to make it or not."

He clenched his teeth together so tight that pain shot across his jaw. The rage inside him was intense, and his mind was filled of images of him and Jesse…and Raine.

For a few moments, they stared at each other in silence, their pain so heavy that Gibson began to whine and eventually slipped away to hide in the shadows.

"This isn't about the bag, Jake." Raine rubbed her hands over the thin robe she wore. "It's so not about the bag."

He shook his head and reached into his pocket, where he retrieved a black-and-white image that he handed over to Raine. "No," he said carefully, because he didn't trust his voice. "It's not."

She took the photo from him and stared down at it for the longest time, her shoulders hunched forward, her body trembling as if she were cold, when in fact the cottage felt like a furnace.

"Why didn't you tell me?" His voice broke and Jake took a step back, the image of a fetus burned into the back of his brain. "I promised Jesse I would be there for you, so why didn't you call me? I know things weren't great when I left. I know that, but Jesus, Raine, I would have come for you if you'd have told me."

"I did," she answered slowly.

"What?" He shook his angrily.

"I tried to tell you."

"When?"

"When I lost the baby, about four months after you left."

The world tilted a little then, and it was all Jake could do to stay on his feet.

"I called."

He stared at Raine, his chest so tight he could barely breathe. He was defeated, and it seemed that he'd failed everyone.

"I'd just miscarried, and…" Raine cleared her throat and spoke quietly. "I called, but a woman answered your cell phone. I heard her tell you that it was someone with a"—she paused and wiped away a fresh batch of tears—"screwed-up weird, hippie name. I heard a noise then, like you'd grabbed the cell off her, so I knew that you knew it was me, and then the line went dead."

Raine walked over to the fire and held her hands out. "You called me eventually and left a drunken message on my voice mail. I think you apologized for everything under the sun, and then I didn't hear from you again."

"Why didn't you…" He was speechless for a few moments. "Why didn't you keep trying? I would have. I'd have come. To be there for you and Jesse."

"I was so hurt, and I felt like I didn't matter to you anymore."

For a long while neither one of them spoke, and when Jake finally managed to put together a few coherent thoughts, his voice was rough and he could barely keep it together.

"Oh my God, I'm so sorry. But Jesus, Raine, no one told me...my parents never said anything. Why would all of you keep this from me?"

Raine glanced away, her voice small. "They didn't know." She paused. "They still don't know."

"What?" he said sharply.

"They don't know that I was pregnant."

Jake ran his fingers through his hair, more confused than ever. "This doesn't make sense. How the hell did they not know you went through with the procedure to have Jesse's baby? I don't... How could you keep that from them?"

Raine's eyes opened slowly, the pain inside them so intense that it was all he could do not to grab hold of her and never let her go. When had things gotten so fucked-up?

"Oh, Jake, I didn't want you to find out like this."

That thin ribbon of pain behind his eyes throbbed harder as the dread in his belly tightened.

"I didn't go through with the in vitro. It wasn't Jesse's."

The roaring in his ears was so loud that at first he wasn't sure what she'd said, and then when the meaning sunk into his brain, Jake stared at her in shock.

And when she whispered again, when she bared her soul and a secret he wasn't prepared to deal with, his heart shattered.

"He was ours. Jake, I lost our baby."

Chapter 26

WHEN RAINE HEARD THE SOFT KNOCK AT THE DOOR, her first thought was that Jake had come back. She tossed the pink blanket onto the floor and rolled off the sofa, hitting her hip against the coffee table. Ignoring the pain, she jumped to her feet and was nearly to the door when she realized that it wasn't Jake.

Jake would never knock. He would walk in, and his large frame and big personality would fill up every nook and cranny in the cottage.

She slid to a stop, her bare feet cold against the wooden floor as she stared at the door, her bruised heart in her throat.

When had things become so screwed up? Was there always going to be something blocking her happiness?

A soft knock sounded again, but she was in no mood to talk to anyone, so Raine turned around, her plan to burrow back under the covers and wallow in her pain.

The look on Jake's face when he'd learned about the baby was seared into her brain, and it was one she was never going to forget. He had stared at her for so long that the silence became unbearable, pounding into her with the strength of a hammer.

He'd glanced at the picture in her hand—the ultrasound of their child—and he'd left without another word.

The whole situation was awful, and there was more than enough hurt and blame to pass around, but the simple truth was that none of that mattered anymore. Raine had already lost so much, and she didn't want to lose Jake, but she wasn't sure how to fix something that was so broken.

"Raine?"

Tiredly, she wrapped her arms around herself and glanced over her shoulder. It was her mother. The woman's timing was crap, as usual.

"Raine, I know you're in there. Can I come in, please?"

Something in her mother's voice sounded different, and Raine bit her lip as she slowly turned around. Gibson sniffed along the bottom of the door and barked a few times, his tail wagging crazily as if the god of dog bones stood on the other side.

"Raine?"

She opened the door and stood back so that Gloria could pass.

Her mother's blue eyes, so like her own, widened when they took in what Raine supposed was a pretty sad sight indeed. She was still dressed in her clothes from the night before. She hadn't brushed her hair or her teeth, and she was pretty damn sure her makeup looked as if she'd just done the walk of shame.

She glanced at her reflection in the window and winced at the sight of her puffy eyes.

"Have you eaten anything? I could fix you a sandwich, or something else, if you like."

Leave it to her mother to ignore the obvious and act as if nothing were wrong.

Raine shook her head. "I'm not hungry."

Her mother was quiet for a few moments, her expression unreadable. She crossed over to the Christmas tree and folded her arms across her chest as she cocked her head to the side. "It's beautiful."

Again silence fell between them. It was big and awkward and so very tiring.

Raine sighed, her eyes on the sofa and the pink blanket, her mind on the little blue pills in her bag. Prescription strength, they'd be good to knock her out until tomorrow, if she took enough.

"Gloria, I'm not feeling real good, so if there is a reason for your visit, can we skip all the stuff in between and just get to why you're here?"

Her mother's hand shook a little as she touched one of the sparkly stars nestled among the fragrant branches. She smoothed her gray skirt and turned to face Raine, that polite, calm expression Raine was so used to firmly in place.

Gloria clasped her hands in front of her as if she didn't quite know what to do with them and exhaled a long, deep breath.

"I want to fix us."

"Excuse me?"

"I think it's time that we tried." She moistened her lips and touched her hair, obviously nervous. "I think it's time that we really tried to… Uh, this is harder than I thought it would be."

Her eyes glistened. With tears.

Disbelief didn't come close to describing what Raine felt. Her life was falling apart. No, it had been freefalling into a pile of shit for the last few years, and her mother wanted to be buddies?

"Oh my God, your timing is as perfect as ever."

"I'm sorry, I'm not sure what you mean."

Raine closed her eyes and took a moment to collect her thoughts. When she opened them, she couldn't help the thin, high-pitched laugh that escaped her lips. It sounded crazy, even to her own ears, and she wasn't surprised to see her mother wince.

"You want to *fix* us," she repeated, sitting on the edge of the sofa because her legs were suddenly weak and she didn't trust that she wouldn't fall on her ass.

Her mother nodded slowly. "I do."

"We're not broken, Gloria, because there is no 'us' to fix. To suggest that means that we were whole at one point, and I don't know what freaking rose-colored glasses you're looking through, but we were never whole."

Raine pushed off from the sofa and stomped over to her mother. "We were never a family, Gloria. We never fit together. You made sure of that."

She saw the hurt in her mother's eyes, but she didn't care. In fact, it fed her anger and pushed her on. If she was going to live through hell, then why shouldn't Gloria?

Gloria held her chin up, though it trembled. "Can't we try?" she said quietly.

"I don't have the energy to deal with your insecurities." She leaned closer, not caring that her mother winced. All she cared about was making someone else hurt as much as she did, and if it was Gloria? All the better.

"You have no idea what I'm going through right now. What I went through after Jesse died and Jake left me."

Raine closed her eyes and grabbed the edge of the sofa. God, she felt weak and used up. And old.

She was thirty years old and felt like she'd lived at least twice that long.

"Let me help you," Gloria pleaded.

"Oh, that's a good one. You want to help me?" She pushed off from the sofa again, which probably wasn't a good thing to do, because she swayed slightly, but when her mother reached for her, she recoiled and shook her head.

"You don't get to come back after all this time and think that a pat on the head and a few meaningless words are going to make a difference in my life. That's not the way it works. You've been living in a dreamworld, Gloria. A hot and hard and foreign dreamworld, mind you, but nothing in your scope of knowledge will make a difference to me."

"I can try," Gloria whispered.

"You don't know anything about me."

Her mother looked horrified. "How can you say that? Yes, I wasn't with you, I was halfway around the world, helping the less fortunate, but that doesn't mean I didn't know what you were up to or keep in touch. Jeanine made sure I knew everything that mattered."

"What's my favorite color?"

Gloria threw her shoulders back. "Purple."

"Wrong, it's blue. How old was I when I broke my left arm?"

Her mother was beat and she knew it. "I don't know."

And still Raine pushed forward. "How old was I when I lost my virginity?"

"Raine, please don't do this."

"Seventeen. How many men have I slept with?"

If she thought that would shock her mother, she was mistaken. It did nothing but deflate her. Defeat her.

The pain inside Raine stretched so tight across her shoulders that she shook out her arms in an effort to alleviate it.

"Two," she said softly, all the fierce attitude suddenly gone. "I've slept with two men. Jesse and Jake."

Tears slipped from her eyes, and when Gloria took a few tentative steps toward her, Raine did nothing to stop her. No poison fell from her lips. There was only the pain.

"When I found out Jesse had died over there, my first thought was that Jake was coming home. Jake would make the pain go away. He'd make things better." She closed her eyes as memories from those turbulent weeks after the funeral settled into her mind.

"But that didn't happen. Things got screwed up and everything changed. We had one moment, a night when we'd both had too much to drink and the pain was just so hard and heavy, and we found comfort in each other. Or maybe it wasn't comfort. It was about feeling alive. But it didn't last. The guilt and pain just made it too difficult. Jake left and I didn't see him for almost a year and a half. And I thought…I thought when he came back that maybe we could work things out. But I don't think it's going to happen."

Raine wasn't aware that her mother had moved closer until she felt her warm touch against her cheek.

"I'm sorry," her mother said.

"So am I."

Slowly Gloria withdrew her hand. "I know you think you don't need me, Raine, and maybe you don't. Maybe I need it more, but it's Christmas. Won't you please let me look after you?"

Raine looked into her mother's eyes and for the first time felt as if she was really seeing the woman. She saw pain but she also saw regret.

"Will you let me try?"

Gibson jumped onto the sofa and growled, a playful challenge, before he tossed his bone onto the floor and ran after it. Raine watched him disappear behind the tree and glanced at the clock. It was nearly four.

"I don't know," she said finally. "I can't promise anything, and maybe I'm just too tired to fight right now. But we can try."

Raine headed for the shower, not really sure what the night was going to bring, but sure in the knowledge that she couldn't hide in the cottage forever. She couldn't hide from Jake. She'd done that for eighteen months, and there was no way she was going down that road again. She wouldn't make it.

As she turned on the hot spray and stripped off her clothes, she thought that maybe a Christmas miracle was possible, and if not, hell, she'd try and find one on her own.

Chapter 27

JAKE HAD BEEN SITTING AT THE BAR IN THE COACH House since noon. He wasn't drunk. In fact, he'd hardly had any alcohol. Not for lack of trying. He just didn't seem able to stomach the stuff right now and had been nursing a tumbler of whiskey for almost an hour.

The bar was nearly empty—which wasn't surprising, considering it was Christmas Eve—and only a few souls were enjoying a last-minute drink or get-together with friends. Behind him, near the DJ booth, sat a boisterous group of college kids, while at the far end of the bar was Mr. Lawrence, owner of the Tackle & Bait. He was doing a crossword in between shooting the shit with Salvatore.

Jake knew he should just leave, but there wasn't anywhere for him to go. Wyndham Place was out—he couldn't face Raine right now—and there was no way he was bringing his parents down with his black mood.

They didn't deserve his shit, not after everything they'd been through.

He hung his head, unable to deal with the overwhelming guilt he felt, and as he thought of Raine, of her alone and dealing with something as awful as losing a baby—his baby—his head fell even lower.

He'd spent the night in his Jeep, driving around aimlessly, and had eventually ended up in the next county, where he'd sat in an all-night diner until he overstayed his welcome, and pointed his wheels home.

The Coach House was as good a place as any to pass the time, and the permanent scowl on his face was enough to drive most people in the opposite direction. Of course, beneath the scowl was a hell of a lot of heartache, pain, and overwhelming guilt.

Lily had already come and gone. She'd tried her damnedest to find out what the hell was going on inside his head, but he wasn't sharing with anyone, not even Lily, and in the end she had realized he wasn't going to spill. Annoyed, she had left, though not before telling him he'd be the biggest asshole on the planet to let his happiness slip away. If he didn't fight for what he deserved.

Jake stared down into the amber liquid and swished it aimlessly. He didn't have the heart to tell Lily that he didn't deserve shit.

"Jake, we close in an hour." Salvatore wiped down the end of the bar and glanced his way. "You gonna finish that drink or stare at it for the next sixty minutes?"

The door flew open behind him and unleashed a cold blast of wind that ruffled his hair, but he paid it no mind. Not even when Salvatore swore—something he rarely did—was Jake even remotely interested in who had just walked through the doors.

"An hour, boys," Salvatore said, shaking his head. "That's it. You've got one hour to convince him to leave, or you can all deal with my wife."

"Okay, Sal."

The deep, raspy voice had Jake turning real quick, though, and he attempted a smile, though he was pretty sure he'd failed by the look in his buddy's eyes. "I didn't expect to see your sorry ass until New Year's Eve."

Cain Black strode over and clapped him on the shoulder before sliding into the seat beside him, while Mac grinned and grabbed the stool on his right.

"Yeah, well, plans change, my friend."

No doubt Mac had had a part in that. Jesus. He wasn't in the mood for an intervention.

Jake glanced at Mac, who was smiling at the bartender, a brunette with big eyes and an even bigger grin and a chest that was well in proportion to both. "I'd watch your step, Mac. That's Sal's daughter, and she's barely legal."

"You're pulling my leg," Mac said. "There is no way in hell that's the little girl who used to—"

"Hey Mackenzie, Merry Christmas."

"—sell Girl Scout cookies to my mom." Mac groaned. "Shit, I feel old."

"Oh my God! Cain, will you let me take your picture?" Angie's eyes looked as if they were going to pop out of her head when she spied the rocker. "Like one with me, please?"

Cain took off his hat and shook out hair that was at least an inch longer than when Jake had last seen him. "Sure, darlin'. How about we get that done, and then you can bring Mac and me some JD on the rocks so that we can catch up with our friend Jake, here."

Angie squealed and practically jumped over the bar, her cell phone out and the picture snapped in under thirty seconds. Sal grumbled from down the way but slid a bottle of Jack toward them. "Merry Christmas, boys, but remember…one hour." He frowned. "And no funny stuff." His eyes lingered on Jake for half a second longer, and then he disappeared into the kitchen.

Cain slid back into his seat and poured out two generous glasses for Mac and himself before turning to Jake. "You look like shit, my friend."

Jake nodded. "Thanks for that, Hollywood."

Cain leaned onto the bar. "I'm not joking. You really look like shit."

Jake felt a spike of anger flush through him, but it left as quick as it came. He was just done. There was no way he was coming back from last night.

"So, I take it Mac called you?"

Cain nodded. "Yeah, he did."

Jake shook his head and glared at Mackenzie. "He shouldn't have done that."

"I'm worried about you, dumbass." Mac held his drink up as if for a toast and then tipped it back, not stopping until the glass was dry.

Jake wished he could drink his pain away, but unlike Mackenzie, alcohol wasn't always his answer. Jake glanced up and saw his reflection in the mirror behind the bar. He saw Cain on his left, while Mac stared back at him from his right. His friends. His brothers.

Except that one was missing. One was never coming back.

That heaviness inside him pressed against his chest something fierce. It hung on, leeching on to his soul and filling his heart with so much pain that he hung his head and gasped as he slid from his stool and took a few steps back.

"I can't do this," he muttered.

"Yeah, well, we don't care." Cain turned around and stretched out his long, jean-clad legs. "You gotta stop this, Jake. It happened over a year ago. You can't stay in that place anymore. You need to move on."

Jake rolled his head and looked at his two oldest friends. He loved these guys. He'd do anything for them, and he knew the feeling was mutual. But they didn't understand how fucked-up everything was.

"You have no idea what the hell's going on."

Cain took a good, long drink from his tumbler and then placed it on the bar. He folded his arms over his chest and nailed Jake with a look that told him Cain wasn't going anywhere anytime soon.

"Well, why don't you enlighten me?"

Something about his attitude pissed Jake off, and he squared his shoulders. "Mac didn't fill you in?"

Jake shot a look toward Mackenzie, but his friend met his glare dead-on and shook his head. "It's not my story to tell."

"It's not a pretty story," Jake said roughly. "In fact, it's damn scary."

"Since when do we care about that shit?" Cain asked. "You're losing it. I can see it in your eyes. You've got that same look, just like you did the summer after Jesse died. There are a whole lot of people who are going to be hurt if you go off the grid again, you got that?"

Cain's voice rose a notch, but luckily no one in the bar was paying them any mind. Even Angie must have sensed that something heavy was going down, because she'd moved to the far side of the bar and was busy cleaning tables, though she threw the occasional look their way.

"This is us," Mackenzie said quietly. "We want to help."

Jake sighed and ran his hands across his temples. Christmas music played in the background, and he glanced to the side, watching an intoxicated couple practically making love on the dance floor while some rocker dude sang about his baby coming home for the holidays.

He wasn't sure how long he stared at them, but it was long enough for his vision to blur and for his heart to crack open as thoughts of Jesse and Raine converged into a chaotic mess.

"I took everything from him," he said so quietly he wasn't sure Cain or Mac heard.

"How can you take something from someone who's dead?" Mac stood, his hands shoved into his pockets as he stared at Jake. "He's dead. He's not coming back, and it sucks and it's fucking wrong. But you know what's worse? Watching you disappear again, and letting something as good as Raine slip away because you feel guilty."

How could he make them understand?

"I know about the baby," Cain said quietly.

His head shot up at that. "And you never told me?" He took a step toward Cain.

"I had to respect Raine's wishes. She wanted to tell you herself, but…"

"But I was being an asshole and never gave her the chance."

"Yeah," Cain replied.

"I took everything from him," Jake said and turned away, suddenly so raw inside he was afraid he'd break down. "Even the baby he wanted."

"Maybe that's how you see things, Jake, but that's not reality. I'm going to say some stuff now, some things that are going to piss you off—"

Jake might have growled like an animal, because Mac reacted instantly.

"It's okay," Mac said, rolling up his sleeves as he

stepped between the two men. The guy was built and had obviously been hitting the gym hard. "I got your back, because no offense, Cain, Jake could kick your ass if he wanted to."

Cain ignored Mackenzie and nailed Jake with a look that promised the hard truth and maybe something else. Maybe redemption.

"Jesse's reality and the rest of the world's weren't exactly in line."

The anger Jake felt flashed hot and hard, but he kept his distance, ground his teeth together, and listened.

"Raine shared a few things with Maggie and me, and I got a clearer picture of what was going on in Jesse's head. And I think a clearer picture of what happened over there." He paused. "Look, I don't know the specifics of the day Jesse died. I don't *want* to know, unless you need me to. But Jake, what I do know is that Jesse is gone and you can't take away something from someone who's no longer here. You just can't."

"Cain…" Jake began.

"Shut up, Edwards, I'm not done." Cain got to his feet. "I think that you're hiding behind what happened to Jesse, blaming yourself for not bringing him back alive, when we all know that's a load of crap. The guy was a highly trained soldier, just like you. Just like the rest of the guys in your unit. Life and death is part of that gig, and you either live with it or you go crazy."

Cain took a few steps until he was almost nose to nose with Jake. "You're running scared, Jake, because everything you want is right in front of you and you've always been afraid to take it. You're hiding behind your dead brother."

"That's fucking bullshit." Jake's hands fisted at his sides, and it was all he could do to control his anger.

"Is it?" Cain asked, taking a step back and reaching for his whiskey. He downed the glass and slammed it on the counter.

"You've loved that girl for more years than I can remember. And from what little I can see, she's crazy about you. So why is Raine"—he checked his watch— "on her way to St. Paul's with my wife, on Christmas Eve, for Christ's sake, while you're sitting in the Coach House feeling sorry for yourself, or guilty, or whatever the fuck it is you're feeling, about stuff that's already over and done with? About things you can't change?"

A strangled sound escaped Jake's throat, and Mackenzie moved in again, this time the lightness in his eyes long gone. "Keep it happy, boys."

Cain tugged his hat back on and waved good-bye to Sal.

"Don't step aside and play the good guy for a ghost. A ghost isn't what Raine needs. You are."

And just like that, Cain was done. He tugged on his leather gloves and nodded to Mac. "You coming?"

"That depends," Mackenzie replied, turning to Jake. "You all right?"

Jake nodded, unable to answer. His chest was still tight and his throat felt as if he'd swallowed a block of lead.

Mackenzie patted him on the shoulder and moved aside as Cain stepped in again. The two men stared at each other long and hard, and when Cain put his hand on Jake's shoulder, something inside Jake loosened. It broke free, and suddenly the tightness was gone.

"You need to make peace with your brother and move on," Cain said roughly. "We can't lose you too."

Jake nodded.

"Are we good?" Cain asked.

"We're good," Jake answered haltingly and then whispered, "Thanks."

"You don't need to thank me for pointing out the obvious. You just need to do the right thing. You need to choose life."

Cain glanced at the door. "You wanna come with us? I'm heading over to the church to meet up with Maggie and Michael, and they're with Raine and her mother, and I'm pretty sure your parents are there too."

Jake shook his head, his mind reeling at the thought that maybe, just maybe, he could make things right.

"Go ahead," Jake said as he tossed some bills onto the counter. "I got something I have to do first." He pulled out his cell and turned it on, wincing when he saw several calls from Raine, and heading out into the cold, he hit speed dial.

—◈◈◈—

The drive out to the cemetery didn't take long at all. No one was on the roads, which was good, because they were on the treacherous side. With the cooler temps rolling in and a crisp breeze that sent snow flying, there were several spots where drifts had crossed the road.

Jake pulled into the entrance, but with several feet of snow blocking his way, he knew he'd have to hoof it the rest of the way in.

It was a clear evening, the kind where the sky is filled with black velvet and sharp, sparkling diamonds. He tugged on his collar as he glanced above him, and not for the first time, he felt small. Insignificant. He headed into the cemetery, his steps bringing him closer to the big oak tree that overlooked his family plot, there at row thirty-six. He had no trouble seeing, thanks to the stars and a cold December moon that hung low in the sky.

He hadn't been out here since the day they'd buried Jesse, and Jake was unprepared for the wash of emotion that rolled over him when he spied the grave.

Snow dusted the top of the dark granite piece, but there were Christmas greens at the base and a candle-holder that was nearly buried under the snow.

He paused just in front and stared down, reading for the first time the words his parents had had inscribed into the granite.

Jesse Edwards
Son. Brother. Husband. Soldier. Never forgotten.

There it was. Laid out nice and simple.

The wind swooped down, ruffling the greens, and Jake shivered, whether from the cold or the onslaught of emotions he wasn't sure. He shoved his hands deep into his pockets and hunched his shoulders against the wind, his eyes riveted on his brother's name.

Jesse Edwards

That feeling in his chest, the one that had been dogging him forever, it seemed, erupted and filled him with heat. And anger. And a vicious need to do something.

He let the anger wash over him, wash through him, and began to pant as his vision blurred with something hot and wet. He scrubbed at his eyes and took a step forward.

"You selfish bastard," he shouted, his voice echoing into the darkness.

Jake turned abruptly and began to pace the length of his brother's grave. All of the blackness, the rage, the pain and anguish from that day filled his head and chest until he could barely breathe. Until he fell to his knees and leaned against the cold, hard granite.

"How could you give up like that? What the hell happened to you?"

But of course there were no answers. Nothing to make him feel better about any of the choices he'd made.

Jake glanced around. There was nothing but death in this place.

He thought of Raine. Of her warmth and smile. He thought of that night they'd been together, just weeks after Jesse's funeral. Of the need they had to connect and to comfort and to…live.

He thought of how he'd felt. As if he'd betrayed his brother. And of how he'd left soon after, leaving Raine alone to deal with the consequences.

Cain was right. He had been hiding behind his brother's death. Blaming himself for the tragic events on that day and using it as an excuse to avoid dealing with the fallout. To avoid taking what he wanted. What he'd always wanted. *Raine*.

Slowly, Jake straightened, his fingers brushing away the snow from the top of the gravestone as he tried to sort out his thoughts.

"I don't know what was wrong with you, brother. Why weren't you strong enough to live?" His voice broke. "Why didn't you live for Raine…for me? Why the hell did you walk out onto that street? Why didn't you fight for what you had?"

Jake shuddered, staring down at the cold granite

and the snow-covered earth that entombed his brother. Such rage welled up inside that for a moment he saw nothing. He kicked the candleholder and sent it flying into the darkness, his breaths coming fast and hard as his chest tightened.

"I'm not sorry that I love her, dammit, I'm not. I'm not sorry that I'm here and you're not, and that's what's killing me, Jesse. The guilt is killing me. I hate that you're gone, but I don't…I don't regret Raine. I can't. I love her."

Silence met his declaration, and as fast as his anger boiled inside him, it slipped away, leaving him empty.

"I love you, Jesse, but I'm done with this. I can't live with this guilt anymore. I came back and you didn't, but it's not my fault. It's no one's fault. It's just what is."

He exhaled slowly. "I hope you're at peace wherever the hell you are, and one day, brother, I'll see you again, but for now…" He wiped his eyes and moved away. "For now, I'm going to live my life, and I'm going to be happy, and I…" He paused and took a step back.

"I hope you're okay with that."

Chapter 28

ST. PAUL'S CHURCH WAS FILLED TO THE RAFTERS. Literally. Every available seat had a body in it, including those in the loft above. The candles were lit, the nativity scene breathtaking, and the children's portion of the event was just ending.

Raine smiled as she spied Maggie's son, Michael. Tucked near the back with his buddy Tommy, he was dressed as one of the shepherds, and while supposedly looking down in reverence at the baby Jesus, he was giggling behind his staff.

"Oh my God, Michael is going to hear it when we get home," Maggie whispered. "He's lucky they let him participate, considering we arrived just a few hours ago, but I'm sure Mrs. Lancaster is regretting it."

Raine nodded, an automatic move, because her attention had already wandered. Again. She clutched her cell phone, thinking of the voice mail she'd retrieved just before the Christmas service had begun.

"I love you and I'm coming for you."

Cain and Mackenzie had arrived just after Pastor Lancaster took to his pulpit, but almost immediately, Cain had been swept away by Mrs. Lancaster and had a guitar shoved into his hands. With Cain on stage and Mackenzie sitting with his mother, Raine had no idea if they'd even found Jake.

The kids began to file out slowly, following her

mother, Gloria, as she sang "Silent Night," accompanied by the soft strains of Cain's guitar. First the angels,
then the wise men, a donkey, a camel, and three sheep
waved good-bye.

Raine wasn't sure when the energy in the church
changed—when the whispers began to overtake the singing. But the hair on the back of her neck stood on end, and
for some reason her heart began to beat faster. Harder.

As if it knew he was there.

She sat on the end of the second pew from the front
and glanced down at the cell in her hands, aware that
everyone on the stage was staring down the aisle. Aware
that her mother had stepped back from the spotlight and
that Cain was strumming something altogether different
than "Silent Night."

She swallowed, her eyes still lowered, and glanced
to the side.

She saw a pair of boots. Big boots. Big, leather, man
boots. They were wet, and snow still clung to the tops of
them along with bits of brown grass and dirt.

And they were pointed straight at her.

Jake.

Did she say his name out loud?

The world fell away then. All of it. The church.
The parishioners. The kids. The baby Jesus, Mary, and
Joseph too.

Slowly she looked up and her heart turned over.
Jake's hair was a disheveled mess, his jaw was darkened
with at least two days' worth of beard, and tiny lines
around his eyes showed just how tired he was. But it
was what was inside them that had her heart beating like
mad. Her face was so hot, she felt scorched.

"I told you I was coming for you," he said roughly.

Raine nodded, the cell still clutched into her hand. "You did."

"I love you," he said and fell to his knee so that his face was level with hers. "I'm not giving you up."

"Okay," she breathed.

"We'll work through this."

His mouth was a whisper away, and she nodded. Or maybe she spoke. Or maybe she did nothing at all. Her mind was such a mess that she had no clue, and when his large hand cupped her chin and his mouth slid over hers, she could do nothing but lean into the man who was everything to her.

Before she knew what was happening, Jake slipped his arms behind her neck and under her legs, lifting her up and crushing her to his chest.

He smelled like winter. Like pine and fresh air. Raine closed her eyes, and for the first time in what felt like forever, she relaxed. He felt like home.

"Hey Edwards, we're in the middle of something here, do you mind?" Cain grinned at them from the stage, and Raine's face went about ten shades darker than it already was when the laughter and whispers grew louder.

Shit. She was bundled up in Jake's arms at the front of St. Paul's during Christmas Eve service with practically the entire town looking on.

Jake turned and she glanced out at the congregation from beneath lowered lashes. Every single face was turned their way.

He took a step and paused, cranking his neck until he spied his parents. "I don't think we'll be stopping by later, Dad."

Steven cleared his throat. "Thanks for letting me know, son."

"Merry Christmas, Mom."

"You're going to leave in the middle of the service?" Marnie asked.

Oh God. Raine's face flamed about three shades past crimson, especially when she caught sight of Lori Jonesberg's sly grin.

"I was thinking about it," Jake answered. "I don't need to be in church to give thanks."

Raine began to squirm, but his hold tightened.

"No," Marnie said softly. "I don't suppose you do."

"Well, if you're going to leave, Edwards, you best get going, because you're holding things up." Cain's mirth was felt by all, and several rounds of giggles erupted.

And then they were striding out of the church with every single eye on them until they disappeared from view and Cain's rich voice broke out in song.

Jake's Jeep was parked in front, and she slid into the passenger side, her body shaking from nerves and the cold. There wasn't one word spoken between them as he drove through the deserted streets of Crystal Lake, though his free hand clutched hers and she held on tightly, not letting go until they pulled into Wyndham Place and then into the driveway that belonged to the stone cottage.

Jake was out of the Jeep in an instant and had her door flung open before she managed to grab hold of the handle. She slid to her feet, and moments later they were inside the cottage. Raine had left the tree lights on, and the warm glow cast shadows in the corners. Gibson was asleep, and for a moment she stared at the puppy, unsure of what to say or do.

She shrugged out of her coat and turned to Jake, watching him as he slowly shed his leather coat. He tossed it on the chair beside the door and then stared at her in silence, running his hands through his hair—a nervous gesture—and something about the thick, brown mess got to her.

She took the few steps between them, reached up, and smoothed the longish waves, her fingers lingering along his jawline as she stared into the eyes of the man she loved. He opened his mouth to speak, but she pressed her fingers there as well, silencing him.

"I don't want to hear 'sorry,'" she whispered, watching the play of light in his eyes. "We've both done things that we're sorry about, and Lord knows there's a lot for us to talk about, but can it wait? Can we just hold each other and know that things are going to be fine? That our love is enough and all the other stuff is just white noise? I'm just…" She let out a long shuddering breath, her hands slowly caressing his cheek. "I'm just done with all the pain and the guilt. I love you, and right now, in this moment, it's all that matters."

"Sounds good to me," he whispered, bending low, his mouth sliding across hers with a gentle swipe as his hard, muscled arms pulled her in close.

For the longest time, they stayed like that, two bodies melted into one, their breaths falling in sync with their hearts.

Eventually their hearts sped up and their ragged breaths filled the silence of the cottage as mouths slid across flesh, and tongues tasted each other. Jake's hands ran across her body as if he were seeing it for the first time, and maybe in a way he was.

Jake slowly undressed her, his eyes reverent, his touch both tender and desperate. When they finally made love in the shadows cast by the Christmas tree, Raine felt him truly break free of the past, as if a bottle had been opened and all the darkness inside him had escaped.

It was in the way he held her. In the way his hands and eyes touched her.

And it was in the words he whispered in her ear.

Later, much later, after they'd made love again and she was snuggled in his warm embrace, Raine couldn't remember ever feeling so contented. So loved and so cherished. She fell asleep, staring into tobacco-colored eyes that were filled with love and sex and need.

And the two of them slept for hours, undisturbed. No darkness. No bad dreams. Just plain old exhaustion to carry them through.

It was nearly nine in the morning when Raine woke abruptly. Gibson was whining at the door, and she carefully extracted herself from Jake's limbs, rolled out of the blanket, and let the dog out.

She grabbed a robe and slipped it over her shoulders, setting the coffee machine up while waiting for Gibson to come back inside. It was snowing once more, big fat flakes that fell slowly from the sky—perfect for Christmas morning—and the lightness in her heart felt amazing.

After letting Gibson back in, she began to hum while cracking eggs into a bowl—French toast sounded mighty good. Raine giggled. She needed an influx of carbs after all the energy she had used up last night.

She was on her tiptoes, reaching up for little container

of cinnamon she'd bought earlier in the week, when two strong, warm arms slid around her waist and tugged her backward. She leaned against Jake's chest, so content and happy, she was afraid to say or do anything in case the spell broke.

"Merry Christmas," he murmured near her ear.

"Same," she said softly, her hands cupped over his as they lay against her belly.

"What are you making?"

"French toast."

"I love French toast."

"I know." She paused and bit her lip, gathering what bit of courage she could find before she turned in his arms. "I need to give you something."

Jake's eyebrows rose and he cursed. "Shit, babe, I'm sorry. I didn't…I mean, I wasn't thinking Christmas and presents or anything like that. I don't have anything for you."

"Last night. What you did was the best present I could ever have had." She moistened her lips and grabbed his hands. "Come with me."

After leading him back to the sofa, she crossed over to the mantel, her fingers trembling, her stomach a crazy mess of nerves. But she had to do this. It was time for all the ghosts to go away.

She saw that Jake knew what was in her hands even before she'd walked back to where he sat. His eyes dimmed a bit and his mouth set into a grim line.

"Where did you get that?"

"Lily," she answered simply.

Raine held it out and waited while he fought some internal battle, and when he finally reached for the brown box, she felt like she'd just won one of her own. She sat down beside him as he stared down at the box, and she waited.

She waited at least five minutes, but eventually he opened it up and stared down at the medal. The Bronze Star. The medal he'd been awarded for his heroic acts the day their unit had been attacked. The day Jesse had died and Lily's brother Blake had been injured.

For the longest time, he just looked at it, and then his body shuddered as his arms swept around her. He pulled her in close, his mouth near her ear as she slipped onto his lap and just held him. His grip was tight, his pain palpable. But eventually she felt him relax, and a shiver rolled over her skin when he spoke.

"Thank you."

"You're welcome," she said softly, stroking his hair. She waited a second and then squirmed out of his arms, smiling when she caught sight of the Rudolph boxers she hadn't noticed the night before.

Jake smiled and shrugged. "My mom."

Her eyebrow slanted at a devilish angle. "So have you been a good boy for Santa?"

"I'm a bad boy, remember?"

Raine nodded, smiling saucily as she reached for the belt that kept her robe closed. "Good. Santa's helper loves bad boys."

She let the robe fall to her feet.

"Yes, good thing," he managed to get out before lunging forward and pulling her back onto his lap.

"We have three hours before your parents expect us for Christmas dinner," she said in between kisses as his hands skimmed her back and landed on her butt.

"Three hours? Babe, that gives us enough time to fool around *and* eat some French toast."

She straddled him and reached for the Rudolph boxers. "Good to know," she whispered and then proceeded to spend exactly two hours and forty-five minutes showing Jake Edwards exactly how much she loved her bad boy.

They arrived at Marnie and Steven's laden with several bags of gifts. And Jake hadn't been wholly honest. He'd done his share of shopping when he was in Boston, which Lily had been more than happy to help him with.

He settled against the wall a few feet from the massive Christmas tree in his parents' family room. His long legs were spread out and Raine was between them, leaning back on him as they watched Lily struggle with the ties on one of the last unopened presents. Gibson rolled onto his belly at her feet, and when she finally freed the package and pulled out an ice-blue silk scarf, she barely got it away from his lunging puppy teeth.

"Wow, this is lovely." Lily smiled, her eyes on Raine.

"I'm glad you like it. It…" The two women stared at each other for several seconds. "It matches your eyes."

Lily folded the scarf and was silent. Jake knew she didn't do real well with this kind of stuff, so he cleared his throat, aware that his parents watched from their perch on the sofa.

"There's one more."

Lily was closest to the tree and reached for the pale peach-colored bag tucked away near the base.

"It's for Raine."

Raine squealed like a kid and Jake's heart caught, suddenly not sure if he'd done the right thing. Shit. He glanced at Lily helplessly. What the hell had he been thinking?

But Lily wasn't looking at him. Her eyes and those of his parents were on Raine as she dove into the bag like a small child.

Her hair swung around her face in a controlled yet mad mess, the waves sexy as they spilled across her cheek. Her skin was flushed, her eyes sparkled, and he knew that if they were alone, he'd have had her out of the jeans and simple red blouse she wore in less than a minute.

His heart began to beat harder, and Jake sat up. He couldn't take his eyes off her, and he didn't realize his fists were clenched so tightly until she glanced up at him.

He stared into her midnight-blue eyes and slowly things loosened. His hands. His chest. His heart.

In her palm was a small box. A small box that changed everything.

Raine slowly made her way back to him. He was aware of the audience watching, but to Jake, in this moment, it felt as if there were only Raine.

She slid along his thighs until she straddled him, her eyes huge and shiny as if there were unshed tears hanging in the corners.

For the longest time he just stared at her, drinking in every detail of her face and remembering what it had felt like to hold her the night before. To cuddle her in the morning. To share breakfast and jokes and the shower.

To be inside her.

To have her hold his heart.

"Are you going to open it?" he asked huskily.

"When did...when did you?"

"Boston."

Her fingers slowly opened the small black box, and she stared down at the simple ring inside. A ring he knew was meant for her as soon as he had seen it. It wasn't flashy. It wasn't over-the-top. It was elegant, classy and...

"Yes," she said breathlessly.

Jake smiled. "I didn't say anything."

"I know," she said and leaned forward, sliding her mouth across his so lightly it made him ache. "But my answer is yes."

Jake's heart felt as if it were going to beat out of his chest. He took the ring and slid it onto her finger, kissing her knuckles and pulling her into his embrace.

He glanced up at his parents—his mom who was slowly dabbing at the corners of her eyes and his father who was grinning from ear to ear—and he finally felt that he was home.

This woman he held had given him everything, and he was going to spend the rest of his life giving back to her.

"O Holy Night" piped through the stereo, while outside the early evening gloom couldn't hide the brilliance of the snowflakes falling onto the lake.

Jake was happy. He was content. And he was finally home.

Pretty much the best Christmas ever.

Epilogue

New Year's Eve...

THE NEW YEAR'S EVE PARTY AT THE COACH HOUSE WAS well under way when Jake and Raine arrived. Maggie and Cain followed them in, along with—surprisingly—Lily. Mac was nowhere to be seen, but then, he'd had a date with a girl from the city. And though he'd assured everyone that he would show up before midnight, Jake wasn't holding his breath.

He guided Raine toward the table they'd reserved, in the back corner.

"Seriously? This is the best you could do?" Lily said drily as she took off her jacket and slid into the booth. She was wearing one of those slinky dresses that did everything to enhance her curves, its metallic shade of silver almost liquid-like. The woman looked as if she were dressed for a club in New York or LA, and with that megawatt little number barely covering her ass, she'd already drawn the eyes of most of the men in the bar.

Which was ironic, considering she didn't like to be touched.

But she sure as hell loved to cause a scene.

Jake sighed and stared down at her. "Don't start, St. Clare, you just got here. Which reminds me." He pulled a bottle of pinot noir from inside his jacket and placed it in front of her. "Don't let Sal catch you drinking from that, or our asses will be toast."

Lily grabbed the bottle and made a face. "I won't as long as you promise to find me something other than a plastic wineglass, because if you don't, I'll be forced to drink straight from the bottle."

He glanced down at Raine, saw the amused smile, and reached down to kiss her before heading back to the bar with Cain. The women weren't exactly buddies, but they shared a certain level of respect that hadn't been there before.

The Coach House was near to bursting—not surprising, considering Cain had agreed to play a set with Shady Aces. The two of them made their way through the crowd, nodding and waving, and when they finally reached the bar, Cain cracked a grin.

"Man, it feels like every single person we know is here tonight."

"That's because every single person we know *is* here tonight, except Mac." Jake grinned and ordered a round of beers, then paused and shot a look at Cain. "I don't remember what Maggie drinks. Is she okay with beer, or would she like some of that cheap Cold Duck Sal keeps behind the bar?"

"Actually, she'll be drinking water tonight."

"Water."

Cain nodded, grinning as he shouted at Sal to bring over a bottle of H_2O.

"Water, as in she wants to DD tonight? Or water, as in she can't drink alcohol."

"Water, as in the woman is carrying my child, so don't be surprised if we have to cut out early because she's so damn tired all the time."

Jake slammed Cain in the shoulder. "Holy shit. Why didn't you say anything?"

"I wanted to, but she said to wait a few more weeks."

Jake took in the silly-ass grin on Cain's face and slapped him on the shoulder again. "Congratulations. I won't say anything." He couldn't lie. There was a bit of bittersweet longing in his words. He thought of Raine and what she'd gone through, and even though they'd discussed their future together, having a child was one thing they'd steered clear of.

Time would heal that wound. He had to believe that.

"Thanks." Cain grabbed the water. "We thought that we'd try after I was done recording this record, but obviously the baby had other plans, because Maggie's almost ten weeks."

Jake slipped into the booth, sliding his long length up against Raine, when Lily cocked an eyebrow and stared at the bottle of water in front of Maggie. She glanced up at him, and though he tried like hell to warn her with his eyes, he knew by now that Lily St. Clare moved to the beat of a different drum and pretty much did or said whatever the hell she wanted.

"So, Maggie, either you're a lightweight or pregnant." Her words were dry, her gaze direct as Maggie blushed to just about the same shade of red as her hair. "Which one is it?"

Maggie's gaze darted around the table, and when Cain grabbed her hand and kissed it, she giggled. "Which do you think?"

"Oh my God, lady! You never said anything," Raine complained, leaning into Jake and threading her fingers through his.

"Well"—her eyes rested on Lily—"I wanted to wait a few more weeks, but I guess there's no point now."

Cain stole a kiss and would have gone in for another, but the squeal of a guitar sounded, and he was being called to the stage.

Jake settled back, his arm around the woman he loved, while Cain and Shady Aces rocked the house something fierce. They performed a wide variety of music, from old blues standards to classic rock to a generous helping of BlackRock, Cain's band.

Cain was in his element, speaking through his guitar and vocals. They didn't take a break—just kept on rocking—and when it was nearing midnight, Jake glanced up, surprised to see his father, his mother, and Lauren Black, Cain's mom. The three of them stood near the dance floor, their eyes on the stage.

His father turned, his warm eyes so much like Jesse's, it was eerie. He smiled and nodded, his arm around Marnie, and Jake answered in kind. He couldn't remember ever feeling this content and just…

Happy.

Cain ended the song and grabbed the mike. "Well, hell, folks, it's nearly that time."

"Okay, I'm outta here."

They all turned to Lily, but she was scooting by Maggie as she grabbed her jacket and shoved her arms into it.

"But it's almost midnight," Raine said.

"I know." Lily picked at her jacket collar and pulled it up under her chin. "It's not really my thing." She smiled and leaned toward Jake, her mouth grazing just near his ear. "You did good."

And then she was winding her way through the crowd, stopping briefly to say her good-byes to his parents.

———∞∞———

Outside the Coach House, the ever-steady fall of snow coated everything in glistening white. Lily wrapped her jacket around her, waiting for the cab Salvatore had called, and was very careful as she stepped forward. She was more than a little tipsy, and she blamed the cheap-ass tequila she'd switched to when the wine ran out.

Ugh, she really needed to talk to Sal about his selection of spirits.

They sucked.

Headlights cut across the dark, and she started forward, her hand on the back door before the cab rolled to a stop. She yanked it open and would have slid inside, but there was a long, masculine leg in the way. It was attached to an equally masculine chest and—as the guy bent forward—the most attractive man she'd ever laid eyes on.

His strong jaw was at odds with the generous mouth, and his cheekbones looked as if they'd been carved from granite. A high forehead, a thick, messy crop of dirty-blond hair, and striking eyes finished off a face that could grace the cover of any men's magazine.

Who the hell was he?

"Are you headed somewhere?"

The tone of his voice struck a chord inside her. And she would think later—much later—that it was the alcohol talking, because surely it couldn't have been anything else.

"That depends," she heard herself say.

What the hell am I doing?

"On what?" He grinned, his smile devastating.

"On you."

The stranger's grin faded, his eyes glittering with something darker. Something hotter. Something a hell of a lot more interesting than anything inside the Coach House.

"Get in," he said.

Lily paused for one second. Hell, she paused for two, because she really wasn't going to listen to him, was she?

"What are you afraid of?" he said dangerously. "I don't bite."

"Promise?"

He didn't answer. Instead he moved over and made space, and before Lily could even process what she was doing, she slid inside.

Lily, the woman who didn't like to be touched.

Lily, the woman who would never get into a taxi with a man who looked and sounded like this one.

And yet she did. She settled into the warmth of the taxi.

And they disappeared into the swirling snow.

———*∿*———

Back inside, Jake would have followed Lily, but Raine tugged on his hand and he finally glanced away.

"Is she going to be all right?"

"I don't know," he answered truthfully.

Just then, the melodic strains of BlackRock's last number one hit, "Never Say Good-bye," rang out.

"Where's my wife?" Cain bellowed. "I need her up

here now, or I'm gonna end up kissing one of these guys when the clock strikes midnight."

Maggie giggled and slid out, leaving just Jake and Raine.

Jake gently ran his fingers across the back of her neck, loving the way she shivered beneath him. "Come on."

The two of them joined a large crowd on the dance floor, and as Cain sang his love song to his wife, Jake held Raine against his body, their bodies moving slowly, in perfect sync with each other.

Sure, he'd caught a few looks, a few whispered words behind hands. Crystal Lake was a small town, and there was bound to be gossip. But he didn't give a rat's ass. He had everything he wanted and more than he deserved.

And as the gentle strains of Cain's guitar fed the soulful lyrics to the song, he and Raine found the perfect rhythm. The perfect dance.

"I could stay like this all night," she whispered into his neck, her breath hot, her hands locked around his waist.

He bent low and whispered, "Babe, we can do this every single night, if you want."

"Promise?"

His heart turned over as he pulled her in closer. He didn't answer.

He didn't have to. Their love was that strong.

Acknowledgments

As always, writing a book is a solitary thing and I love that my cat, Gibby, and my gorgeous retriever, Shelby, kept me company while writing this book. Whether it was at four in the morning or nine in the evening, they were always there, watching, so thanks for that.

I wrote most of this book in the summer, which was weird considering it was a Christmas book, but there was something cool about writing winter scenes while parked on the dock at a cottage in Muskoka. Thanks to my family and friends, for not forgetting about me even though I wasn't there half the time. You guys know I love you!

As always, a book doesn't just happen on its own. Much thanks to Sourcebooks publicity team, their sales team, the art department, and to my editor Leah Hultenschmidt. You guys are wonderful and professional to work with!

Lastly, thanks to my readers, especially the ones who take the time to write. I always love hearing from you, so please don't stop!

Look for the next book in Juliana Stone's
acclaimed Bad Boys of Crystal Lake series

the Day
he
Kissed
Her

Coming April 2014

Coming home is the only way to heal his heart

Mackenzie Draper thought he had everything he ever
wanted, but he knew he needed to head back home
one last time to conquer the demons from his past. For
Lily St. Clare, the charming small town she just moved
to is a haven. Big cities only want to eat you up and
spit you out. Neither Mac nor Lily was expecting to
stay very long…until the day they found each other,
and one amazingly red-hot night followed. But old
wounds almost always leave a mark, and Mac's scars
run deeper than most. With her flirty charm, Lily could
be exactly what he needs—if he's willing to give love
one more chance.

And in case you missed it, read on for an excerpt from
the first book in the Bad Boys of Crystal Lake series

the
Summer
he came
Home

Now available from Juliana Stone and
Sourcebooks Casablanca

Chapter 1

CAIN BLACK HADN'T BEEN HOME IN TEN YEARS.

At the age of twenty he'd packed his guitar—a beat-up Gibson Les Paul—said his good-byes, and left. Always a rebel, he'd had no trouble disappointing half the town, and as for the other half? Hell, they'd expected it of him.

Cain Black—the star quarterback who'd had the arrogance to turn his nose up at a full ride to Michigan State University. The nerve, some said, after everything the town had done to support him and his mother. He'd left for Los Angeles one hot summer night in July and hadn't looked back until now, and—truthfully—he'd rather be anyplace other than Crystal Lake.

He ran fingers through the thick waves atop his head and cracked his neck in an effort to relieve the tension that stretched across his shoulders. Damn, but his muscles were tight, his legs stiff. He placed a booted foot on the top step of the Edwardses' porch and paused. He'd been traveling for hours and would just about kill for a bottle of Jack Daniel's, except he was fairly certain it would knock him on his ass. He was dead tired and knew he'd either crash hard or catch his second wind.

He smoothed his hair, trying to tame the waves a bit. It wasn't as long as it used to be, barely touched his shoulders these days. With the earrings and the nose ring long gone, he was almost respectable.

Or, at the very least, as close to some kind of respectability as he was ever going to get.

He glanced at his forearm. The edge of an elaborate tattoo peeked out from under the hem of his sleeve. It was the only thing left over from his hell-raising days, and that was way before *LA Ink* and Kat Von D had brought tattoos into the mainstream.

Now everyone and their mother had one.

Cain blew out hot air, tugged his shirtsleeve down a bit more, and glanced around. It was surreal, standing here after all this time. How many nights had he and the boys hung out, shooting the shit and dreaming of a future that would rock their reality?

He shook his head, a bittersweet smile tugging at the corner of his mouth. Too many nights to count.

His thoughts darkened, and he clenched his teeth tightly as the reason for his return hit him in the gut. Not everyone's future had turned out as planned. The unimaginable had happened, and it was a sobering reality check.

One that had brought him full circle. Back to Crystal Lake.

Back to this porch.

He glanced up at a pristine blue sky and a plane caught his attention—its drone a melancholy sound that echoed into the stillness. A warm breeze caressed his cheek, bringing with it the smell of summer—of freshly mowed lawn, flowering bushes, and warm lake water. He closed his eyes and the scent took him back. Memories rushed through him: Fourth of July celebrations that lasted the week. The annual boating regatta that filled the lake with hundreds of revelers. Christmas out at Murphy's sugar shack. Tailgate parties and football. Beach nights with the boys, a guitar, a couple of girls, and a case of beer.

He saw the kid he'd been—the teen who'd dreamed large and let nothing stand in his way. Hell, none of them had. The twins, Jake and Jesse, had realized their dream to serve their country, while Mackenzie had fought his way out from beneath his father's fists to make a life in the Big Apple.

Ten years gone and it seemed like yesterday. Like nothing had changed.

The Edwards family abode was a large, redbrick Georgian with a long rambling driveway lined with petunias in varying shades of violet. At the moment, every available space of blacktop was occupied. There were at least thirty cars parked in the driveway, and several had pulled onto the grass near the road.

He'd left his rental on the street, because if memory served, Mr. Edwards was pretty anal when it came to his lush green lawn.

Cain reached for the door, but something held him still. His fingers grazed the cool burnished-steel handle and he faltered. He hated hypocrisy, and at the moment it felt like his throat was clogged with its bitter taste. He was so far off the grid, he felt like he didn't belong anymore.

He took a step back instead. Christ, could he do this?

Less than twenty-four hours ago he'd been on stage in Glasgow. BlackRock—the band he fronted—had snagged the opening slot on the Grind's latest tour and had performed in venues all over Canada, the United States, and Europe. It had been the chance of a lifetime—one he'd been waiting years for—and the exposure had been more than a gift, it had been a godsend.

The tour had been a grueling, eye-opening experience with more than its fair share of drama, yet every drop of blood had been worth it. The record label was happy, and the buzz was incredible. BlackRock was a band on the rise, and after years of sacrifice, his dream was within reach.

It was a dream that had taken him from this town ten years ago, and sadly, it had taken a funeral to bring him back.

The door opened suddenly, and a small boy ran out, yanking it closed behind him. He skidded to a halt, barely missing Cain, his shiny shoes sliding across the well-worn wooden planks. He looked to be about six or seven and had a mess of russet curls, and large blue eyes that dominated his face. The child was dressed for church—black dress pants, white button-down shirt— and he clutched a bright piece of fabric in his hand that was a shade darker than emerald green. The boy's eyes widened as his gaze traveled the tall length of Cain.

"Who are you?" His young voice wasn't so much surly as defiant.

Cain cracked a smile. The kid had spunk. "I'm Cain."

"Oh." The boy's brow furled. "I don't know you."

"No, I suppose you don't."

The kid angled his head, peered around him, and frowned. "Why are you standing out here by yourself?"

Good question. "I just got in a few minutes ago." He nodded to the boy's hand. "What's that?"

The little guy's mouth tightened as he unclenched his fist. His face screwed up in disgust. "It's a tie. My mom made me wear it, but I hate 'em." He glanced at the long settee off to the side. "Thought I'd hide it so I didn't have to wear it the rest of the day."

Cain laughed out loud. "Good call. I'm not really a tie man myself."

"You won't tell her?" The kid grinned and ran to the settee, where he promptly stuffed the offending piece under the seat. He carefully placed the cushion in the exact way he'd found it and stepped back. "Do you think she'll know?"

"I'm pretty sure she won't."

Cain walked over to the boy and paused. They stood in front of a large bay window, and he heard voices— muffled of course, but he knew there was a good-sized crowd in the house.

"Did you know him?"

The child's question hit a nerve, and Cain clenched his jaw tight, fighting the emotion that beat at him. *Know him? He was like a brother.*

"What did you say your name was?" he asked the boy instead.

His reflection in the window didn't look promising. He'd been on a plane for hours, and then there'd been the long drive from Detroit. He hadn't showered since before the show in Glasgow. His jaw was shadowed, his clothes rumpled—the black shirt, faded jeans, and heavy boots were not exactly appropriate either.

He looked like shit and knew he'd hear it from his mother, but until now none of that had mattered. His only thought had been to get home in time for the funeral, which he'd failed to do. As it turned out, he'd been damn lucky to make the reception.

"My name's Michael." The boy's eyes were huge as he looked up at Cain. He shoved his small hands into the pockets of his pants and scuffed his shoes along the worn wooden floorboards. "Mom says he was a hero. I never met a hero before." He squared his shoulders. "*Did* you know him?"

Christ, but the kid looked earnest. His pale skin was dusted with light freckles, his round cheeks rosy.

"Because I didn't."

Cain looked inside but couldn't see shit. The reflection of the sun didn't allow it.

"Yeah, I did." A wistful smile crossed his face, and he glanced down at the kid. "Your mom's a smart lady. He was a bona fide hero." He nodded. "I was about your age the first time I met the Edwards twins."

The young boy smiled, but it faded as he glanced toward the door. "I should go. My mom is gonna wonder where I am."

They both turned when the front door opened and a slender woman stepped onto the porch. She wore a simple black skirt cut to just above her knee, a fitted blouse in a muted moss green, and low-heeled shoes. Her hair was held back in a ponytail—one that emphasized the delicate bone structure of her face—and was dark, a shade between crimson and brown, more like burnished amber shot through with bits of sun. Her skin was the color of cream, and when she turned toward them, Cain felt a jolt as their eyes connected.

Hers were blue—like liquid navy—feathered by long, dark lashes and delicately arched eyebrows. She was, without a doubt, one hell of a looker. A little on the thin side for his tastes, but Cain's interest was piqued.

Her eyes widened for the briefest of moments, and then she turned to the boy, eyes narrowed and lips pursed. "Michael John O'Rourke! What are you doing out here"—her voice lowered—"and *where* is your tie?"

She had a slight Southern drawl that rolled beneath her words. It was melodic and soft.

"It was tight and, uh, I took it off and I, um…" He tapped his foot nervously and shrugged. "Well, I'm not sure where I left it."

The boy shot a quick look his way, and it took some effort for Cain to keep a straight face.

The woman sighed. "Michael, this is a serious occasion." She walked over to them, ignored Cain, and bent forward to fix a stray curl that rested upon the boy's forehead before fastening the top button of his shirt.

Her scent was subtle, fresh with a hint of exotic. Cain liked it.

"I know, Mom. But, like, can't I be serious without a tie?"

A ghost of a smile tugged the corner of her mouth and Cain smiled. "He's got a point." Cain motioned toward his tieless shirt.

She straightened, though her hand never left her son as her eyes traveled the length of him. Gone was the smile. The lady was all business. "And you are?"

Cain opened his mouth and then closed it. What to say? Obviously she wasn't a townie, because he'd sure as hell have remembered someone like her. For the moment he didn't feel like sharing his relationship with Jesse, didn't feel like owning up to his hell-raising days.

"A friend of the family," he answered instead.

She grabbed her son and pushed him toward the door. The boy opened it and a soft swell of voices spilled outside. He ran inside, but the woman paused. She looked at Cain as if he had two heads.

"Aren't you coming inside, then?"

Her abrupt tone kick-started him into action. Cain exhaled and followed in their footsteps.

The Edwards home boasted a grand foyer—the focal point, a massive centered staircase that led to the upper level. He took a second and glanced around.

The walls were no longer taupe and had been done over in pale, cool greens. The wood accents—the railing and trim—once oak, were now dark ebony, and the ceramic floors had been replaced with a funky hardwood. It was similar to what was in the house he'd shared with his ex-wife, but damned if he remembered what it was called.

Music wafted from the back of the house, and he assumed a good many people were gathered outside on the deck. It was the first week in June, so the weather was warm and the Edwardses' yard was renowned for its landscaping, pool, tennis courts, and prime lake frontage.

It was the sweetest spot on Crystal Lake and one not many could afford.

There were quite a few folks talking quietly. He felt their interest. It was in the understated whispers and covert glances directed his way. Cain ran his hand over the day-old stubble that graced his chin and winced. Shit, he should have at least shaved.

The woman and little boy disappeared among the crowd, and he took a step forward, suddenly unsure of himself. He was surrounded by faces he recognized, yet he felt like an outsider. Again he fought the sliver of doubt.

Maybe he should have stayed away. Sent a card or a flower arrangement.

"Cain, you came."

The whispered words melted his heart. Years fell away as he turned and gazed down into Marnie Edwards's face. She was older, of course, her face fuller, with time etched into the lines around her eyes and mouth. Her dark hair was elegant, hitting the curve of her jaw in a blunt cut. She wore a smart black suit, with a dash of red in the scarf draped loosely about her neck.

Marnie opened her arms, and he grasped her small frame close to his. She trembled against him. "I knew you would."

Grief welled inside him. Hard, like a fist turning in his chest. He couldn't speak; his throat felt like it was clogged with sawdust. So he just held her, took her warmth and strength into his body, and closed his eyes.

"Cain, thank you for coming. It means a lot."

Cain looked up, kept Marnie secure in his arms, and nodded to Steven Edwards. Pain shadowed the older man's eyes, and Cain swallowed hard. "Sir, I tried to get here for the funeral, but…"

Steven Edwards nodded. "I know, son."

"Jesse would be so happy to know you're all together." Marnie wiped her face and slipped from his embrace. "Mackenzie and Jacob are out back somewhere." She crossed to her husband's side. "You should go see them."

"Is my mother…" His voice trailed off as he struggled to gain control over the emotions inside. "I tried to get hold of her earlier, but she didn't pick up."

Marnie smiled warmly. "She's here somewhere, helping with the food, I think." She glanced up at her husband. "It's good now. We're all home." Marnie motioned toward the back of the house. "Go, the boys are waiting."

Cain nodded and slipped through the small groups of people gathered in the hall. Muted voices and snatches of conversations followed him as he entered the kitchen and headed toward the patio doors. He recognized a lot of the faces, smiled, said hello, but didn't stop to talk.

The deck was crowded, and conversation halted as he stepped outside. Hot sunlight filtered through the vine-heavy pergola overhead, and the scent of lilac filled the air. The bushes alongside the pool house had grown a lot. They were in fact twice the size he remembered and were full of fragrant white and soft purple-colored blooms.

His gaze wandered past the deck. There was no one here he wanted to talk to. Bradley Hayes, a classmate from back in the day, nodded and headed in his direction. They'd never been friends, and he sure as hell wasn't in the mood to pretend.

Cain turned abruptly and took the stairs two at a time to the patio below.

He cleared the bottom step, grabbed a cold beer from the nearest waiter, and took a long, refreshing draw. He glanced out over the backyard as his hand absently wiped the corner of his mouth. The tight feeling in his gut pressed harder, and his skin was clammy.

Cain was used to being the focus of attention but this was different. These weren't fans. They were old neighbors, teachers, acquaintances, and some he'd considered friends a long time ago.

Were they judging him? Was he the prodigal black sheep, returned?

He squared his shoulders. None of them were the reason he'd come back.

Two men caught his eye, and he moved methodically

through the crowd of mourners, nodding to those who called greetings, yet his gaze never left the duo several feet away from everyone.

The man on the left was dressed in a suit, his tall frame draped in expensive Armani. Cain knew this. His closet was filled with the crap. His newly minted ex-wife, Natasha, had insisted he wear nothing but the Italian designer whenever he accompanied her to one of her damn premieres. She'd spent wads of cash dressing him up like one of her West Coast buddies. After she had left, he'd considered getting rid of the lot, but hell, it had cost a fortune and he didn't see the benefit in throwing money away.

The man on the right was decked out in full military dress.

Cain stopped a few feet away, and they both turned at the same time to face him.

Silence fell between the three, their eyes locked on each other as a world of pain united them.

Armani raised his beer, a tight smile settling on his face, though his eyes remained shadowed as he spoke. "You look like shit."

The soldier stepped forward.

"I'm sorry…I…" Cain struggled to form a coherent sentence but faltered. Two arms enveloped him in a bear hug that was crushing and welcoming and hard, in the way it was among men.

The pain he'd felt for days, ever since he got the news, grabbed him, twisting his insides until he nearly choked from the intensity. Mackenzie stepped back, gave them some room, and Cain fed off the strength and energy that was Jake Edwards.

After a few moments Jake let go, grabbed another cold beer from the bucket at his feet, and tossed it to Cain—who nearly dropped the one he already had. Mac scooped one for himself, and they wandered down to the beach.

There were no words spoken. The easy silence of their youth enveloped them as if the passage of time meant nothing.

They'd buried one of their own today.

There was nothing else to say.

New York Times and *USA Today* Bestselling Author

The Bridesmaid

by Julia London

―⁓―

Two mismatched strangers on a disastrous cross-country trek

Kate Preston just moved to New York, but she has to get back to Seattle in time for her best friend's wedding. Joe Firretti is moving to Seattle, and he has to get there in time for a life-changing job interview. But fate's got a sense of humor.

Kate goes from rubbing elbows on the plane with a gorgeous but irritating stranger (doggone arm-rest hog) to sharing one travel disaster after another with him on four wheels. Joe thought he had his future all figured out, but sometimes fate has to knock you over the head pretty hard before you see that opportunity is standing right in front of you…in a really god-awful poufy bridesmaid dress.

―⁓―

Praise for Julia London:

"London's ability to draw real-life characters and settings is superb…her characters cope with life's curveballs and keep on trucking."—*RT Book Reviews*

For more Julia London, visit:

www.sourcebooks.com

A Shot of Sultry

by Macy Beckett

~~~

Welcome to Sultry Springs, Texas: where home can be the perfect place for a fresh start.

For West Coast filmmaker Bobbi Gallagher, going back to Sultry Springs is a last resort. But with her career in tatters, a documentary set in her hometown might be just what she needs to salvage her reputation. She just can't let anything distract her again. Not even the gorgeous contractor her brother asked to watch over her. As if she can't handle filming a few rowdy Texans.

Golden boy Trey Lewis, with his blond hair and Technicolor-blue eyes, is a leading man if Bobbi ever saw one. He's strong and confident and—much to her delight—usually shirtless. He thinks keeping his best friend's baby sister out of trouble will be easy. But he has no idea of the trouble in store for *him*…

~~~

"A heartwarming, humorous story of second chances…sweet at its core. A strong continuation of this promising series."—*Publishers Weekly*

"Brimming with rapier wit and heartwarming moments… Packed with humor and heart."—*Fresh Fiction*

For more Macy Beckett, visit:

www.sourcebooks.com

Sultry with a Twist

by Macy Beckett

—⁓—

Welcome to Sultry Springs, Texas:
where first loves find second chances…

Nine years after June Augustine hightailed it out of Sultry
Springs with her heart in pieces, one thing stands between
her and her dream of opening an upscale martini bar: a bogus
warrant from her tiny Texas hometown. Now she's stuck
in the sticks for a month of community service under the
supervision of the devilishly sexy Luke Gallagher, her first
love and ex-best friend.

If Texas wasn't already hot enough, working side-by-side
with June would make any man melt. Luke wants nothing
more than to strip her down and throw her in the lake—the
same lake where they were found buck naked and guilty as sin
all those years ago. In their heads, they're older and wiser. But
their hearts tell a different story…

—⁓—

For more Macy Beckett, visit:

www.sourcebooks.com

Surrender to Sultry

by Macy Beckett

Feeling the Heat

How do you stay under the sheriff's radar in a town that prides itself on knowing everyone's business? Leah's not sure it's possible, but she's determined to avoid Colton Bea for as long as she can. Seeing him again would be too heartbreaking—and she knows from experience his bone-melting kisses are way too tempting.

Colt still hasn't forgiven Leah for her sudden disappearing act ten years ago. He may no longer be the hellion he was in high school, but he's still willing to play dirty to get what he wants. And he won't let Leah get away again. Armed with chocolate éclairs, a killer smile, and an adorable niece, he will make sure that this time the love of his life has plenty of reasons to stay.

"This heartwarming tale will pull at the heartstrings yet still leave the reader with a sense of satisfaction."—*RT Book Reviews*, 4 Stars

"Fans will appreciate Beckett's humor and the reappearance of old friends."—*Publishers Weekly*

For more Macy Beckett, visit:

www.sourcebooks.com

The Officer and the Secret

by Jeanette Murray

If there's one thing he hates, it's a secret…

Coming home after a rough deployment, Captain Dwayne Robertson wants some stability in his life, and finds it in the friendship he's forged with Veronica Gibson while he was away. But her past is a well-guarded mystery, and Dwayne doesn't know if he can deal with a woman who has something to hide…

and she's filled with them…

Veronica Gibson doesn't want anyone to know about her bizarre upbringing. She's finally escaped her missionary parents and would be enjoying her independence if she didn't feel so insecure about fitting in. She can easily envision a glorious future with Dwayne—but can she build a new life on a web of lies?

Praise for Jeanette Murray:

"Her characters and their challenges are relatable, and will inspire readers to fight for what they want in their own lives."—*RT Book Reviews*

For more Jeanette Murray, visit:

www.sourcebooks.com

The Officer Breaks the Rules

by Jeanette Murray

———

Some rules are meant to be broken.

He's ruled by loyalty…

Every man knows that you don't date your best friend's little sister, but Captain Jeremy Phillips can't seem to convince Madison O'Shay to stay away. And he can't convince himself to stop thinking about her, either.

She's ruled by love…

Madison knows exactly what she wants… and whom. But she won't give up her career in the Navy for any man, not even Jeremy.

They're both about to learn that in the game of love, it's all about breaking the rules.

———

"If you are looking for sexy, edgy, gripping series that will keep you invested and turning pages, look no further. You will absolutely love this one."—*Guilty Pleasures Book Reviews*

"I just loved *The Officer Breaks the Rules*. I fell in love with the characters from the first book in the series and continued to fall in love with them in this book."—*Night Owl Reviews*

For more Jeanette Murray, visit:

www.sourcebooks.com

The Officer Says "I Do"

by Jeanette Murray

He's a Marine…she grew up on a commune.

He always puts duty first…she's a free spirit with an unshakable belief in Fate.

He loves routine and order…she brings chaos and creativity everywhere she goes.

They're either going to balance each other perfectly— or drive each other completely, utterly insane…

On a wild pre–deployment celebration in Las Vegas, Captain Timothy O'Shay encounters free–spirited beauty Skye McDermott, and for once lets down his guard. Now his life is about to take off in directions he never could have imagined…

"The clever dialogue will tickle your funny bone while the characters, the chemistry, and sensual love story will have you begging for more. An easy recommend and a new favorite writer for me."—*The Long and Short of It*

"Funny, charming and sexy…It's all a girl could want and then some!"—*The Romance Reviews*

For more Jeanette Murray, visit:

www.sourcebooks.com

One Day in Apple Grove

by C.H. Admirand

———

Welcome to Apple Grove, Ohio (pop. 597), a small town with a big heart.

Caitlin Mulcahy loves her family. She really does. But sometimes they can drive her to her last shred of sanity—from her dad ("I'm not meddling, I just want what's best for you") to her eight-months-pregnant older sister to her younger sister, who will do just about anything to avoid real work. Cait just needs to get away, even if for only an hour.

When she sees someone in need of help on the side of the road, of course she's going to pull over. She might even be able to fix his engine—after all, the Mulcahy family is a handy bunch. She's not expecting that former Navy medic Jack Gannon and a little black puppy named Jameson will be the ones who end up rescuing her…

———

"For fans of Susan Wiggs and Janet Chapman."—*Booklist*

For more C.H. Admirand, visit:

www.sourcebooks.com

A Wedding in Apple Grove

by C.H. Admirand

———〜〜〜———

He's not so sure about small town life.
She can't imagine living anywhere else.

Welcome to Apple Grove, Ohio (population 597), where everyone has your best interests at heart, even if they can't agree on the best way to meddle. When the townsfolk of Apple Grove need handiwork done, there's no job too small for the Mulcahy sisters: Megan, Caitlin, and Grace.

Specializing in hard work and family loyalty, tomboy Meg Mulcahy has left behind any girlhood dreams of romance. Enter newcomer Daniel Eagan, looking to bury his own broken heart and make a new start. He's surprised—and delighted—by the winsome girl with the mighty tool belt who shows up to fix his wiring.

But Dan's got a lot to learn about life in a small town, and when Meg's past collides with her future, it may take all 595 other residents of Apple Grove to keep this romance from short-circuiting.

———〜〜〜———

"Sexy and fun… Admirand's series will be popular, especially with fans of Susan Wiggs and Janet Chapman."—*Booklist*

For more C.H. Admirand, visit:

www.sourcebooks.com

A SEAL at Heart

by Anne Elizabeth

———

He lost just about everything on that mission…

Being a Navy SEAL means everything to John "Red Jack" Roaker, but a mission gone wrong has left his buddy dead, his memory spotty, and his world turned upside down. His career as a SEAL is threatened unless Dr. Laurie Smith's unconventional methods of therapy can help him.

Maybe she can show him how to get it back…

Laurie's father was a SEAL—and she knows exactly what the personal cost can be. She can't resist trying everything to help this man, and not only because she finds him as sexy as he is honorable.

As the layers of Jack's resistance peel away, he and Laurie unearth secrets that go to the highest levels of the military—and the deepest depths of their hearts…

———

"A romance with real heart, from a talented
writer who has deep personal insight into what
it takes to be a Navy SEAL."—*New York Times*
bestselling author Suzanne Brockmann

"Two wounded souls find healing through love…
Readers will find this book an accurate reflection of
what's happening in the world today and perhaps
be uplifted by its message of hope."—*Booklist*

For more Anne Elizabeth, visit:

www.sourcebooks.com

About the Author

Juliana Stone's love of the written word and '80s rock have inspired her in more ways than one. She writes dark paranormal romance as well as contemporary romance and spends her days navigating a busy life that includes a husband, kids, and rock 'n' roll! You can find more info at www.julianastone.com.